D1012241

MY MEE-TAH-WEEN

"There are many things in this world that can be described as sad," Black Wolf said thickly.

He stopped and slid his arms around Maddy's waist and swung her around to face him. "But I am no longer sad," he said. "I have *you*. You are my happiness, my hope for the future. With you at my side, everything is possible."

"I'm not sure how I feel, knowing that you depend on me so much," Maddy said, searching his eyes. "It's such a responsibility."

"Our love and what comes from it should never be a responsibility, but something wonderful to be rejoiced over," Black Wolf said, twining his fingers through her hair, bringing her lips to his. *"Mee-tah-ween . . ."*

Maddy sighed with heady pleasure when his lips came down on hers and kissed her.

Other *Leisure* and *Love Spell* books by
Cassie Edwards:
TOUCH THE WILD WIND
ROSES AFTER RAIN
WHEN PASSION CALLS
EDEN'S PROMISE
ISLAND RAPTURE
SECRETS OF MY HEART

The *Savage* Series:
SAVAGE HEAT
SAVAGE DANCE
SAVAGE TEARS
SAVAGE LONGINGS
SAVAGE DREAM
SAVAGE BLISS
SAVAGE WHISPERS
SAVAGE SHADOWS
SAVAGE SPLENDOR
SAVAGE EDEN
SAVAGE SURRENDER
SAVAGE PASSIONS
SAVAGE SECRETS
SAVAGE PRIDE
SAVAGE SPIRIT
SAVAGE EMBERS
SAVAGE ILLUSION
SAVAGE SUNRISE
SAVAGE MISTS
SAVAGE PROMISE
SAVAGE PERSUASION

SAVAGE WONDER

CASSIE EDWARDS

LEISURE BOOKS   NEW YORK CITY

A LEISURE BOOK®

August 1998

Published by

Dorchester Publishing Co., Inc.
276 Fifth Avenue
New York, NY 10001

If you purchased this book without a cover you should be aware that this book is stolen property. It was reported as "unsold and destroyed" to the publisher and neither the author nor the publisher has received any payment for this "stripped book."

Copyright © 1998 by Cassie Edwards

Cover Art by John Ennis

All rights reserved. No part of this book may be reproduced or transmitted in any form or by any electronic or mechanical means, including photocopying, recording or by any information storage and retrieval system, without the written permission of the Publisher, except where permitted by law.

ISBN 0-8439-4414-5

The name "Leisure Books" and the stylized "L" with design are trademarks of Dorchester Publishing Co., Inc.

Printed in the United States of America.

I wish to dedicate Savage Wonder *to the following fans who have become very special to me:*

> *Deborah Bass*
> *Pam Guy*
> *Vera Koppler*
> *Jane Herron*
> *Terry Hill*
> *Debbie Frazier*
> *Maureen Bishop*

> *Love,*
> *Cassie*

DARE TO DREAM

"Without a dream, your soul dies,"
an Indian once told me,
but I just laughed it off,
going out into the world to see.
As a child, I would have believed him.
As an adult I thought I knew more.
I took every chance, and many a risk,
And opened every door.
But as I grew older
and experienced life as it came,
I grew not richer nor wiser
And still nothing yet to gain.
Another of his sayings hit me—
"It is a good day to die,"
and pondered at the Indian's wisdom,
for he knew much more than I.
Now I dare to take the challenge
to breathe life into my soul,
to take the chance I'd not yet made,
And make a dream my goal.

                              —Janene Helm,
                                Poet and friend

SAVAGE WONDER

Chapter One

Rough winds do shake the darling buds of
   May!

                    —William Shakespeare

The Ohio River Valley—1879
May—The Moon When the Ponies Shed

Standing high on a knoll overlooking the Ohio
River, Chief Black Wolf stared up at the sky. He
was troubled by the thunderstorm that was approaching from the west. The thunder clouds
were black, rolling, and full of many voices and
lightning. Behind the black clouds the Thunder
Warriors were riding wildly on their horses in
the sky.

Tall and muscled, and dressed only in a breechclout and moccasins, Black Wolf stood tall. His
waist-length, raven-black hair blew away from
his shoulders and whipped in the wind. His
heart pounded as he felt an impending doom
bearing down on him and his Oglala people.

He saw it in the clouds. He saw it in the river,
which was swollen and treacherous.

He felt it deep inside his heart. This island, which had been a home for his people for too short a time, might no longer be a safe haven for them.

"But, Grandfather, why?" he whispered, peering heavenward. "Must this island also be taken from my people?"

After Black Wolf's cousin Chief Crazy Horse had died at Fort Robinson in Nebraska, Prancing Wolf, Black Wolf's father, who was then the proud chief of the small band of Oglala Sioux, had been forced to make decisions that would change the lives of his people forever.

Those decisions had been forced upon him by the arrival of the *wasichos*, white men. At first, the Oglala had been willing to be the *wasichos'* guides on land that the white men were not familiar with.

But that kindness, that foolishness, had stopped when the *wasichos* began the destruction of all that was holy to the Sioux!

They destroyed and drove away many beautiful native birds. They changed the landscape. They unmercifully slaughtered the buffalo.

When Black Wolf's father no longer saw hope for his people in their homeland, he led them far away from the prison-reservation life forced on them by the United States Government.

Then they found the huge island that lay in the Ohio River, halfway between Illinois and Kentucky, and the Sioux saw that it was filled with forest animals, and also black soil for grow-ing their food. It was as though the island had beckoned to them to stay and live off it!

Overjoyed to have finally found a place they might be able to call their own, the Sioux had built their homes there. It was a land that the *wasichos* would not want. Always before, the greedy, land-hungry *wasichos* had taken huge tracts of land from the red man, not small por-tions.

A keen sorrow swept through Black Wolf as he recalled that his mother had not made the journey to this new land. She had died after only a few short weeks out on the long, difficult trek from their beloved homeland in Nebraska.

Black Wolf had known that her death had come from a broken heart, for he knew how much his mother had grieved at leaving the land that had been hers and her people's since the beginning of time, and the graves of her beloved ancestors. She had feared most of all that the graves would be desecrated and used by the *was-ichos* for farmland and cattle grazing.

Her fears had gnawed at her heart until they had completely devoured it. It pained Black Wolf to remember his frail mother dying in her husband's arms.

And now her beloved husband had died also. Black Wolf's father had been murdered, and no trace of the killer had ever been found. His death had come from a knife wound in his belly.

Black Wolf had been named chief shortly after

his father's death, and now the decisions for his people lay solely in his hands. *He* was now in total charge of their destiny. And today he had a serious decision to make.

He stared at the roaring river, which was already so swollen it was eating away at the banks of the island, one clump of earth, one loose rock, at a time.

Would it rise enough to swallow the island, he wondered desperately, as though it were some ugly, monstrous, hungry being? Should he move his people to safety just in case?

If so, to which side of the river should he encourage them to go? Illinois? Or Kentucky?

The Illinois side had not been good to his people. His father had died there.

But if Black Wolf had to make this choice, he would choose Illinois, so that he would have a better chance of one day finding his father's killer!

Thunder rumbled and rolled like many drums, shaking the ground beneath Black Wolf's feet. Lightning flashed in lurid streaks overhead.

Black Wolf's spine stiffened as he watched a portion of a white man's house float past him in the river, bobbing from side to side, then pitching strangely forward. His eyes widened when he saw a squealing pig sweep by him in the thunderous roar of the water.

As it had these past several days, soon the rain would come again, its big drops splashing down on the painted robes of the girls and women and the finery of the braves and elderly warriors of his village.

Again Black Wolf studied the banks of the island. Panic seized him when he saw just how much the water had risen while he had been pondering what to do. In a matter of moments, much of the shoreline, where the canoes were beached, had disappeared into the hungry jaws of the river.

He stiffened as he saw his people's birchbark canoes rocking precariously back and forth in the water, threatening to become dislodged, soon to float away!

Black Wolf looked heavenward again and saw the rolling black clouds drawing closer at a much more rapid speed than before. It was now a world of clouds!

The wind had picked up and was howling like a pack of wolves sending off their mournful cries on a lonely night. The wind was so strong, it threatened to dislodge Black Wolf's solid footing.

Knowing that all things came from above, Black Wolf took the time to prepare himself, spiritually, for what was to come. He lifted his eyes and hands heavenward and prayed to Grandfather, the Great Spirit. He made vows to the four quarters that he would, to the best of his ability, protect his people.

"Give me power, Grandfather," he cried, his voice lifting in the wind through the clouds overhead. "Give me power and wisdom to lead my people to safety! Give me the strength and swiftness of those that have wings! *Ha ho! Ha ho!*"

Feeling stronger because of his prayers, and confident that whatever happened now was how it should be, Black Wolf turned and stared at his village.

The buffalo hide tepees were pitched close together. Some were spewing curls of cooking smoke from their smoke holes, their black, fringed smoke flap ornaments whipping in the wind.

Near the lodges a crude corral of buffalo hair rope held the band's pony herd. The horses showed their nervousness as they shook their thick manes and pawed at the earth.

Another streak of lightning that struck a tree on the far side of the island and sent quick flames into the brisk wind brought Black Wolf out of his reverie.

He broke into a hard run and hurried to his village.

He went to the village crier's tepee and, panting, sweat streaming from his brow, stepped inside.

"Go!" he cried. "Carry the word among our people that we should abandon the island. Tell everyone to take what they can in their canoes. Put the horses on the rafts that have been prepared for the possibility of a time like this. Go, Sun Spirit! Spread the word! Quickly!"

Sun Spirit nodded, threw off the blanket that

was wrapped around his thin, old shoulders, then left the lodge with Black Wolf.

As Sun Spirit made his rounds in the village, crying out his message of doom, Black Wolf began helping everyone. In a panic, his people ran around, doing what they must to save themselves, as well as taking whatever could be placed in their personal canoes.

Forgetting his own possessions in his worry about the safety of his people, Black Wolf helped everyone, and then, one by one, led the horses to the rafts and secured them with ropes to the sides of the small river craft.

He watched as his people began carrying the lodge poles and folded buckskin coverings of their lodges to another raft, carefully laying one against the other.

Black Wolf then began making trips in his canoe to and from the island to the Illinois side, helping move as many of the women and children as he could to safety on higher ground.

His heart ached when he heard some of his people loudly mourning the loss of their new village, this place they had grown to love as their home. It was hard to accept another loss in their lives, especially their land. It was as though history was repeating itself.

Would it ever end? Black Wolf wondered in despair.

As he rowed one more time across the river to the island in his empty canoe, he looked over his shoulder at some of those who were on the Illinois side, putting their arms across each other's shoulders, wailing, *"Hownh, Hownh!"*

Others called for spirit power, saying, *"A-hey! A-hey! A-hey! A-hey!"*

Suddenly a huge limb came rushing through the water and collided with Black Wolf's canoe, spilling him overboard.

The current was so strong he was swept quickly away, taking him from the sight of those who had witnessed what had happened.

Everyone stared in panic-stricken silence at the river. Its wide-open jaws had swallowed their beloved leader. He was gone.

He . . . was . . . gone!

Black Wolf fought to stay afloat. He bobbed up and down in the river. He coughed and strangled on water that was forced down his throat each time he was pulled under the surface again by the force of the current.

His muscled arms finally kept him afloat long enough to get him closer to shore, and he reached land far downriver from where his people had last seen him. As he crawled exhaustedly onto the muddy, rocky embankment, the roaring wind whipped a limb from a tree, sending it down onto Black Wolf's head and knocking him unconscious.

As he lay there motionless among the rocks and mud, the river roared on past him. The lightning flashed. The thunder roared. . . .

Chapter Two

Listen! the mighty Being is awake
And doth with his eternal motion make
A sound like thunder—
                    —William Wordsworth

Madeline Penrod shoved the wet scrub brush in circles along the wood floor of her cabin, the suds bubbling dark and dirty around it. When Maddy heard a growl of thunder outside in the distance, she reciprocated with a low groan.

"Mud and more mud," she whispered, blowing a damp strand of her golden hair back from her face. She prayed that it wouldn't rain again. Not only because of the mud her ten-year-old sister constantly tracked into the house, but also because of the threat of a flood that seemed almost certain if it rained again.

When her father had first built this cabin so close to the Ohio River, none of the family had thought about the possibility of floods. They had come from higher country in Kentucky where sometimes people even prayed for rain in the spring.

But in southern Illinois, one prayed for anything but rain in the spring, for it came in buckets, pouring from the heavens.

"Hi, Maddy, I'm back," Jaimie said as she ran into the cabin. She grabbed a rifle that always stood at the side of the door for quick protection if anyone came that posed a threat to the two sisters who had been left alone to fend for themselves. Their mother had died while giving birth to a child one year before, the baby having been stillborn. Only recently, their father had been knifed to death in the dark shadows of the forest.

"Jaimie, where on earth have you been?" Maddy asked, dropping the scrub brush into the bucket of water. She grimaced when some water splashed onto her face. She wiped it away with the hem of her apron, then pushed herself up from the floor and stretched as she clasped her hands to the small of her back.

"I've been mushroom hunting," Jaimie said, running a hand up and down the smooth, cool barrel of the rifle. "Didn't find none, though."

She screwed her face up into a frown as she glanced from Maddy to the wet floor, then to Maddy again. "Sis, you should quit fussin' over the house so much," she said. "Come on outside with me. Get some fresh air. Let me teach you how to shoot Pa's rifle. You should learn ways to defend yourself. It might take both of us to fend off Indians should any ever decide to attack."

Maddy was half hearing what Jaimie was saying. She sighed heavily as she stared at how her sister was dressed. Jaimie was so unlike herself. Maddy always wore feminine cotton dresses. Through the week they were plain. On Sundays, when she attended church, she wore fancier, lacier finery.

"Jaimie, I shouldn't have allowed you to buy those boy's breeches and shirts at the general store in River Town," Maddy said with an edge in her voice. "I don't know what I was thinking to allow you to take the scissors to your hair, clipping it so short you now truly look like a boy."

" 'Cause you got tired of hearin' me fussin' all of the time about how my long, red hair got so tangled while outside ridin', shootin', or workin' in the garden," Jaimie said playfully, her green eyes dancing. "That's why, Sis."

"Yes, I know," Maddy said, again sighing. She wiped her hands on her apron, then ran her long, slim fingers through her golden hair. "Sometimes I wish *my* hair was shorter, but one tomboy in our family is enough."

Maddy went to Jaimie and gently touched her freckled face. "I must confess, little sister, I was getting very tired of washing the mud out of your dresses and having to iron so many. Your roughhousing ways made it necessary for you to change into a clean dress more than once a day," she said, laughing softly. "Plain denim breeches and cotton shirts are much easier to tend to."

"Then why don't you wear them, also, Sis?"

Jaimie asked, then quickly changed the subject when Maddy gave her an annoyed look. "All right, no more fussin' over clothes, but still, Sis, I wish you'd listen to what I say about the importance of your learning how to handle firearms. I listened carefully to Father's lessons. *You* shied away from guns like they were poison, never expecting that Father could be taken so quickly from us at the age of forty."

"Yes, Father was way too young to die," Maddy said, stepping away from her sister.

She went and stood at the open door and looked up the hill, where beneath a beautiful birch tree lay three graves, the final resting places of her parents and stillborn brother.

"Maddy, Pa built our cabin too close to two Indian tribes . . . the Sioux, who live on an island downstream from our cabin, and the Shawnee, who have a village not far upriver from River Town," Jaimie said sadly. "Our father was knifed to death by someone. Indians are known for the huge knives they carry sheathed at their waists. I believe one of them killed Pa."

"Indians aren't the only ones who carry knives," Maddy said, turning to face Jaimie. "White men, Jaimie. There are many deranged white men who go around killing for the fun of killing."

She grabbed the handle of the water bucket and struggled to drag it toward the door. "As for Indians?" she said, giving Jaimie a glance as she walked past her. "I don't think much about them. If I tend to my own business, the Indians will surely tend to theirs."

She stopped and rubbed the muscles of her right arm with her left hand as she gazed at Jaimie. "And as for who might have killed Pa?" she said, her voice breaking. "Jaimie, I just don't allow myself to think about it, since I doubt we will ever know."

She gave Jaimie a playful shove. "Now scat, little sister," she said, laughing. "You've muddied my floor enough for one day. Be sure to remove your shoes the next time you come in."

Maddy stepped outside with Jaimie. Her eyes were drawn to the sky when she heard another low rumble of thunder.

She shivered when she saw the big, black, rolling thunder clouds approaching overhead.

She gasped and jumped when a jagged streak of lightning lit up the darkening sky.

Then she sucked in a deep breath as a flock of split-tail swallows suddenly swooped down around her, sweeping low, then high in a frenzy of flight.

"It's an omen," she said, giving Jaimie a quick, frightened look. "Mama said swallows are holy. When they act peculiar as they are today, what do you think it means?"

"Hogwash," Jaimie said, her eyes also following the path of the swallows. "It means nothing. There aren't such things as omens. Birds are birds. Nothing more."

"Look at the river, Jaimie," Maddy said, her

eyes widening when she saw how high it was. The edges of the banks were already covered. She hugged herself. "Sis, today I think we have more to fear from the river than anything else. Should it continue rising, we could lose everything."

Maddy again looked uphill at the graves. At age nineteen, she had been thrust into the responsibility of keeping a household for herself and her sister. She suddenly felt old before her time.

Her thoughts went to Farris Boyd and how he could take her and Jaimie away from all of the drudgery, fear, and worry that came to her every morning upon her first awakening. He had asked her to marry him.

From what he had told her, he had a beautiful home outside of River Town. She had never actually seen it, for she had yet to go anywhere with Farris Boyd.

Actually, she detested him. She hated the very ground he walked on!

As for everyone else, and how they felt about him, as far as she knew, he was a respected man. He was the sheriff of River Town. Some even called him a hero because he'd killed Crazy Horse, the famous Sioux Indian leader.

But that was exactly why Maddy loathed the very thought of his being her husband. It turned her stomach the way he bragged about having bayoneted Crazy Horse to death, and the way he bragged about having killed many Indians, men, women, and children alike, while he rode with the cavalry.

Farris wasn't much to look at, either. Maddy couldn't imagine herself waking up every morning to the sight of a bald-headed man who was twice her age. Besides, his face was scarred from chickenpox, and he limped from an old arrow wound that he had received during the war.

The mere thought of the times this vile man had tried to steal a kiss from Maddy made her shudder.

Gunfire and her sister's laughter brought Maddy out of her deep thoughts. She turned and watched, grimacing as her sister shot another tin can from the top of a fence, the can flipping up into the air with a hole directly in the middle.

Before Jaimie got another shot off, Maddy went to her and took the rifle from her. "If you truly want to make yourself useful today, go down to the river and see how much it has risen this past hour," she said, glad now that she had thought to place a marker in the ground that showed how many inches the water might rise.

"Glad to, Sis," Jaimie said, running toward the river.

Maddy gave one more long look at the clouds in the sky, gave a slow look at the river, then returned to the cabin and propped the rifle back in its resting place.

Before throwing out the mop water, she fell to her knees and scrubbed up the mud that Jaimie had tracked in.

Once the floor was spotless again, at least for a little while, Maddy took the bucket outside and dumped it out to the right of her door, where the ground quickly absorbed it.

After turning the bucket upside down and leaning it against the house to dry, Maddy watched Jaimie as she checked the measurements.

"It's risen a foot in the last hour!" Jaimie shouted.

"A foot?" Maddy whispered, paling at the realization of just how quickly the river was rising. She had never seen the Ohio so vicious and uncontrollable.

She turned and looked at the cabin, worried anew about it. At this rate, the water would soon be lapping at the doorstep.

Fearing the worst, Maddy went inside and started packing valuables in boxes. She knew where she and Jaimie would go. A while back, while Jaimie had been out on her horse exploring, she had found a cave on higher ground. They could stay there until the threat of the flood passed.

They certainly couldn't go to River Town. If their cabin washed away, River Town would already be gone, for it had been built right on the banks of the river to make it easier for those who came and went daily in their boats to trade at the largest town in this area of southern Illinois.

If the river did continue to rise, River Town might soon be a thing of the past . . . a memory!

Again Maddy thought of Farris Boyd. She knew that if he started worrying about her welfare, she would have him to contend with as well.

She just wished he'd leave her be!

When she married, she wanted the man to be someone she would look forward to kissing, to sleeping with, to being held by.

So far she had not met anyone who caused her to take a second glance. She sometimes wondered if it would only be in her dreams that she would find such a man as that!

She dropped a box of books when a clap of thunder shook the floor of the cabin beneath her feet.

The wind was howling ominously down the fireplace chimney and around the outside corners of the cabin. The sky was growing darker and darker as the clouds rolled closer.

Fearing for Jaimie's safety, Maddy ran out of the cabin, but before she got the chance to shout Jaimie's name, she turned at the sound of an approaching horse.

She went stiff when she saw that it was Farris Boyd on his white stallion, riding toward her.

"Please, oh, please, not now," Maddy whispered to herself, curling her fingers into tight fists at her sides.

Chapter Three

Pain has an element of blank;
It cannot recollect
When it began, or if there were
A day when it was not.

— Emily Dickinson

Having never seen the Ohio so wild, Jaimie walked slowly beside the river, staring at the debris swept along by the raging water.

She could hardly believe her eyes when she saw an outhouse turning and tossing in the current as it swept on past her. Her eyebrows rose when she saw a broken raft tumbling past her in the swift current.

It was clear that the river was no small threat this time. There was going to be a full-blown flood in the area, which meant that her home would surely be swallowed by the river.

Seeing a flood for the first time in her life was so intriguing, she could hardly take her eyes off it!

Not paying any attention to where she was

walking, Jaimie stumbled over a limb that had fallen from a tree.

She fell clumsily to the ground, and what she fell next to, half hidden beneath a bush, made her throat go dry and an instant fear leap into her heart.

"An Indian!" she gasped, glued to the spot as she stared at him. "An . . . unconscious . . . Indian!"

Scarcely breathing, and feeling safe as long as the Indian was unconscious, Jaimie got to her knees and crawled closer to get a better look. Thus far she had only seen Indians from a distance. What an opportunity to be able to see one up this close. And he would not even be aware of it. To Jaimie, Indians were a mystery; their lives and customs were so different from her own.

Her eyes widened when she saw a huge lump on his head, with blood seeping from it.

Her curiosity sent her gaze lower. There was no denying how handsome the Indian was with his aristocratic face, strong nose, and sharply chiseled features.

Her gaze moved still lower. He was strongly muscled; his bare copper chest was smooth and tapered down to a lean waist.

Her face grew hot with a blush when she saw the warrior's breechclout, a piece of clothing that did not cover much of the man's lower anatomy.

She felt as though she were trespassing on his

privacy by staring at his attire and jerked her eyes quickly elsewhere, to a small bag dangling from the waist of his breechclout.

Her fingers trembling, she dared to reach a hand over to the Indian and touch the small buckskin pouch. Her father had told her many tales of Indians before they had moved to Illinois. He had told her about Indian medicine bags which contained an Indian's special magic objects.

She wondered what might be inside this Indian's medicine bag. Feathers? Claws? Beaks? Or perhaps even some valuable precious stones?

Then her gaze shifted away and she gasped when she saw a huge knife sheathed at the Indian's waist at his right side. In her mind's eye she recalled having seen her father with the lethal knife wound in his belly. Could this be the very knife that had downed her father? she thought sullenly.

Was this Indian a cold-blooded murderer?

Without thinking, Jaimie grabbed the knife from the Indian's sheath and moved quickly to her feet. As she held the knife and stared down at the Indian, she was uncertain what to do.

She glanced over at the river as it roared and splashed by her. If the Indian wasn't moved soon, the water would drag him out into the river and he would drown.

Again she gazed at the man. She just couldn't leave him there for the river to swallow as it rose along its banks. She must do the humane thing and at least drag him to higher ground. Just like herself, he was a human being!

She would hope that if things were reversed, and he found *her* unconscious and at the mercy of a raging river, he would help *her*.

Yet she was afraid to become involved with Indians, especially if this one might have killed her father.

What if helping him brought more Indians to their homestead?

Would they think that Jaimie had hit the Indian over the head?

Surely they weren't versed in English well enough for Jaimie to make them understand that she had only found him, not harmed him.

She stared at the knife. She stared at the Indian. She stared at the river.

Her hands trembling, she replaced the knife in the warrior's sheath. She didn't want to be killed because she had taken the Indian's knife from him. He couldn't harm her with it while he was unconscious.

Her Christian upbringing guiding her every move now, Jaimie squatted down and tried to drag him away from the river, but she soon discovered that he was too heavy.

Not knowing what to do, she rose slowly to her feet. She decided that she had no choice but to go and get her sister's help. Maddy had never spoken against Indians. In fact, she was horrified that Farris Boyd had killed the great Sioux chief, Crazy Horse.

Maddy even defended Indians every time anyone mentioned that one of them might have killed Jaimie's and Maddy's father!

But Jaimie knew that Maddy just didn't want to believe that the Indians in this area were hostile. It made living near them easier. It made a person sleep better.

"Yes, Maddy will want to save this Indian's life," she whispered.

She ran along the riverbank until she saw her cabin through a break in the trees.

She stopped dead in her tracks when she saw Farris outside the cabin on his white stallion, talking to Maddy. Jaimie's spine stiffened and her eyes narrowed.

No!

She couldn't let Farris know about this Indian needing help. Farris might take delight in killing him as he had killed Crazy Horse!

And even if Farris didn't kill the Indian at first sight, it wasn't best to bring those two men together.

If the Indian survived his head wound and he knew that he was in the presence of Crazy Horse's killer, he wouldn't think twice about killing Farris when his strength returned.

And if either man shot the other, a full-scale war could break out between red and white-skinned people in this area.

A war was the last thing anyone needed.

Yes, it was up to Jaimie to do what she could

to prevent such a catastrophe as that. There had been enough killing.

Jaimie turned and ran back toward where she had left the Indian. When she got close enough to see him, she stopped short when she saw that he was conscious.

But she could tell that he was too weak and disoriented to stand when he tried and his knees buckled beneath him, sending him back down on the mud and rocks.

Her heart thudding, Jaimie inched closer to the Indian until she was standing over him.

When he raised his head and their eyes met and held, Jaimie knew almost for certain that this Indian was no one's enemy. She saw a deep kindness in his dark, unwavering eyes.

But she soon saw something else.

Pain!

Jaimie fell to her knees beside him. "I'm your friend," she said softly. "I want to help you."

She hoped that he could understand her. She scarcely breathed as she watched his hands, hoping that what she had read in his eyes was right . . . that he *was* a kind man . . . someone who would not go for his knife and try to kill her.

Black Wolf gazed with blurry eyes at the young white brave, glad that the boy did not see him as an enemy. Black Wolf needed someone he could trust, for he knew that he had lost much blood from his head wound. He was too weak to fend for himself.

He realized the danger of the river being so close. He felt lucky that he had not already died in its depths.

Grandfather in the sky was giving him a second chance!

"*Oh-oh-way-shee-chah?*" he said, reaching his fingers to the wet blood that covered the knot on his head, wincing when touching it sent sparks of pain through him.

"What?" Jaimie murmured, lifting her eyebrows. "What did you say? I . . . I . . . only speak English. Surely you know some of the language, for it is obvious that you know that I am not here to harm, but to help you."

"Young, friendly brave, I speak the English language well enough," Black Wolf said, slowly nodding. "I shall use it whenever possible when we are speaking to one another. I accept your friendship as I offer mine to you. Never fear me because of my skin color. I am *chah-shah-ee-yo-tahn.*"

"You are what?" Jaimie asked, again confused by his Indian language, yet recalling that he had called her a "brave," which meant that he thought she was a boy.

She wasn't insulted by his mistake.

But she would remedy his misconception when she didn't have so many other pressing things on her mind.

"I told you in my language that I am a man of honor, someone to be trusted," Black Wolf said. He closed his eyes and swallowed hard when his

34

head began a deep throbbing which made him feel dizzy and ill.

"What is your name? Mine is Jaimie. How is it that you are here?" Jaimie asked, finding it so exciting to be there with an Indian, actually talking with one.

More and more, Jaimie found it impossible to think that this Indian could have killed her father . . . unless he only played the role of an innocent, friendly man.

She had to remember that this might be possible and keep on her guard at all times while with the stranger.

"My name?" Black Wolf said, appearing to Jaimie to be searching inside his mind how to answer her.

Then he nodded and spoke. "I am *Oh-glah-lah-khchah*, Oglala Sioux," he said. "My name is Black Wolf. You ask what happened and how is it that I am here?"

Black Wolf inhaled a deep, nervous breath, then his eyes widened with remembrance. "My people," he gasped out, the blurring of his memory lessening, making him recall why he had been in the river, almost drowning in its depths.

He had been attempting to move his people from their island to safety!

"I . . . must . . . return to my people," he said, his fingers clawing at the ground as he tried to rise to his feet. "The river will soon swallow whole our island! The river threw me from my canoe and sent me away from my people!"

"Your island?" Jaimie said thickly. "Sioux? You are one of the Sioux who make their residence on the island downriver?"

Black Wolf scarcely heard what Jaimie was saying. He was desperate to get back on his feet and find his way back to his people!

But his knees were still too weak to hold him up for long. Again he crumpled back down to the ground, his eyes and head lowered in his grief.

"I don't think you know just how far the river carried you," Jaimie said, now understanding too well what had happened to this warrior.

She looked downriver, then bent down to her knees and placed a gentle hand on Black Wolf's cheek. "You're too weak to return now to your people," she said softly. "There are surely others there who will see that they are taken to higher ground, as I am here to see that *you* are taken to safety until you are stronger."

Black Wolf felt the warmth of the child's hand on his cheek and heard the compassion in his voice. He was touched deeply that a boy of this young age should care so much for someone of a different skin color. It made him realize that the young brave had not been raised by prejudiced parents who hated all men whose skin was red.

He raised his eyes to meet the pleading in Jaimie's as Jaimie lowered her hand from Black Wolf's cheek and placed it on his arm.

"Come on," Jaimie encouraged. "I must get

you far from this river. I know of a cave. I'll take you there. I'll then get matches for a fire, and blankets and food."

Black Wolf rose shakily to his feet and leaned against Jaimie as she slowly led him up the hill.

Jaimie cast a quick glance toward her cabin, which she could see through the cluster of trees they were walking beneath. She wanted to make sure Farris would not see what she was doing.

"How . . . much . . . farther . . . ?" Black Wolf asked, gasping as he slipped and fell to the ground.

On his knees, he hung his head, almost blinded by the pain in his head.

"Not far," Jaimie murmured, falling to her knees beside Black Wolf. She reached over and took his right hand. "Come on. It's so important that I get you to the cave before—"

She stopped short of saying that she was afraid that Farris might ride in this direction once he finished speaking with Maddy.

At all costs, Jaimie must not let Farris know about the Indian!

Black Wolf was aware that the child had not finished what he was saying, and he was astute enough to know that the child had stopped short on purpose.

At any other time Black Wolf would have pressed to learn what the boy had been about to say. But right now he was having moments of lightheadedness that threatened to send him back into the dark void of unconsciousness. All that was important at this moment was getting to the cave and resting.

All he wanted now was to close his eyes and escape from the pain that was overwhelming him.

He forced back a feeling of nausea, not wanting to humiliate himself by vomiting in front of the young brave. He was humiliated enough that he even needed the young brave's help.

His pulse racing, his whole body consumed by pain and weakness, Black Wolf forced himself back to his feet. He welcomed the arm of the child as Jaimie offered it to him, and once again they trudged slowly up the hill.

"We're almost there," Jaimie said, trying not to show just how hard it was to keep the Indian on his feet; his weight felt like a ton of stone against her small frame. Sheer willpower kept her going until she finally reached the cave.

"We've got some brush to go through at the mouth of the cave," Jaimie softly explained as briars plucked at her breeches when she helped Black Wolf through the undergrowth. She winced when she saw small streams of blood rolling down Black Wolf's bare legs from scratches made by the briars.

She breathed a sigh of relief as she finally got Black Wolf safely into the cave. She led him over to a spot where she had made many campfires.

Maddy was unaware that Jaimie had gone there many times to sit by the fire to enjoy thinking about the exciting stories her father had told her as they fished together. She had relished those moments alone in the cave, reliving cherished memories. Sometimes she missed her father so terribly much, her insides ached from loneliness.

"I'll not be gone for very long," she said, brushing everything from her mind but the business at hand.

She helped Black Wolf settle down on the cave floor beside the cold ashes where she would soon have a fire roaring to help warm the Indian's flesh. Then she hurried from the cave, hoping that Farris was no longer at the cabin.

Surely Maddy had sent him packing soon after his arrival.

That man was the last thing either of them wanted to be bothered with!

Especially now, now that a more interesting man had entered their lives, for Jaimie would show the Indian to Maddy. Surely Maddy would be as intrigued by Black Wolf as she!

Thinking about the Oglala warrior's handsomeness made Jaimie smile. "Maddy might be even more intrigued than I am by the Indian," she whispered, glad when the cabin came into view. But her smile faded when she saw that Farris was still there.

She stopped and hid behind a tree as she waited for him to leave.

When he finally did ride away, Jaimie noticed how fast he was going.

She smiled, knowing by his hasty exit that

Maddy had once again got the best of the arrogant, ugly man. She waited until he was out of sight, then rushed on toward the cabin, waving and shouting Maddy's name.

Chapter Four

Bards of Passion and of Mirth,
Ye have left your souls on earth!
Have ye souls in heaven, too,
Double lived in regions new?

—John Keats

Still too stunned by Farris's insistence that she marry him, Maddy was only scarcely aware of Jaimie shouting her name as she ran toward her. Maddy still stood at the door watching the point where Farris had disappeared over the crest of a hill.

The demands that Farris had made on her today frightened her so much, an uncontrollable shiver raced across her flesh. When Farris had said that she *must* marry him and she had flatly ignored him, he had said that as long as she and Jaimie lived alone, without the protection of a man, their lives could be in danger.

He had said that if the floods ruined the Indian villages in the area, there would be redskins everywhere seeking shelter. They could come and force themselves on Maddy and Jaimie.

When Maddy had stood her ground and told Farris that she wasn't afraid of Indians, or anyone, for that matter, Farris had laughed sarcastically and told her that she had neglected her history lessons if she didn't have enough sense to be afraid of redskin savages.

After Maddy had once again told Farris that she could fend well enough for herself, and that she most certainly didn't want the likes of him as a husband, he had finally ridden off so angry and humiliated that she knew this wasn't the last she would see of him.

He was not the sort of man to take no for an answer, or to let go of something he wanted.

"Maddy, why was Farris here?" Jaimie asked, running up to her, panting. She took a step away from her sister when she saw how pale and frightened she was. Jaimie knew that Farris was the cause.

"What'd he say to you this time, Sis?" Jaimie asked, almost afraid to hear the answer. Hate was not a strong enough word to use when describing her feelings for Farris Boyd. A persistent man, he had worn out his welcome long ago at Jaimie and Maddy's doorstep.

"He told me that I'd marry him or else, then rode off," Maddy said, still staring into the distance. "He warned me against Indians. He said that if they got flooded out and were forced to leave their homes, they might come and . . . and . . . take advantage of us."

Those words struck a chord of apprehension

in Jaimie's heart. Now she thought perhaps it was best *not* to mention Black Wolf, not just yet, anyhow. Not until Maddy was more settled, and her nerves restored.

"Where have you been, Jaimie?" Maddy asked, noticing that her sister had come from a direction other than the river. She noted, especially, the flush of her sister's cheeks.

"Where?" Jaimie said, fumbling with a frayed edge of one of her breeches pockets. "Oh, I was just checking things out, you know, the higher water. I could see better from the crest of the hill."

"Oh, I see," Maddy said, again sighing. She gave Jaimie a soft gaze. "Jaimie, you've got to be careful going so far from home. Never . . . never . . . forget what happened to Father. You can't trust strangers as easily as we used to . . . before Father was killed."

"Yes, I know," Jaimie said, swallowing hard. She looked over her shoulder in the direction of the cave where she had left the Indian. *He* was a stranger. Worse than that, he was an Indian, yet she wanted to help him.

She just hoped that Maddy would, also. Jaimie had felt a sudden bonding with the warrior. She wasn't afraid of him.

"Hurry inside, Jaimie," Maddy said. "We've things to do."

Jaimie followed Maddy into the cabin. Her eyes widened when she saw all of the packed boxes.

She gave Maddy a slow look. "Sis, are you lettin' that pipsqueak of a man scare you from our home?" she asked warily. "Are you runnin' from Farris?"

"No, sweetie," Maddy said, giving Jaimie a smile across her shoulder as she wrapped the last piece of her beautiful china, which had been her mother's prized possession, in a dishcloth. "I'd never let that man force me out of my home. It's the river, Jaimie. We must get to higher ground, and *now*. If the river continues to rise at such a rapid rate, our cabin will soon be under water. We must save as much as we can."

Jaimie helped pack more boxes, then ran to the barn and hitched her bay gelding to a buckboard wagon, tied Maddy's strawberry roan to the wagon, and then their lone cow, and hurried them back to the cabin.

Huffing and puffing, Jaimie and Maddy loaded their belongings into the wagon . . . even managed to balance and tie the small fishing boat on the top, then took one last look at the cabin before leaving for the cave.

"It's so sad that we have to leave it," Jaimie murmured, tears filling her eyes. "Pa put so much of himself into building it. So did we, Maddy. Remember how Pa made building fun instead of a chore? I can still hear his jokes . . . and his laughter."

"Me too, Jaimie, but Pa should've known never to build this close to the river," Maddy said solemnly. "I wondered about it at the time, but

I never openly questioned anything Pa did, so I didn't say anything to him."

"Sis, everything will be all right," Jaimie reassured her. "We'll build a new home on higher ground when this is all over. You'll see. Things will work out for us. Together, you and I, we'll make our new home something even more special than this one."

"But it won't hold the memories of Ma and Pa like this cabin does," Maddy said. A sob lodged in her throat as, in her mind's eye, she recalled the happier times right after they had arrived from Kentucky and everything was new and exciting for the family.

She would never forget how when the cabin was so fresh and new and smelling of cedar, they would all sit beside the fire eating popcorn, and how she and Jaimie would take turns playing checkers with their father while their mother sat contentedly close by, embroidering.

All of those wonderful nights had been shattered when their mother had given birth to a stillborn son, and then followed him to the grave.

"Come on," Maddy said, her voice thick with emotion. She climbed onto the wagon seat, watching Jaimie hop onto the seat beside her. "Let's get to that cave, Jaimie. We can get a fire built and spread our blankets beside it."

Maddy forced a nervous laugh as she slapped the reins, which sent the bay gelding into a trot toward the hill a short distance away. "Jaimie, we can pretend it's a picnic, can't we?" she said. "I've brought enough food to last a lifetime."

Jaimie gave Maddy a nervous glance, then scarcely breathed as they came closer and closer to the cave. She hoped now that Black Wolf was gone. It would make things much easier for Jaimie and Maddy, especially if Farris came back again looking for Maddy. Jaimie just couldn't allow Farris to see the Indian!

Jaimie didn't understand why, but she felt a strange sort of bond with the Sioux warrior. She most certainly didn't want to see harm come to him.

One thing was in their favor. As far as Jaimie knew, Farris didn't know about the cave. And it was large enough to take the wagon inside it, as well as the animals. When she had explored it that first time, after making a torch from dried grass and twigs, she had found just how far the cave went back into the ground . . . so far she hadn't walked its full length.

There was even a small stream that ran along one side of the cave, which would yield as much water as they needed to survive from day to day.

Finally at the mouth of the cave, Jaimie still said nothing to Maddy about Black Wolf. She crossed the fingers of both of her hands behind her back, wishing Black Wolf had improved enough to be on his way, although knowing that if this were true, she would search for him when the flood was over. She would find him and make his acquaintance again under more favorable circumstances.

She could envision him now . . . the surprise in his eyes . . . when she told him that she was a girl instead of a boy!

That thought made her smile as Maddy stopped the horse just outside of the cave and jumped from the seat.

"Let's get this done, Jaimie," Maddy said, trying to see through a strand of hair that had fallen across her eyes.

She glanced heavenward and grimaced when she discovered that the black clouds, heavy with rain, were now overhead.

She jumped when a lurid streak of lightning ran in a quick zigzag from cloud to cloud, erupting in loud crashes of thunder.

"Hurry!" Maddy cried, leaning against the wind as they carried their fishing boat up beneath trees only a few feet from the cave and secured it with a rope wound around one of the trunks.

Maddy then carried the first box through the thicket of briars into the cave, wincing as the sharp prickers grabbed at the skirt of her dress.

Jaimie quickly followed with another armload, her heart thumping as she waited to see if Black Wolf was still there.

She had promised to return and build him a warm fire.

Never had she thought that she would be

bringing more than matches and blankets with her!

Maddy used her feet to find her way in the darkness. "We've got to get a lamp lit," she cried, feeling slowly around with her feet. "Hurry, Jaimie. We must be able to see what we're doing and we must get it done before the rain begins and ruins everything in the wagon."

The sky was now so dark it seemed more like midnight than afternoon, making it impossible for Jaimie to see whether Black Wolf was still there.

Her heart thudded like a sledgehammer inside her chest as she took a kerosene lamp from the box she had carried into the cave.

Jaimie grumbled to herself as she fumbled around inside the box for the kitchen matches, sighing with relief when she finally found them.

Her pulse raced as she took the chimney from the lamp and screwed the wick up into place, then struck the match and placed it to the kerosene-soaked wick.

The sharp gasp behind her from her sister was enough for Jaimie to know that the light from the match was enough for Maddy to see the Indian stretched out, unconscious, on the floor of the cave. He was so close to her feet that if she had gone another inch she would have tripped over him.

"My Lord, Jaimie!" Maddy cried as she stared at the man. "It's . . . an . . . Indian! And, Jaimie, he looks *dead*. Look at the blood in his hair.

Oh, Lord, see the large lump on his head!"

In a rush of words Jaimie told Maddy about Black Wolf, how she had found him, and how she had helped him to the cave.

"He's not dead, Sis," Jaimie said, falling to her knees beside Black Wolf. "But he *is* unconscious."

Her heart sank to see Black Wolf's helplessness, realizing how shallow his breathing was.

Still too startled to move, her heart thumping wildly within her chest, Maddy studied the Indian, her gaze becoming fixed when she saw the huge knife sheathed at his waist.

In her mind's eye she was recalling the knife wound in her father's abdomen.

Although she had never truly thought an Indian responsible, here was an Indian close to their home with a knife in his possession!

"Jaimie, *hurry*! Take his knife," Maddy said.

She glanced at Jaimie as her sister gave her a quick look but made no move to do as she was told.

"Jaimie, good Lord, did you hear what I said?" Maddy screeched. "Take the knife from the Indian!"

A visible shudder ran through Maddy. "That might be the very knife that killed Father," she said. "No other Indian has been seen this close to our house."

"Sis, that's because the river never delivered one to our doorstep before," Jaimie softly argued.

"Jaimie, this isn't the time to be stubborn," Maddy said, her jaw tightening. She took the lantern from Jaimie and held it closer to the Indian. "Take the Indian's knife."

"Sis, I think it's best to leave it where it is," Jaimie said.

She proceeded to tell Maddy how she had earlier grabbed Black Wolf's knife, and then, on second thought, returned it to his sheath, and why.

"If we disarm him, his friends might blame us for attacking him, should they come looking for him," Jaimie murmured. "Although no knife has been used on him, they might think we hit him over the head with something and *then* disarmed him. It's best to look as though we helped, not harmed him."

"Maybe you're right," Maddy said, her fear having given way to curiosity the more she looked down at Black Wolf.

Maddy set the lantern down, then moved to her knees beside Black Wolf.

Gingerly she touched his head wound, then drew her hand away from him and gazed at his face.

The flames of the lantern wafted a soft, golden glow on Black Wolf's copper face, and Maddy could not deny just how handsome he was with his sculpted features and hooded eyes like an eagle's. His arms were muscled and big like two oak trees!

When her gaze swept lower and she saw how

scantily he was dressed, in only a brief breech-clout and moccasins, she felt the heat of a blush rush into her cheeks.

Seeing that her sister was as mesmerized by Black Wolf's unique handsomeness as she had been herself, Jaimie fell to her knees beside her. "Sis, his name is Black Wolf," she murmured. "He is an Oglala Sioux. He's from the island downriver. While he was helping move his people from the island to higher ground, his canoe capsized. He was sent swiftly down the current. I found him unconscious on the riverbank. I . . . I . . . saw his helplessness, and when he awakened, and I discovered that he was no threat to us, I brought him to the cave. Sis, we must help him. The short time we talked, I discovered that he is an honorable, trustworthy man. When I look at him I don't even see the color of his skin. I see a man . . . in trouble."

"You listened well in your Sunday school classes when Mrs. Pratt taught us that the color of the skin doesn't matter, that it is the heart that one must pay attention to," Maddy said, reaching over to draw Jaimie into her arms. "I'm proud of you, little sister, so very proud of you."

"Then we will take care of him?" Jaimie asked, drawing away from Maddy to look her directly in the eyes. "We will give him food? We will share our blankets and fire with him until he is well enough to return to his people?"

"Yes, we will do all of that, and even more," Maddy said, again gazing at Black Wolf, who

51

looked so innocent and childlike as he lay there unconscious. "I shall also see to his wound."

"Thank you, Sis," Jaimie said, easing back into Maddy's arms and giving her a fierce hug. "Oh, thank you."

"You said he is a Sioux?" Maddy said, stroking her fingers through her sister's short red hair.

"Yes, Oglala," Jaimie said, enjoying the pampering from her sister for the moment, because soon there would be no time for such hugs and simple conversation. These next few days would test their true ability to survive.

They would also have to find ways to keep Farris from knowing where they were.

She smiled as she remembered the pirate books she had read by the fire. Pirates sometimes made their hideouts in caves such as this. Some even left their trunks filled with jewels and money hidden in caves.

Then her thoughts wandered to the books she had read about reckless outlaws who also sought such caves for their hideouts.

She would make believe that this was hers and Maddy's hideout . . . and also Black Wolf's!

"Jaimie, remember Farris bragging about slaughtering so many Sioux, especially Crazy Horse, who was said to be the greatest chief of all?" Maddy said, feeling Jaimie stiffening in her arms at the mention of Crazy Horse. "Jaimie, since this man is a Sioux, we must make certain that Farris never knows about him being here. While Black Wolf is so disabled, he would not be able to defend himself against such a man as Farris, who'd surely kill him at first sight."

Jaimie nodded.

"Jaimie, we must get Black Wolf well and gone *soon*," Maddy said.

She prayed to herself that she wasn't making a mistake in helping the Indian.

What if he *was* the one who'd killed her father?

She shook that thought from her mind almost as quickly as it entered. "We must hurry now, Jaimie, and get the rest of the things in the cave," she said, gently shoving Jaimie away from her.

"And also the wagon and the animals," Jaimie said, running with Maddy from the cave. "We must keep them hidden from Farris."

"But where?" Maddy asked, hugging herself against the force of the wind as it whipped around her. She felt the first drop of rain on her face.

"I've studied the cave before today," Jaimie said, grabbing the reins. "It's huge, Sis. Huge enough to house not only us, but the wagon and the animals. Come on. We'll take everything in the cave at once, then unload the wagon at our leisure instead of rushing to do it before the rain comes."

"But the briars?" Maddy said, shoving her hair back from her face as the wind whipped it across. "I hate to tear the horses' flesh."

"Better a few scratches than leaving them outside for Farris to find," Jaimie said, already leading the bay gelding toward the cave entrance. "Come on, Sis. This is the best way."

Maddy laughed softly. "Jaimie, so often you amaze me," she said, walking beside her sister into the cave. "Sometimes you seem older than me."

"Maddy, only when it comes to decisions that have nothing to do with housework or cooking," Jaimie said, smiling over at her. "I listened to Pa's teachings about the outdoors while you listened to Ma's about things indoors. That's where the difference lies, Sis."

"Always before, I felt you were wrong not to want to learn things women need to know about housekeeping and cooking," Maddy said, the lamplight revealing to her that the Indian was still unconscious. "But now? I welcome the differences between us."

They worked together and soon had a fire built, then began unloading the wagon before taking it and the animals farther into the cave.

While they labored together, Maddy kept looking at Black Wolf. Her throat tightened with a fear she did not wish to feel when she thought she saw a slight movement in his closed eyes.

Was he awakening?

If so, how would he react when he discovered that things had changed in the cave since he had last been awake?

For certain he would not expect someone to be setting up housekeeping!

Chapter Five

Nymph of the downward smile and sidelong
  glance,
In what diviner moments of the day
Art thou most lovely?

—John Keats

Slowly emerging from his unconscious state,
Black Wolf heard voices speaking softly somewhere near him. In flashes of memory he recalled the white boy and how the young brave
had befriended him.

The child had left the cave to get matches for
a fire, blankets, and food. He had returned, and
with him he had brought the things he'd promised. Black Wolf sensed the comfort of a blanket
on his body, the warmth of a fire, and the smell
of food.

Black Wolf was keenly aware that the child
had brought more than those things to the cave.
Someone had come with him. One of the voices
Black Wolf now heard belonged to a woman.

Black Wolf was skilled at interpreting voices

and inferring what kind of person they belonged to, whether the person speaking was of a kind and gentle nature or someone who was deceitful and not to be trusted.

This woman's voice came to him in soft, gentle tones, which meant that the one speaking was surely as trustworthy and kind as the child. Her speech was lilting like music. And when it was mingled with laughter, it seemed to reach deep inside Black Wolf's heart, bringing his eyes slowly open so that he could see the face that belonged to the voice.

Although his head was throbbing unmercifully, Black Wolf could see well enough. His eyes focused on a lovely, petite white woman with long, flowing golden hair and brilliant, friendly green eyes.

He also saw that the woman was slight in build. She was so tiny that she looked almost fragile.

By the light of the fire he could see the exquisite features of her face. Pinkish in complexion, it was oval in shape, with perfectly sculpted lips and a nose that was tiny and slightly turned up at the end.

Her green eyes were widely set and somewhat slanted, with a fringe of thick lashes above them.

When she laughed again, ah so softly and gently, she revealed to Black Wolf straight, white teeth.

His gaze swept slowly lower and he noted how she was dressed. Like the other white women he'd seen, she wore a simple cotton frock that reached to the floor. He knew that beneath that dress was skin that would be as soft as a rose petal, and breasts ample enough for a man's hands to cradle.

Again he silently observed how the woman and the child behaved toward one another. He could tell by the way they spoke to one another that there was much respect and love between them. He had to believe that this woman was the boy's sister. She was not old enough to have mothered a child his age.

The closeness he witnessed between the woman and child made him think of another brother and sister, which brought the heartache he always felt when he thought of his beloved sister.

Many years ago, his people had learned by harsh experience that the *wasichos* were not to be trusted. At first they had foolishly believed they could peacefully coexist with the white pony soldiers. After a cavalry officer had taken it upon himself to send his soldiers into battle with the Sioux in a surprise attack on Black Wolf's village, everything changed. That day Black Wolf's ten-year-old *tahn-kah*, younger sister, had died in Black Wolf's arms, a pony soldier's bullet in her breast.

A sudden panic grabbed Black Wolf's heart when he thought of his people and the pain they were experiencing today. This time it was not the *wasichos*, but Mother Nature who had betrayed them by sending ravages of water to their new homeland.

Had his people succeeded in getting across the river before the storm hit in its full fury?

He was aware now of great blasts of thunder outside that shook the cave floor beneath him. At the cave entrance he could see great bursts of light from the lightning, and sheets of rain so thick he could scarcely see beyond it.

It was now even hailing, the great balls of frozen ice bouncing just inside the cave's entrance.

In his mind's eye Black Wolf could see the island being swallowed whole by the river. He could see his people at the mercy of the river and the rain without adequate shelter.

Guilt flooded him that he was dry and safe in the cave beside a warm fire, with food cooking that would surely be offered to him.

As he tried to lean on an elbow to get up, he became quickly aware of his weakness. He fell back to the floor in terrible pain. He fought back the groans that came with pain. He did not want to appear weak to the woman and child!

Maddy heard movement behind her.

She turned and her breath was momentarily stolen away when she discovered that Black Wolf was awake. Their eyes met and held. Something strange happened to Maddy in that instant and it had nothing to do with fear.

Instead, she was mesmerized by the Indian's deep, dark eyes.

She shook herself quickly from her reverie, reminding herself that their two worlds were vastly different in all respects. When they came in contact, his people and hers always collided, the Indians usually coming out of the collision the losers.

No white woman could ever dare trust an Indian, for surely their resentment toward all whites ran deep.

And although Maddy truly doubted it, she must always remember that this Indian *might* be guilty of having killed her father!

Yet he was human and he was injured. She could never turn her back on anyone in trouble, no matter what the color of his skin.

Her pulse racing, Maddy went to Black Wolf and knelt down beside him. "How are you feeling?" she asked softly, her gaze going to his head wound. The blood was now dried and caked in his hair, but at least it was no longer flowing freely from the wound.

Black Wolf was uncertain about how to react to this woman's apparent interest in him when he had not dealt with any *wasicho* for many years now, except when forced to trade for supplies to help sustain his people through harsh times.

His people had always been self-sufficient before the arrival of the *wasichos* in their homeland. Since then, the Sioux had been forced to depend increasingly on *wasichos* for their survival, especially after the slaughter of the vast herds of buffalo that had supplied so many of the essentials of life to the Sioux.

Now, Black Wolf was so weak he could not even stand up to return to his people, and he was at the mercy of the *wasichos*, but this time it was different. This woman and her brother did not seem to hold hate in their hearts. They had had nothing to do with the past atrocities against his people.

"You can speak English, can't you?" Maddy asked, her eyes once again locked with Black Wolf's.

"Sis, he can speak English as well as you and I," Jaimie said, coming to kneel down beside her. "Black Wolf, why aren't you answering my sister? You know that we are your friends."

"Yes, friends," Black Wolf said, his voice drawn. "I do see you as friends."

"How are you?" Maddy asked, finding his deep, masculine voice as appealing as his handsomeness. "Does your wound hurt you very much?"

"The pain in my head is not what concerns me," Black Wolf said, glancing at the cave entrance and seeing that the rain was still falling in thick sheets.

He looked again into Maddy's eyes. "The true pain is here," he said, placing a hand over his heart. "I hurt for my people. Once again land has been taken from them, but this time not by the hands of the *wasichos*, but instead by the river. By now it surely covers the island upon which my people trustingly made their homes."

"I'm sorry," Maddy murmured, his pain, sorrow, and regret touching her deeply.

She looked toward the cave entrance. "I believe by now Jaimie and I have also lost our home," she said sadly.

She nodded toward all that lay around inside the cave. "What we were able to save is all that is left of our belongings," she murmured.

Then she looked again into Black Wolf's eyes. "But that is nothing to compare to what happened to your people," she murmured. "So many homes were lost to you. Not only one cabin."

"*Hetchetu-aloh*, that is so," Black Wolf said solemnly. "Black Wolf's title of chief is not powerful enough to hold back a river."

"You are a chief?" Maddy asked, her eyes wide.

She looked him quickly up and down, then gazed at him in puzzlement. "I thought elders of Indian tribes were chiefs," she said guardedly. "You . . . you . . . can't be more than twenty-five years old."

"You judge age well," Black Wolf said, finding it good to have cause to smile. "But add three winters to the age you guessed and you will have my true age."

"You are twenty-eight?" Maddy murmured.

"Yes, and you are . . . ?" he asked, more and more captivated by this lovely, gentle woman.

"Nineteen," Maddy said.

For a moment everything became quiet in the

cave as Maddy and Black Wolf seemed to enter a trance while gazing into one another's eyes.

Jaimie saw the strange fascination forming between her sister and the Indian and was not sure how to feel about it.

She leaned quickly closer to Maddy and broke the spell. "I am ten," she said to Black Wolf. "But Pa always said that I behave as though I am much older."

"Pa?" Black Wolf said. "What is the meaning of this word 'pa'?"

He was glad to have cause to think of something besides the woman, for it was not right to allow himself to have special feelings for her. He had vowed long ago not to become infatuated with a woman, *any* woman, white *or* red-skinned, until he was much older, so that he could direct all of his faculties only toward his people's welfare.

But never had this decision been challenged inside his heart as it was being challenged now. This woman, whose eyes seemed to reach clean into his soul, was bringing sensations alive inside him that he had forced to remain dormant for too long.

"When I speak of Pa, I speak of our father," Jaimie said.

"Where is your *ahte*, your father?" Black Wolf asked, looking from Maddy to Jaimie. "Where is your mother? You said that you have come to the cave to escape the river. Are your parents coming later?"

He saw how those questions seemed to bring much sadness into the eyes of both the woman and the child. It was the same sort of look he probably wore when someone asked him about his parents, who were no longer alive.

Maddy felt uncertain how to answer him; for a brief moment she thought it was safer to make this Indian believe that she and Jaimie weren't alone in the world.

Yet she quickly felt it was wrong to think this way about Black Wolf. He had given them no reason not to trust him.

But how could he? she argued with herself. He was disabled by a head wound.

But after he was well, what then?

"Pa and Ma are both dead," Jaimie rushed out, drawing a quick look from Maddy.

Jaimie glanced down at the knife that was exposed where the blanket on Black Wolf was folded away from it.

Then she looked solemnly at Black Wolf. "Pa was murdered," she said softly. "Ma died while giving birth to a child."

Maddy wanted to scold Jaimie for being so open with a perfect stranger, yet it was done and there was nothing that could be said to change it.

She gazed at Black Wolf to see his reaction to this information about her family. Did he see their vulnerability as useful to him? Or did he sympathize with them at being orphaned?

"*Hoon-hoon-hay*, my heart is heavy over you

and your brother's loss," Black Wolf said, directing his words to Maddy. "I, more than once, have suffered such losses. Not only are my parents now in the spirit world, but also my beloved sister."

"Oh, I'm so very sorry," Maddy said softly; then she looked quickly over at Jaimie as she realized that Black Wolf had referred to her as a boy.

She smiled at Black Wolf as she slid an arm around her sister's shoulders and drew her closer. "Jaimie isn't a boy," she murmured. "She is my *sister*."

Black Wolf leaned on an elbow, his eyes raking slowly over Jaimie. "*Tahn-kah*? She is your *tahn-kah*, younger sister? A girl who wears boy's clothes?" he said wonderingly. "A girl whose hair is cut even shorter than Sioux braves and warriors wear their hair?"

"It is Jaimie's preference to wear such clothes," Maddy said, sighing deeply. "And I foolishly agreed to her taking scissors to her hair."

"In time the hair will grow back," Black Wolf said, cringing when a blast of thunder echoed through the cave and streaks of lightning flashed at the cave entrance.

Exhausted from talking, and weary with worry about his people, Black Wolf had no choice but to lie back down. For certain he wasn't going anywhere. His legs would not hold him up just yet.

But just as Jaimie's hair would grow back, so would the strength return to his legs. He was a strong, virile man who had always exercised often to keep his body vigorous.

"I can see that you are tired," Maddy said, pushing herself up from the floor. "Just lie there and rest. Soon supper will be ready. And of all the belongings I brought to the cave, I made sure my first aid kit was among them. I'll bathe your wound and then medicate it."

"Why are you and your sister being so kind to a red man . . . someone most *wasichos* hate?" Black Wolf dared to ask, touched deeply by their caring.

"You have used this word *wasichos* more than once," Maddy said guardedly. "What does it mean?"

"*Wasichos* means whites," Black Wolf said blandly.

"I see," Maddy murmured, then once again knelt down beside him. Their eyes held as she tried to explain her feelings to him.

"I'm not familiar with your religion, but my religion is taught from a book we call the Bible," she said. "In the scriptures it is said that all people should be treated the same, that all people are as one people in the eyes of the Lord. The color of the skin does not matter. The Bible teaches that everyone should love one another. It speaks against warring and prejudice."

"The talking leaves of your Bible hold much wisdom. What it says makes it a good book,"

Black Wolf said, his eyes drifting closed as his weariness consumed him. "*Ee-shtee-mah*, sleep. I must sleep."

"Here's the first aid kit, Sis," Jaimie said as she came to Maddy with a small black bag. "I'll go and get fresh water from the stream at the back of the cave. Also, I'll check on the horses to see if they are restless."

"Then, Jaimie, when you return you might bring Black Wolf a bowl of vegetable soup," Maddy murmured, opening the bag and taking gauze and tubes of ointment from it.

Black Wolf's eyes opened and Maddy saw that again they locked with hers. "I think Black Wolf would rest much more comfortably if he ate before he went to sleep," she said softly.

Jaimie nodded and rushed away, soon returning with a basin of water.

As Maddy gently washed the blood from Black Wolf's hair, she was keenly aware of his eyes still watching her.

Her heart raced under such close scrutiny from such a handsome and virile man.

For the first time in her life she was familiar with how it felt to desire a man! She tried to fight this strange wanting, but the longer she was with him, the deeper it went inside her heart.

She was glad when she had finished medicating his wound and Jaimie took over, slowly spooning vegetable soup between Black Wolf's willing lips.

Maddy took this opportunity to be alone with

her thoughts and strange mood. As she stood at the entrance of the cave, gazing down toward their home, and now seeing only the roof peeking through the rain, tears filled her eyes.

She turned and gazed at Black Wolf as Jaimie continued to feed him soup. She hugged herself and trembled sensually, knowing that they were going to be thrown together for some time before the river started receding.

A thrill soared through her at the thought of being with Black Wolf like this yet she knew that once they left the cave, they would part and go their separate ways. She wasn't sure now if her life would ever be the same again . . . not after having met Black Wolf.

She turned quickly and gazed at the rain and thought of her parents' and brother's graves, thankful that they were located on high enough ground not to be threatened by the flood waters. She wouldn't allow herself to believe that Black Wolf could have killed her father. He seemed too kind . . . too compassionate, unless it was a clever ploy to make her and Jaimie trust him!

Chapter Six

O! Let me have thee whole, all—all—be
    mine!
That shape, that fairness!
               —John Keats

The rain was still falling hard as Farris Boyd
scrambled to the roof of the jail in River Town.
He reached it just in time to keep from being
swept away in the wild current of the Ohio
River.

Panting, the color drained from his face and
water dripping from his black suit, Farris stood
on the roof. Even now the river was lapping dangerously around it.

Hardly able to believe what he was seeing, he
watched people float past in the river, screaming, their eyes wild.

Small boats were everywhere, with people
plucking loved ones and belongings from the
water.

No one had realized the true danger of the rising water. Only now did the townspeople begin to understand the devastation it could wreak on their small community.

Nor had Farris envisioned anything like this when he had moved to this small river town. It had seemed a perfect place to sink his roots, to take up residence, a place where it had been easy to pretend to be the perfect gentlemen so that he could acquire the title of sheriff without much of a fight.

After having seen Maddy on the streets of River Town, and then on Sundays in the town's pretty little Baptist church, he had known that he had come to the right place at the right time to find the perfect woman to be his wife.

And he would do anything now to have her.

Anything!

He had just returned to the jail after Maddy's refusal to marry him when the river had come crashing over the banks of River Town, soon consuming the small community as though it were its dinner.

Farris had paid no heed to how much the water had risen when he had ridden into town, his thoughts too filled with Maddy and how foolish she was to reject his offer of marriage.

She had so little.

He had so *much*.

Having brought his inherited riches with him from the sale of his late father's vast Louisiana plantation, and filling his mansion with the valuable possessions of his late mother, Farris had thought that it would be easy to persuade . . . to *lure* . . . some lovely lady into sharing it all with him.

When he had seen Maddy that first time, walking down the main street of River Town, he had thought he was looking at some lovely vision. Surely no woman could be as pretty and delicate as Madeline Penrod!

He had begun to pursue her that very moment as he went to offer to help her with her armful of packages. She had accepted his help and had even seemed interested in him at first, but he had known the very moment her feelings had changed . . . when he had bragged about his killings during the war, how he had willingly entered the Indian villages and killed whoever stood on two feet, women and children as well as the warriors.

Still, he had not given up on Maddy. He had even gone far beyond what was normal to have her.

He had murdered her father so that she would feel helpless without any man to help fend for her and her younger sister. Still she ignored him as though he were the plague. But now? If she lost everything in the flood? He smiled to think that finally she would be at his mercy.

The trembling of the small, weak building beneath Farris's feet brought him from his deep thoughts. Then, moments later, when he heard the creaking of the timbers of the jail and felt it shifting, panic seized Farris.

He began waving his hands and shouting to be rescued.

All but one person ignored him, for most who had learned to know his true character thought him a violent man obsessed with killing. He had bragged too much about how he enjoyed massacring whole villages of Indians. He always ended each tale with the grisly description of how it had felt to sink the bayonet of his gun into Chief Crazy Horse's body.

Only recently had he realized that no one listened anymore.

Kenneth Clark, Farris's deputy, fought the raging current as he edged his boat close to the roof of the jail.

"Come on, Farris!" he shouted, his muscles straining as he tried to keep his boat steady. "Jump in! I'll get you to higher ground!"

Slipping and sliding as he inched his way down the steep angle of the wet, slippery roof, Farris kept his eye on the small boat. The rain slammed against his face; the wind threatened to topple him sideways.

"Hold it steady, Kenneth!" he shouted. "Damn it, hold . . . it . . . steady!"

His feet slid from beneath him, sending him rolling the rest of the way down the roof; luckily, he landed in the boat.

He accepted Kenneth's hand and was soon sitting behind him and holding on for dear life as his deputy rowed toward the hill at the far edge of town, where others had gone to seek safety.

Finally on higher ground, where people were standing in clusters in the rain, silently watching everything they owned being swallowed whole by the river, Farris jumped from the boat and stood apart from the others.

Trembling from the chill, he too, stared dumbfoundedly at the lost, drowned town.

"I'm goin' to go help find others who are stranded!" Kenneth shouted at Farris over his shoulder, already moving back toward deeper water in his boat.

Not offering to help, Farris nodded.

All that Farris could think about was Maddy. Had she gotten to higher ground in time? Or had she drowned along with so many other people?

Hardly able to stand such a thought, Farris ran with his limping gait through the crowd toward the horses that had been rescued. He was glad when he found his proud steed among the horses. He grabbed the reins of his white stallion and swung himself into the saddle.

Ducking his head against the fierce winds and rain, he rode off in the direction of Maddy's house. He knew that she couldn't actually be in her cabin, for if River Town was covered by water, her house would be, too.

He wondered where Maddy and Jaimie might have gone to seek shelter? He would search until he found them.

He smiled when he thought of how it would be when he approached Maddy with the offer of his home again. He could just imagine how eagerly she would say yes to him when she thought of the home he had described to her countless times.

Yes, she would be anxious to get out of the weather, the darkness of night. She would willingly go with him to his home, which stood high above the flood line . . . a home that offered warmth, good food, clean, beautiful, dry clothes that had been his mother's, and a comfortable, luscious feather bed.

His loins grew hot as he envisioned how Maddy would look in a sheer chemise as she sank slowly into the feathers of the bed. Her golden hair would be hanging in lovely waves down her back as she held her hands out to beckon him to join her there.

Yes, surely she would be so grateful to him for rescuing her from a cold, wet night without a roof over her head that she would willingly pay him back for his services.

"I want only one thing for payment, Maddy," he shouted into the wind. "You! Your luscious body!"

He looked overhead.

Night was falling, soon to cover the river valley with its cloak of black.

"Damn it, now I'm going to have a hell of a time finding her," he grumbled to himself.

He sank his heels into the flanks of his horse and pushed his steed at a harder gallop along the higher, drier land.

"I *will* find her," he whispered to himself. "No

rain, no flood waters, nothing will stand in my way. I will have her tonight in my bed."

His patience had run out, and if Maddy wouldn't go willingly to his house, by God, he would force her at gunpoint.

He shrugged idly, thinking that even if he did have to force Maddy, in the end she would be grateful, for no amount of telling her about his home was anything like actually seeing and living in it.

Yes, she would feel as though she were a princess who had been offered a place on the throne beside her king!

Laughing raucously, he rode onward.

Chapter Seven

I fear thy kisses, gentle maiden,
Thou needest not fear mine;
My spirit is too deeply laden
Ever to burthen thine.

—Percy Bysshe Shelley

Maddy paced at the entrance of the cave. Night had fallen and still it rained. The water was even now creeping higher toward the cave. Should the water reach the cave, everything Maddy owned would be destroyed. She would be forced to leave it behind and scurry for even higher ground. The only higher ground that was left nearby was the cemetery.

Maddy glanced over her shoulder at Jaimie, who was sitting with Black Wolf, asking him about his people.

She was touched that Black Wolf didn't seem to mind being quizzed by a curious ten-year-old.

In fact, her curiosity seemed to be helping him get past these troubled moments by speaking of his people. There was pride in his voice as he talked about them.

"My people's warriors only began to fight the *wasichos* when we realized that the hoop of the Sioux nation was broken and there was no longer a center. Fighting was required or the Sioux would disappear as had the buffalo," Black Wolf said. In his mind he was recalling much of his past, and it made his heart ache.

"Black Wolf, himself, too often saw the *wasichos'* fire boats float down the Missouri River loaded with dried bison tongues," he said sadly. "The rest of the bodies had been left to rot in the sun."

Black Wolf stared into the flames of the fire as he continued to talk, not only to Jaimie, but to himself, and perhaps the ghosts of his past.

"The Sioux's cause then became a righteous one," he said thickly. "It was for the preservation of our race." He gave Jaimie a slow gaze. "For this the Sioux are being put down in history as the most warlike of all tribes."

"What did you mean by saying the Sioux's hoop was broken?" Jaimie asked, inching even closer to Black Wolf. "What sort of hoop?"

"Everything an Indian does is in a circle, and that is because the Power of the World always works in circles and everything tries to be round," Black Wolf softly explained, feeling other eyes on him as he spoke of things that needed to be said. He wanted this child and this child's sister to understand about him and his people.

Even if their relationship did not go beyond this cave, he would forever be a part of their memories and hearts. They might spread the truth about his people. Most *wasichos* ignored the Sioux. Whenever the Sioux and *wasichos* had met in council, it had been as though the Sioux were speaking to a wall that had no life . . . no feelings. The Sioux's words had just floated away in the wind, worthless!

He looked up and found Maddy gazing at him, a look of savage wonder in her expression as their eyes met and held.

This woman caused the beat of Black Wolf's heart to become like distant thunder in his ears. He could feel the throbbing in his chest.

A part of him wanted to jump up and run away from such feelings. Another part of him wanted to reach his arms out for her and comfort her and tell her that with the changes in her life today came hope.

He had learned long ago that if there was a tomorrow, there was always hope. One just had to learn how to reach for it and grab it one day at a time!

"Tell me more," Jaimie said, glancing from Black Wolf to Maddy, noticing once again the strange way they looked at one another. She had to believe it was the fascination two people from different cultures felt for one another.

Nothing more.

Not unless this was how people behaved who were fascinated with one another for other reasons . . . like a man and a woman who were discovering intimate feelings for each other!

Jaimie's voice drew Black Wolf from his reverie, and he looked quickly away from Maddy, but his heart continued to throb. He forced himself not to envision this delicate, beautiful woman in his arms, his lips exploring hers, his hands filled with her breasts. . . .

"In the old days, when the Sioux were a strong and happy people, all our power came to us from the sacred hoop of the nation, and so long as the hoop was unbroken, the people flourished," Black Wolf said, focusing his thoughts and eyes elsewhere . . . on the dancing flames of the campfire instead of the woman who still watched him.

"The flowering tree was the living center of the hoop, and the circle of the four quarters nourished it," he went on. "The east gave peace and light. The south gave warmth. The west gave rain. And the north, with its cold and mighty wind, gave strength and endurance. This knowledge came to us from our religion."

He smiled over at Jaimie, whose eyes were wide and curious as she continued to listen attentively. "You see, *tahn-kah*, little sister, everything the Power of the World does is done in a circle," he said. "The sky is round and so are all the stars. The wind in its greatest power, whirls. Birds make their nests in circles. The sun and moon come forth and go down again in a circle. Tepees are round like the nests of birds. The nation's hoop is a nest of many nests where the Great Spirit meant for the Sioux to hatch their children."

He looked quickly away from Jaimie and lowered his eyes. "But the *wasichos* have broken the circle," he said solemnly. "Our power is all but gone."

"I'm so sorry," Jaimie said, swallowing hard. "I wish it were different for your people. When I hear tales of how the great Sioux chief Crazy Horse died, I feel so sad."

Black Wolf looked quickly over at Jaimie. "Crazy Horse?" he said thickly. "Yes, you would know of my cousin Crazy Horse. Everyone, both of white and red skin, knows of the great man he was and how his life was ended as though he were no more than a snake crawling on the ground."

When Maddy heard Black Wolf say that Crazy Horse was his cousin, the color drained from her face. Again she thought of Farris and how he had bragged about having killed the powerful Sioux chief. And here, with Maddy, was that slain hero's cousin.

Panic filled her to know just how much danger Black Wolf would be in should Farris know that he was related to the very man Farris had loathed.

She started to tell Black Wolf of this danger, but then thought better of it. The less he knew, the better. It would be up to her to make sure that Farris never found Black Wolf while he was with her.

She felt much compassion, and something even deeper, for this man.

She had a need to protect him and wished now that she had listened to the teachings of her father about weapons. With so much awry in hers and Jaimie's lives, knowing the art of firearms would have come in handy.

Now she might have to learn while doing!

She turned and watched the rain and the rising water as Black Wolf again spoke in a low, soft tone to Jaimie.

"My cousin was but thirty winters when he was murdered at the soldiers' town on the White River," Black Wolf said slowly. He was growing tired, and his head ached now as he talked. Yet there was more that needed to be said to this child whose heart was open to the plight of the Sioux.

It was a rare thing . . . to find someone white who truly cared about the red man!

"He died so young," Jaimie said solemnly.

She recalled how Farris Boyd enjoyed bragging about having killed Crazy Horse. Surely if Black Wolf knew that Farris was near, he would not stop until he found a way to avenge his cousin's death.

But not wanting Black Wolf to get into trouble with the law, Jaimie would not tell him about Farris.

"My cousin was a special man who dreamed and went into a world where there was nothing but the spirits of all things," Black Wolf said, remembering how as a child he had sat in the council circle and listened to his cousin speaking of things only few knew or experienced.

"That is, the real world that is behind *this* one," he quickly added. "Everything we see here on earth is something like a shadow from *that* world. My cousin went there on his horse in that world. When he returned to his people on this earth he shared his feelings. He said that while he was there in that other world, his horse and himself and the trees and grass and the stones, and *everything*, were made of spirit. Nothing was hard. Everything seemed to float. His horse was standing still, yet it danced around like a horse made only of shadow."

"He told you this?" Jaimie asked, eyes wide. "Your cousin Crazy Horse told you of this experience in the spirit world?"

"He repeated the tale often to anyone who would listen and he spoke of it proudly," Black Wolf said, nodding. "This vision gave my cousin his great powers. When he went into a fight, he had only to think of that world to be in it again so that he could go through anything and not be hurt."

He looked away from Jaimie and looked up at Maddy just as she turned and gazed at him. "But the day my cousin died, all of his powers had already been taken away by the *wasichos*," he said solemnly. "His death came quickly."

The sound of oars splashing in water and Farris shouting Maddy's name made her heart skip a beat. Surely he had seen that her cabin was under water; he must be searching for her and Jaimie. As far as Maddy knew, he knew nothing about the cave.

Our boat, Maddy thought, paling. Should Farris see her boat, then he would know how to find her and Jaimie.

She hoped it was hidden well enough in the dark shadows for him not to see it.

"The fire!" she then gasped. "If he comes this close, he will see the light from the campfire!"

Her heart pounding, Maddy hurried to the fire and poured coffee on it in an attempt to put it out.

"Maddy, what are you doing?" Jaimie cried, leaping to her feet and going to her sister. "Why are you putting the fire out?"

"Grab a blanket and help me! We must get the fire out!" Maddy said. "And keep quiet! We don't want him to hear us!"

"*Who*, Maddy?" Jaimie asked in a panic as she grabbed a blanket and began smothering the flames of the fire with it.

"Farris," Maddy said.

Black Wolf heard the panic in Maddy's voice as she and Jaimie put out the final flames of the fire. "Who is this Farris person?" he asked, his voice low but loud enough for them to hear.

Afraid that he might know Farris Boyd, Maddy went quiet.

So did Jaimie.

The coals in the circle of rocks glowed enough for Black Wolf to see the guarded expression in both Maddy's and Jaimie's eyes.

He sensed a tenseness that went along with their sudden silence. His jaw tightened.

"In my lifetime I have known only one man who went by the name Farris," he said, his teeth clenched. "It is a name I will never forget. It is the name of the man who brags of killing my cousin!"

He leaned on an elbow and gave Maddy a steady stare. "Is this Farris you mentioned the same man?" he asked, his voice tight.

Maddy's and Jaimie's continued silence was answer enough for Black Wolf. He struggled to his feet, his head feeling as though it were the size and weight of a huge boulder, pulling him back to the floor of the cave.

"Maddy, what is this man to you?" Black Wolf asked, holding his head in his hands.

"A pest," Maddy blurted out.

Again he gazed up at her, seeing that she still stood as stiffly as the last time he'd looked at her. "In what way is he a pest?" he asked solemnly.

She explained how Farris was determined to marry her and how she loathed him and would never marry him, not even if he was the last man on earth.

Hearing of the loathing Maddy felt for Farris Boyd made Black Wolf smile. He was glad to know that she had no good feelings for the man.

And it was good to know that Farris was in the area. Black Wolf couldn't go after the man now. But once Black Wolf's life and the lives of his people were back in order, he would make the evil man pay for his wrongful deeds against the Sioux people.

For certain, Black Wolf didn't want this woman and her sister involved in his vengeance. The woman and the child had become too special to him . . . especially the woman, whose voice was as soft and sweet as a breeze in spring.

"He's gone," Maddy whispered, sighing heavily.

Her knees weak from having stood there so tense for so long, she crumpled down on a blanket and held her face in her hands. When she felt a gentle hand on her shoulder, she looked slowly up into Black Wolf's compassionate dark eyes.

He had found the strength to come to her to give her comfort. Scarcely breathing, she moved into his gentle embrace.

Her mouth agape, Jaimie stared at them.

Chapter Eight

Your kiss, those hands, those eyes divine,
That warm, white, lucent breast—
                                    —John Keats

The damp breeze blowing in from the cave opening caused Jaimie to shiver. "Maddy, surely it's safe to build another fire," she murmured. "Surely Farris has gone far past the cave by now. There'd be no need for him to come back in this direction. Please, Maddy? Can't we build another fire?"

So cold that her own teeth were chattering, Maddy nodded. "Yes, we'll have another fire," she said, already on her knees, laying firewood in a crisscross fashion on the shimmering coals of what was left of the earlier fire.

She then took small twigs and arranged them between the larger logs. Bending lower, she blew on the hot coals, sending sparks to the dry twigs. Soon small paths of flame were edging along the larger firewood, sending off warmth and light.

Maddy turned and gazed at Black Wolf. It was good to see him sitting upright, a blanket clutched around his shoulders. That had to mean that he was no longer feeling as disoriented and weak as before.

But just as she thought that, he stretched out again on the floor of the cave, visibly shivering.

Her brow furrowed with concern, Maddy grabbed another blanket and took it to him. She shook it out onto the floor beside him. "Do you have the strength to roll over on the blanket?" she asked softly. "You won't be as cold if you have something between yourself and the cold floor of the cave."

More and more amazed by this woman's compassionate caring for him, Black Wolf gazed up into her eyes, his heart pounding hard when her eyes held his.

Knowing that he could not indulge his feelings now, especially feelings he had for this woman whose skin was white, Black Wolf wrenched his eyes from Maddy's and nodded.

"Yes, I can move onto the blanket," he said thickly. "Thank you for spreading it for me."

"You just look so cold," Maddy said, her pulse racing because of that brief embrace when their eyes had spoken a message they never dared speak aloud.

She was falling in love with this man, even if she had known him for only a short while. There was something about him that reached right inside her heart. Perhaps it was his vulnerability now that he was injured . . . his helplessness.

But she thought not. She believed it was because he was the man she had secretly sought all of her life . . . the man who made her insides feel deliciously warm and wonderful as no man before him had made her feel.

Black Wolf used what strength he had to move over onto the blanket, stiffening when Maddy knelt over him and gently tucked the blanket around him more closely.

"There, there," she murmured, as though she were talking to her small sister, not a grown man who was a powerful chief. "Now doesn't that feel better?"

When Black Wolf gave her another lingering look, unnerving her, Maddy scurried to her feet and sat down beside the fire with Jaimie.

She realized her hand was trembling when she handed Jaimie the coffee pot. "Jaimie, go and get some fresh water," she said, her voice quivering as much as her hand. "I'll . . . I'll . . . make us some more coffee. That should warm our insides."

"Maddy, are you comin' down with something?" Jaimie asked, gazing at Maddy's trembling hands. "Oh, Maddy, don't get sick on me."

Maddy gave Jaimie a weak smile. "Sweetie, I'm not sick," she whispered. She held her hands out for Jaimie to see. "See? They're no longer shaking. I'm fine, Jaimie. Just fine."

"It's just that you are behaving so peculiar," Jaimie said, raising an eyebrow.

She leaned into Maddy's face, glanced over at Black Wolf, then gazed into Maddy's eyes. "Ever since you saw the Indian, you've been behaving differently," she said in a whisper. "Maddy, deep down, are you afraid of him? Or . . . or . . . is it something else?"

Maddy felt a hot flush rush to her cheeks. "Jaimie, quit it. Now *quit* it," she whispered harshly. "Just do as you're told. Go and get me water for the coffee. And, Jaimie, stop worrying about me so much. It's as though sometimes you forget who is the elder between us."

"Sometimes you seem so vulnerable," Jaimie whispered back so that Black Wolf could not hear her. "Maddy, you seem to need looking after. I want to protect you. I love you, Maddy. I *love* you."

"As I love you," Maddy said, wrapping her arms around Jaimie, drawing her into her embrace. "We've got to look out for one another. I won't let you down, Jaimie. I never have. I never will."

Maddy eased away from Jaimie. She smiled. "I'd sure like to have that cup of coffee, little sister," she murmured. "Now scat. Get me that water."

Jaimie giggled, rushed to her feet, stopped long enough to give Black Wolf a studious stare, then ran on past him.

"How long has Farris Boyd been in the area?" Black Wolf asked, struggling to a sitting position. He fought back the nausea that came with sitting upright; the pounding in his head was so strong he could hardly tolerate it.

When Maddy turned and saw that he was sitting up again, she felt somewhat encouraged. But when she looked into his eyes, she knew that he was not all that well. She could see much pain there. And sometimes he would wince as though pain was shooting through his wound.

She went and knelt beside him. "Farris?" she said softly, wishing she could reach over and stroke his copper brow in an effort to comfort him. Although that would be only a simple act of compassion, she kept her hand to herself. "Farris has not been in the area for long. I caught him watching me one day while I was in town getting supplies. I foolishly allowed him to assist me with my packages since my arms were burdened with so many. And then he didn't approach me again until that next Sunday as I was leaving church. He came and introduced himself to my father and Jaimie. After that he made several visits to our home. Pa didn't take to him, nor did I or Jaimie."

She swallowed hard and lowered her eyes, then looked at Black Wolf again. "Pa didn't have as long to know Farris as I did; he never realized how loathsome he truly is," she said softly. "My father was found dead in the forest. Jaimie found him while she was out exploring one day."

Maddy covered her mouth with a hand, choked back a sob, then continued telling Black Wolf about her father. Black Wolf felt her anguish as though it were his own, for not long ago, he had experienced the same loss as Maddy when his own father died.

"How did your father die?" he asked guardedly when she was through telling him all that she seemed to want to disclose about her father, and her life in general.

"A knife wound," Maddy said, the words bitter as they crossed her lips.

She glanced down where the knife was still sheathed at Black Wolf's side, yet hidden from view by the blanket.

She then gazed into his eyes again. "Someone stabbed my father . . . in the belly," she stammered out. "I'm not sure how long . . . he . . . lay there before he died."

Wanting to comfort Maddy, yet not sure if she would be offended by the offer of his arms around her a second time, Black Wolf kept them beneath the blanket. "I am sorry for your loss," he said, his voice breaking.

"Thank you," Maddy murmured, wiping tears from her eyes with the backs of her hands. "Everyone was so kind to me and Jaimie after the death of our father. The women from the church brought us food. The men came and did the chores Pa would never again do. And . . . and . . . Farris? Even he came and offered his services."

She frowned and her jaw tightened. "But it quickly came to mean more than that," she said tightly. "It became quite apparent that the only reason Farris came around offering help was because he wanted *me* in return, as though I were payment to him for his kindness."

As Maddy continued to talk, Black Wolf's mind went back to her description of how her father had died . . . by stabbing. Since his own father had died in the same way, Black Wolf wondered if the same man might have done the killing.

Could the same knife have snuffed out the lives of both of their fathers?

And from what she had said about Farris, and how her father had taken a dislike to him, Black Wolf wondered if it might have been Farris who had knifed her father.

Could he have killed her father to pave the way for him to marry Maddy? Could he have killed Black Wolf's father just because he couldn't resist killing a Sioux if he had the opportunity?

Yes, Farris was capable of anything dark and sinister, especially killing a father to get to his daughter!

Panic seized Black Wolf. Now that he knew Farris was nearby, he realized that his people, as a whole, were vulnerable. Farris could do much harm to many under the conditions now forced upon his people by the ravages of the Ohio River.

Not only were his people without the security of their homes, but also their chief.

"*Heh-eee,*" he cried, startling Maddy so much she fell over backwards.

When she saw how Black Wolf struggled to

get to his feet, then fell back down, panting and grabbing at his head, wincing, she scurried over to him and held him in her arms.

She became quickly aware of how his whole body was trembling. He was so distraught that she could actually hear an occasional sob come from somewhere deep inside him.

"My people," he cried. "I . . . must . . . get to . . . my people!"

Jaimie heard Black Wolf's loud cry as she was on her way back from the stream, the pot filled with cool, clear water. It sent a strange sort of dread through her.

She broke into a mad run, then stopped suddenly when she found Maddy holding Black Wolf as he leaned into her arms. Maddy was slowly rocking him as she talked softly to him.

It was at this moment that Jaimie knew she had lost a part of her sister to the Indian.

And from the way the Indian was responding, allowing a white woman to hold and comfort him, she knew that he felt the same bonding with Maddy as she felt to him.

Jaimie didn't know how to feel about this. She had never shared her sister with anyone but their parents.

Yet on the other hand, wouldn't Maddy's closeness with the Indian bring someone else into Jaimie's life, also?

Since their parents' deaths, things had grown so quiet in their house. When their mother and father were both alive, there was always laughter, hugging, and sharing.

Jaimie had known many sad moments when her despair over missing her father was almost too much to bear.

For Maddy's sake, Jaimie had fought the despair . . . the loneliness for her father . . . as best she could.

Yet it was still there every morning when she awakened. It was there every night when her father was not there to listen to her prayers or kiss her good night.

Perhaps it was all right for Maddy to be feeling something special for Black Wolf, Jaimie thought. For if Jaimie were somewhat older, she might, herself, have fallen in love with the handsome Indian.

That thought brought a smile to her lips.

She hurried onward and prepared the coffee as Maddy and Black Wolf eased apart and talked further.

"Are you certain you don't need to lie back down?" Maddy asked, her arms still warm from holding him, her heart filled with the wonderful feelings blossoming inside her.

"I need to stand . . . to *walk*," Black Wolf said, frustration thick in his voice. And not only over not being able to go to his people. He was still reeling in shock at his feelings for Maddy, afraid to allow himself to feel so intensely for someone whose skin and customs did not match his.

Especially now. He should have room in his

heart only for his people and their plight!

It was not fair that just as his people had finally found contentment, their roots planted deeply in the soil of the island, they should be swept away from it all. Now they would be forced to seek a new place . . . a new life . . . elsewhere.

No, the woman had no place in his world at this moment in time.

Perhaps she never would.

"I know how concerned you must be over your people, Black Wolf, but you must accept that you are in no condition to do anything about their plight," Maddy said, giving Jaimie a smile when the smell of coffee brewing wafted toward her.

She placed a gentle hand on Black Wolf's arm. "Having enough rest is important for your recovery," she murmured. She gave Jaimie another glance. "And, Black Wolf, a cup of coffee will do you wonders."

"While this man Farris looks for you, he might find my people," Black Wolf said, frowning as he gazed at the cave entrance.

"Farris has too much on his mind now to take time to harm your people," Maddy murmured. "And he is only one man. Just how much havoc can he wreak, alone, among your people? Please relax, Black Wolf. Rest. As soon as we can, Jaimie and I will take our boat and go see if we can find where your people have made camp."

"No," Black Wolf said flatly. "*I* will go."

"If you insist, yes, *you* will go," Maddy said softly. "But not without me and Jaimie. We will go with you."

Their eyes met and held, then shifted quickly when Jaimie brought them each a cup of coffee.

They drank the coffee in silence, then settled in their separate bedrolls beside the fire for the night.

Maddy and Jaimie listened as Black Wolf again began softly talking about his people and how it had been for them before the white wars . . . and about his cousin Crazy Horse. He spoke again of how Crazy Horse had died before his time, at the age of only thirty winters.

"Always when I heard anyone speaking of Crazy Horse, I envisioned an old, scholarly man," Maddy murmured.

"Yes, he was but a young warrior when he died," Black Wolf said thickly. "He had so much life left to live when the bayonet slammed into his body."

He swallowed hard. "But Crazy Horse was not the only one who died so young," he said thickly. "So many red-skinned warriors died young, leaving widows and children to fend for themselves."

Maddy was feeling herself being drawn more and more into loving Black Wolf. She vowed to herself that she wouldn't allow Farris to harm him. Although she had, until her father's death, depended on someone else to keep her safe, living alone had built strength and character within her.

Somehow she would be there for Black Wolf, to keep *him* safe!

The thought of Farris possibly sinking a bayonet into Black Wolf's body made her feel sick all over.

Black Wolf's words drifted off as he slid into a deep sleep.

Maddy couldn't sleep for looking at Black Wolf as the fire's shadows danced on his sculpted features. Yes, if it became necessary, she would protect this man with her life.

He had already suffered too much injustice at the hands of whites.

Chapter Nine

Love pour'd her beauty into my warm veins.
—John Keats

Black Wolf awakened to the pleasant aroma of *paezhuta-sapa*, coffee, and scrambled eggs cooking over the campfire. He sat up and gazed toward the fire, his eyebrows rising when he didn't see either Maddy or Jaimie.

He smiled when he guessed where they might be, taking care of a personal chore that he, himself, needed to tend to. He tested the strength of his legs by stretching them and found they were no longer so weak.

He lifted his head and was glad when doing so didn't make it resume its hideous pounding. A full night of undisturbed sleep had been beneficial in his recovery.

And realizing that he was not yet fully recovered, he knew not to stretch his limits too far today.

But he did have something planned . . . something that had to be done, yet would be hard, since he could not deny his feelings for the lovely white woman.

And the child.

Jaimie intrigued him no end—a girl with the behavior of a boy. He had not yet witnessed her skills with firearms but he guessed that she was probably a crack shot with a rifle, for surely her father had taught her such skills since he had no sons to tutor in such a way.

Pushing thoughts of the child and Maddy from his mind, he gazed at the cave entrance and was relieved to see sunshine. Heavenly, blessed sunshine was flooding the open space instead of torrents of rain. That would make what he had planned easier. He hoped his wound would not keep him from what must be done.

Maddy and Jaimie rushed into the cave, laughing, then stopped short when they saw that Black Wolf was awake and sitting up, his eyes seeming more alert today.

"Good morning," Maddy said, going to kneel beside Black Wolf, her pulse racing as their eyes met and held. "How . . . how are you this morning?"

"Better," Black Wolf said, wrenching his eyes from the mystical lure of hers. He shoved the blanket aside and rose slowly to his feet. "I must step outside for a moment to tend to private business."

"You'll find a beautiful day awaiting you," Maddy said, rising and stepping away from him as she watched him finally make it to his feet. He was somewhat unsteady, but nevertheless standing. She understood what he meant by "private business," for she and Jaimie had just taken care of their own private needs behind some bushes.

She watched Black Wolf inch his way toward the cave entrance, seemingly testing each step as he took it. She grimaced when he suddenly reached up and grabbed at his head, as though a sudden pain had shot through his wound.

"The water has even receded somewhat," she said, trying not to show that she had noticed his discomfort.

Her eyes followed his every step, herself feeling his strain, for it was clear to see in the corded muscles of his legs just how hard it was for him to remain steady on his feet.

"Black Wolf, it's safe to take our boat to search for your people today," she said, not revealing her secret fear. The river would, indeed, be safe enough for travel, but only if they didn't run into Farris, who might resume his search for Maddy today.

She saw no need to worry Black Wolf about that. She was worried enough for both of them. She knew what Farris was capable of. He would take much delight in killing Black Wolf, especially if he guessed that Maddy had feelings for the Sioux chief that she could never feel for Farris Boyd!

"You do want to go today and search for your

people, don't you?" she asked guardedly when he did not respond to her remark.

When he turned and gazed at her, she tried to read the strange look in his eyes. They seemed filled with a yearning that reached right inside her heart.

She couldn't understand why he did not respond to her but instead turned his back to her again and went on outside the cave.

"He's in a strange mood today," Jaimie said as she came and stood beside Maddy.

"Well, wouldn't you be, also, if you were a powerful Sioux chief whose whole world had been turned upside down by the Ohio River?" Maddy asked, sighing heavily.

"Sis, *our* world has been turned upside down and *we* aren't in a dark mood," Jaimie softly argued.

"*We* don't have a whole village of Indians who depend on us for leadership, now do we, little sister?" Maddy said, patting Jaimie playfully on the cheek. She nodded toward the fire and the pan of scrambled eggs and coffee that awaited them. "Come on. Let's fill the plates and pour the coffee. We'll have them ready when Black Wolf returns. Maybe after he eats he'll feel somewhat better."

"He didn't seem at all eager about leaving with us today, Maddy, to go and look for his people," Jaimie said, skipping over and plopping down on a blanket beside the fire.

"I'm sure that he doesn't care much for the

idea of having to depend so much on us 'ladies'," Maddy said, smiling at Jaimie as she sat down beside her. "You know how men can be. Too many of them believe women are to be seen, not heard. Pa never approved of Ma speaking her mind about things. He only seemed to change his attitude about females when you came along. I think he tried to make you into a boy since he began doubting he would ever have a son."

"Is that why he took more time with me than you?" Jaimie asked, pinching off a piece of egg and slipping it into her mouth.

"Now don't act so innocent, Jaimie," Maddy said, nervously eyeing the cave entrance. She knew that it shouldn't take this long for a man to relieve himself in the bushes. "You know that's why Pa took the time to teach you how to shoot and ride like a man."

"Maddy, why are you looking at the cave entrance like that?" Jaimie asked softly, following Maddy's line of vision. "Are you thinking what I'm thinking? That . . . he . . . isn't coming back? He's been gone for too long to do his business, hasn't he?"

"Yes, far too long," Maddy said, jumping to her feet. She ran to the entrance of the cave and stepped outside into the sunshine. Her spirits sank when she saw that not only was Black Wolf gone, so was her boat.

"He's taken our boat," Jaimie said, breathless as she ran outside and stood beside Maddy. She looked quickly up at her sister. "He's gone, Maddy. He's gone."

"He most certainly is," Maddy said, placing her hands on her hips as she slowly scanned the flooded land. She groaned and dropped her hands to her sides, doubling her fingers into tight fists. "But look who *is* here this morning, Jaimie, rowing his boat toward us."

When she heard the splash of oars and saw the disgust in her sister's eyes, Jaimie turned and looked. Her eyes filled with fire. "It's that pest again," she snapped out, kicking at the loose rocks at her feet, spilling several into the water, which was not that far from the cave entrance.

Maddy felt trapped. Farris would realize where they had been hiding, and now the cave could never be a place of refuge for her again. Maddy sourly watched him as he beached his boat only a few feet away at the edges of the dry land fronting the cave.

"Thank God!" Farris cried as he came running toward Maddy.

She grimaced and stiffened when he reached out for her and grabbed her into his arms. As he clutched her desperately, she tried to get away, but no amount of wriggling would loosen her from his tight hold.

"Thank God, Maddy, I thought you and Jaimie had drowned," Farris said. "I'm so glad you are all right. I searched last night for you even in the darkness. I hardly slept for worrying about you."

"Farris, as you can see, Jaimie and I are quite

all right," Maddy said, finally managing to yank herself free. "Now you can be on your way. Go and do what you must elsewhere. I'm sure there are others who would welcome your assistance."

Farris's nose twitched as the delicious aroma of coffee and cooked eggs came to him from the cave. He looked toward the cave entrance, his eyes widening when he saw it behind the tangles of briars and bushes.

He gave Maddy a questioning stare. "A cave?" he asked. "You found a cave? That's where you've been all along?"

Maddy and Jaimie exchanged frustrated looks, then Maddy nodded and gazed at Farris again. "Yes, this is where we came when the river became too much of a threat to our home," she said softly. "Jaimie found the cave one day while she was out doing her usual exploring. It's been a godsend for us."

She looked nervously past him, hoping that Black Wolf would not return. Moments ago she had wanted nothing more than to see him coming back for her and Jaimie. Now she hoped he would stay away, at least until she could send Farris packing!

"Do I smell coffee?" Farris said, running a hand over his bald head as he smiled at Maddy. "Do I smell eggs? I didn't take the time for breakfast before I resumed my search for you this morning."

Panic seized Maddy when she realized that

Farris was going to invite himself into the cave for breakfast.

The blankets!

The bedrolls!

Anyone could tell by a glance that more than two people had slept in the cave the night before.

Maddy caught Jaimie's eye and gave a nod toward the cave when Farris was not looking.

Jaimie seemed to understand. She had probably thought of the same thing when she realized that Farris was not going to leave right away. She slipped past Maddy and Farris and went inside the cave. Hurriedly, she rolled up Black Wolf's blankets, getting them stacked with hers and Maddy's along the cave wall just as Farris came inside with Maddy.

"Well, ain't this nice and cozy?" Farris said, his gaze moving slowly around the cave. The fire's glow gave off enough light for him to see all of Maddy's belongings. "One could live quite comfortably here for quite a spell, now couldn't one?"

"I hope we won't have to," Maddy said dryly.

Panic filled her eyes when she saw the three plates of eggs and the three cups of coffee.

It was too late for her to do anything about it. As Farris sat down he immediately saw the plates and cups. He stared at them for a long moment, then gave Maddy a frown as she sat down beside Jaimie on the far side of the fire, away from Farris.

"Who was keeping you company before my arrival?" Farris asked, his eyes going suspiciously from Jaimie to Maddy.

"Sis saw you coming way before you saw us and came in and told me to prepare a plate and pour a cup of coffee for you," Jaimie blurted out. "Wasn't that kind of my lovely sister, Farris?"

"Yes, very," Farris said, giving Maddy a sly, knowing grin. "And I appreciate it, Maddy. Is your kindness toward me today a way to apologize for your rudeness yesterday?"

Maddy felt herself getting deeper and deeper into a situation she might lose control of.

And she had to get Farris out of the cave. Black Wolf could return at any moment.

"My kindness toward you today is the same as it would be toward anyone during a crisis like the one we are now suffering," Maddy said stiffly. She took a plate of eggs on her lap and grabbed a fork. "Let's eat before it gets much colder. And then you can be on your way, Farris, and find someone who needs helping more than Jaimie and I. As you can see, we're fine and we will be until the flood waters recede."

Farris scooped several bites of eggs into his mouth, followed by large swallows of coffee.

And then something else caught his eye. He lowered the fork from his mouth and set the half-eaten dish of eggs down beside him as he rose and went to where Maddy had left the first aid kit open, with bandages and ointment on the ground beside the bag.

"And who did you use this on?" Farris asked,

stooping and picking up a roll of bandage. He stared at the open bag, then turned and looked at Maddy. "Who was here besides you and Jaimie, Maddy?"

"No one," Jaimie blurted out, going to gingerly take the bandage from him. "Sis used it on me. Right after we arrived at the cave, I . . . I . . . got bit by a spider."

Farris's eyes narrowed as he looked over at Jaimie. "I see no bandage on you anywhere," he said warily. "Where is the spider bite?"

Again Jaimie thought quickly. She pretended to be bashful as she lowered her eyes. "My bite is in a place I can't show you," she murmured. "It's . . . on my . . . fanny."

Tired of the game Farris was playing, Maddy went to him and yanked on his arm so that he was forced to turn and look at her.

"Now listen here, Farris Boyd, I don't appreciate your coming here today implying this and that when all my sister and I want is to be left alone to ride this flood out so that we can proceed with our lives," Maddy said hotly. "It's bad enough that we lost our cabin. We don't need someone like you making things more miserable for us. Please leave, Farris."

"Come with me," Farris said, his eyes pleading with her. "This isn't a safe place for you. You know that, because Jaimie already got bit by a spider. Surely there are poisonous snakes in here. There might be rabid bats. I want to take you to my house. It's on dry land. The river water will never reach it. It's beautiful, Maddy. My mother's things are there. They are so pretty, they'll take your breath away."

"Farris, as I've told you countless times before, I don't need your fancy house nor your mother's fancy things," Maddy said, sighing. "I just want a normal home with normal things. As soon as we can, Jaimie and I will rebuild. We'll build this time on higher ground. Farris, you are wasting your time here. We don't want any part of you or your life. Where's your pride, Farris? Surely you have none, not if you can beg a woman like you are begging me."

"I'll never give up," Farris said, believing that this refusal was just another attempt to postpone what, in the end, she would have no choice but to do. She *would* be his wife!

"I thought not," Maddy said, stiffening. She gave Jaimie a quick glance, then set her jaw as she again looked at Farris. "There is one thing that you can do for me and Jaimie that would be appreciated."

"That is?" Farris asked, his eyes gleaming.

"We feel stranded," she murmured, hating to ask anything of this man, for she knew that in his eyes she would now owe him.

But she would have to swallow her pride and fight that battle when the time came. Now all that was important was to find Black Wolf and make sure he was all right. Chances were that once he'd gotten out in the boat, the exertion of rowing had been too much for him. She hated to think of what might happen to him if he passed out in the boat and was carried away by the current.

Not only was his life in danger if that happened, she knew that she would never see him again. And she must. She loved him.

She must have a boat, no matter how she got it.

"Where is your boat?" Farris asked warily. "Surely you knew that it was as important to bring it to higher ground as it was to bring your belongings."

Maddy and Jaimie gave each other a quick, nervous glance.

Then Maddy took *her* turn lying to Farris. "We did bring it to higher ground, but the river managed to wash it away when we weren't looking," she said softly.

"All right, then, Maddy, I'll bring you a boat, but only if you promise to allow me to court you once things are back to normal," he said huskily. "What could it hurt, Maddy? All I'm asking of you is to give me a chance, a *real* chance."

Maddy felt trapped, but she knew that she had no choice but to appear as though she would agree to his terms.

"Yes, I'll do as you say," Maddy said, ignoring the gasp her promise elicited from Jaimie. "Once all of this is behind us, you may court me."

"Now that's more like it," Farris said, chuckling. He left quickly, leaving Maddy and Jaimie in strained silence.

"Why did you do that?" Jaimie finally blurted out, her eyes showing her disbelief at what her sister had done.

"For Black Wolf," Maddy said, crumpling down onto a blanket beside the fire. For long moments she stared at the flames. Then she glanced over at Jaimie as she fell to her knees beside her sister. "We've got to find him, Jaimie. Don't you see the danger he could be in? If he collapses in that boat—"

"Don't say anymore," Jaimie said, inhaling a nervous breath. "I understand."

They sat in silence until Farris returned. And after he showed that he had kept his word and had brought her the boat, he reminded her of what he expected of *her*.

He yanked her into his arms and tried to kiss her.

Maddy shoved him away.

"I won't be patient too much longer," Farris grumbled. "Once the water recedes, you'd best be prepared to stand before a preacher with me."

"That's not what I promised you," Maddy cried, paling. "I only promised to allow you to court me."

"Courting leads quickly to a preacher's doorstep," Farris said, then swung around on a heel and left.

Feeling cold and drained inside, Maddy now knew that her plans to stay and rebuild close to her parents' graves had just been altered. She couldn't stay in the area if Farris was always going to be there to force himself on her in one way or another. She most certainly wouldn't allow him to court her, not for one minute!

Her thoughts returned to Black Wolf. She wished that it were he wanting her to be a part of *his* life, no matter if it was forbidden for a man with red skin and a woman with white skin to marry!

She now knew without a doubt that he was not the sort of man who went around killing innocent men like her father.

But he *was* a guilty man . . . guilty of stealing an innocent, lonely woman's heart!

Chapter Ten

Come, slowly, Eden!
Lips unused to thee,
Bashful, sip thy jasmine,
As the fainting bee.

—Emily Dickinson

Looking for his island, Black Wolf rowed the boat slowly up and down the river.

When he finally found where it had been, only the tops of the trees were visible through the water.

With a deep sadness in his heart, and dizzy and weak from the exertion of rowing the boat through the troubled Ohio waters, Black Wolf searched for traces of his people along the shore.

He searched every stretch of higher ground where those who had fled the ravages of the water might have sought safety and shelter.

The only survivors he saw were people with white skins.

Like their island, his people had disappeared!

Forlorn, filled with sorrow, his head throbbing, Black Wolf knew that he could go no farther without stopping to rest. If he lost consciousness while on the river, he might lose his life.

This time if he capsized, he would surely sink like a heavy stone to the bottom of the water, for that was how he felt . . . like a lump of rock. His head felt as though it had swollen to twice its size.

Groaning, finding each pull of the paddle through the water an effort now, Black Wolf was glad when he finally reached dry land.

Tumbling over the side of the boat into waist-high water, he managed to drag the boat with him until he had it beached safely beneath a huge oak tree. Its shade was welcome as Black Wolf sank down onto the ground and rested his back against the huge trunk of the tree.

Hanging his head in his hands in despair, he muttered a soft prayer.

A sob lodged in his throat as he thought of how his people were no longer under the safe wing of their chief.

Yes, they were now surely scattered, with no one in this unfriendly land to help them . . . with no future.

When he heard the splash of paddles in the water, he looked quickly up.

When he discovered Maddy and Jaimie coming slowly down the river in a boat, their eyes searching the shore, he was torn by conflicting feelings.

He truly didn't want to bring Maddy into his

world of despair and danger, for he knew that it was forbidden for a white woman to be with an Indian. Her reputation would be ruined if she was seen in the company of a red-skinned man.

And then there was Maddy's sister, Jaimie. Although her skin was white, there was so much about Jaimie that reminded Black Wolf of his sister, who was now a part of the spirit world.

His sister had been the same age as Jaimie at the time of her death. She had followed Black Wolf as though she were his shadow, learning the pursuits of boys instead of girls.

Black Wolf had humored his younger sister, and had taught her how to use a rifle and a bow, how to hunt and fish . . . everything that young braves should know.

He had hoped that his sister's knowledge of weapons, and her ability to fend for herself, might help keep her safe from the onslaught of white people, who, for the most part, seemed determined to rid the land of all red-skinned men, women . . . and children.

It hadn't been enough.

Nothing had been enough. Far too many of his people had died at the hands of the soldiers.

Thinking it best to put distance between himself and Maddy and Jaimie, not wanting to see them hurt because of their acquaintance with him, Black Wolf struggled to his feet and found the strength to get the boat back in the water again.

But the pounding of his head disoriented him.

He stumbled and fell. He landed in the water.

As the boat floated away from him, Black Wolf fought against the current as it began carrying him away; but once again he felt himself losing the battle with the dark river.

He swallowed great gulps of water as he was sucked beneath the surface. Then he was tossed up again as though the river had belched him out of its belly.

Suddenly catching sight of Black Wolf, Maddy was seized with panic. "No!" she screamed, then dove headfirst into the water as Jaimie steadied the boat, her eyes wild as she watched first Maddy, and then Black Wolf.

Jaimie was paralyzed with fear that she might lose them both in the river!

Maddy fought against the draw of the current and of a whirlpool sucking at her feet.

Her father had taught her how to swim almost as soon as she knew how to walk, and she was a strong swimmer.

Not allowing herself to take her eyes off Black Wolf, Maddy swam hard until she finally reached him. Her heart pounding, the filthy water stinging her eyes and throat, she grabbed Black Wolf around his neck and managed to take him to dry land.

Panting, soaked through, they stretched out on the ground.

Maddy's insides warmed suddenly when she felt a hand circling hers. The knowledge that it was Black Wolf's made her heart melt with rapture.

"Again you touch my heart deeply by your caring ways," Black Wolf said, his voice drawn and tired from his exhausting moments in the river. "Thank you . . . thank you."

Maddy turned to her side and gazed into his eyes. She reached a hand over and gently touched his cheek. "Yes, I care," she murmured. Her jaw tightened. "Black Wolf, why did you leave without telling me? Surely you knew you weren't strong enough."

"I did not want to make my struggle your struggle," Black Wolf said thickly. "It is not right to draw you any further into my life. My people have again lost everything. It is my responsibility as their chief to find them and make things right for them once more."

He reached up and took her hand from his face and held it over his heart. "Do you feel the pounding of my heart?" he said thickly. "It is not because of my weariness as much as it is because of my feelings for you. They run deep now . . . far deeper than the treacherous Ohio. I do not want to bring the hardships into your life that being the woman of a Sioux warrior would bring. You must go your way. I will go mine."

Maddy had listened with a trembling heart to everything he had said and knew now that he *did* have special feelings for her.

And she was touched deeply by the fact that he wanted to protect her from the life he had been forced to live because of the manipulations of evil, greedy white people. He knew that she would not fit well into his life. The white community would make it almost impossible for them to be together.

At this moment, she didn't care about what anyone might say or do. She just knew that she would do anything to be able to stay with Black Wolf, forever.

She would go up against anyone who tried to interfere.

"If I told you that I wished nothing more than to stay with you, what would you say?" she asked softly.

Her words, which revealed her feelings for him, made Black Wolf's heart sing.

Yet he still feared for her should he allow her to stay with him. "*Mee-tah-ween*, my woman, I would say you are foolish," he said thickly.

"It is foolish to love?" Maddy asked, swallowing hard, for this was the first time she had ever come so close to telling a man that she loved him.

She had never loved before. But this man, this wonderful, gentle man made it so easy to love.

"I say it is not the time to speak of love when so much has gone awry in both our lives," Black Wolf said, hating to fill her heart with disappointment when he knew how she felt about him. It was the same way he felt about her.

He loved her. He needed her. Oh, how badly he wanted her!

"Then I shall speak of it later when things are right again in our lives," Maddy murmured, not to be dissuaded from the love that she now felt with every fiber of her being.

Just then Jaimie beached the boat and ran up to Maddy. She fell to her knees beside her. "Sis, are you all right?" she asked, stark fear in her voice. "Black Wolf! Are you hurt?"

Realizing that her stillness had frightened her sister, Maddy sat up quickly and drew her into her arms. "I'm sorry, Jaimie," she murmured. "I didn't mean to scare you. I . . . we . . . Black Wolf and I . . . were worn out. We were resting before . . . before . . . heading back to the cave."

"We're going back there even knowing Farris might return while Black Wolf is with us?" Jaimie asked. Leaning away from Maddy, she looked quickly over at Black Wolf as he moaned while pushing himself up from the ground.

"We will return to the cave at least long enough to dry off and for me to change into something else," Maddy said, rising and turning to Black Wolf. "Please stay with us. You know you aren't well enough to be alone. We can return to the cave long enough to get some belongings and move our animals where there is plenty of grass to sustain them while we are gone. Then we can leave and find safer shelter elsewhere. Black Wolf, you aren't well enough to go on a lengthy search for your people. Trust me. As soon as you are well enough for extensive travel, Jaimie and I will go with you and help you find your people."

Black Wolf frowned as he gazed first at the river and then at Maddy, knowing very well that she was right. And although he still didn't want to bring hardship into her life because of her alliance with him, he felt he had no other choice but to accept her help.

"We will stay together," Black Wolf said, nodding.

Feeling triumphant, and oh, so very happy, Maddy had to fight against flinging herself into Black Wolf's arms. Instead she placed an arm around his waist and led him to the boat she had borrowed from Farris. Her own had floated away in the river after Black Wolf fell out and was surely gone forever.

After arriving at the cave, they dried off and rested for a while. Then they loaded up as many of their supplies as they could in the boat.

Jaimie took their two horses and cow and tethered them beneath a tree. Hating to leave them, afraid someone might steal them, she stroked the horses' manes, one at a time.

"I hope you will be safe," she whispered, then went to the cow and hugged her. "You too."

She hurried back to Maddy and Black Wolf and boarded the boat, taking one last look in the direction of the animals as the boat moved off into the middle of the river.

Sad over having to leave so much behind, Maddy headed the boat back upstream, away from River Town and, she hoped, the threat of Farris Boyd. When Black Wolf asked to take the paddle, Maddy refused him. She knew that he wasn't well enough.

And although every pull of the paddle through the water hurt her arms and shoulders, she forced herself to go on.

She kept her discomfort from Black Wolf. She wanted to prove to him that she could be more than the weak little thing almost everyone thought she was.

From now on, she must be stronger. Life was no longer easy. Each day brought new challenges.

They traveled until the sun began to set behind the distant hills. Along the way they saw many homes that sat back from the river, which had not been disturbed by the flood but had been abandoned anyway, the people having feared the worst.

Maddy spied a cabin that she recognized. It belonged to an old man she knew well. He was an elderly man whose beard was snow-white like Santa Claus's, and he had acquired the nickname Santa because of his appearance. He had chosen the life of a hermit over associating with people.

Maddy's father had come across the old man one day while her father was on a hunting excursion. He had found Santa delirious after having lain alone in the woods for two days, his foot caught in the jaws of a steel trap.

Her father had removed the trap and had taken the hermit to his cabin and doctored his foot.

Maddy would never forget the long hours she had spent worrying about her father when he did not come home that day at the expected time. She had thought that he had met with foul play.

When he had arrived home and explained about the old man and his injuries, Maddy had returned with her father for many days after that to help the old man. She had fed him broth while he was delirious with a raging fever.

She and Jaimie had taken turns sitting at his bedside and keeping him company when he finally passed the danger of losing the foot from gangrene.

When her father had been killed, Maddy had gone and told Santa. Afterwards, he had stayed with her and Jaimie until they had recovered enough from the shock of their father's death to fend for themselves, alone.

"He surely won't mind us stopping off for one night," she whispered to herself, heading the boat toward shore.

After the boat was beached, they knocked at the cabin door, but there was no response. A keen fear swept through Maddy that something might have happened to Santa. But the river had not reached his cabin. It was high and dry.

And she just couldn't imagine him being like the others who lived along the river, who had left because of their fears of what *might* happen.

Slowly she inched the door open and stepped inside. Everything seemed in place, as though nothing was wrong, except that Santa wasn't there. She had to surmise that he *had* fled to higher ground.

Knowing Santa so well, she knew that he wouldn't mind if she, Jaimie, and Black Wolf stayed in his cabin for the night to get some much needed rest. Santa was a kind-hearted man despite his desire to live as a hermit.

"You seem to be familiar with this cabin," Black Wolf said as he saw the ease with which Maddy went into the cabin and started a fire in the fireplace.

"I am familiar with being here," Maddy murmured, smiling at Black Wolf over her shoulder.

She explained to him how she knew Santa and how often she had been in his cabin.

Later, she made sure the boat was hidden in a storage shack behind the cabin so that, in case Farris came downriver searching for them, he would not see his boat moored on the banks of the river.

After night fell, and Maddy had prepared food from her supplies, and everyone had settled down before the fire, comfortable for the moment, Maddy gave Black Wolf a quick glance, and then Jaimie.

She then looked overhead at the loft, where Jaimie had begged to sleep. Back at their home in Kentucky, Jaimie had slept in the loft bedroom. Maddy could tell by Jaimie's melancholy expression that she was also thinking back and feeling lonely for those times when their family had been together and happy.

When Jaimie yawned and stretched, Maddy went to her and took her by the hand, urging her to her feet. "I readied things earlier for you in the loft," she murmured. "Go on, Jaimie, and sleep there."

Realizing that her departure would leave Maddy and Black Wolf alone, Maddy gave Black Wolf a nervous glance, then walked Jaimie to the ladder that led up to the loft. She hugged Jaimie, then playfully swatted her behind.

"Get on up there and let's not hear another sound out of you until morning," she murmured.

Jaimie yawned again, then went on up to the loft.

Seeing how quiet Black Wolf had become, Maddy felt a bit unnerved.

She grabbed two blankets from her belongings. One she gave to Black Wolf and the other she kept for herself.

Feeling his eyes on her all the while, Maddy went and stretched out on the floor close to the fire.

Black Wolf had been watching Maddy go through the ritual of preparing food for them, washing the dishes afterward, and then engaging in small talk with her sister before the roaring fire.

He had watched Maddy lead Jaimie to the loft ladder, thinking Maddy would join her sister there, then raised an eyebrow when Jaimie went up the ladder alone.

And now, with Maddy having curled up in her blankets for the night so near to him, and looking so ravishingly beautiful with the fire's glow on her cheeks, it was taking all of his willpower not to go to her and whisk her into his arms.

There was an urgency building inside him to hold her . . . to kiss her . . . that he had never felt with any other woman.

But still he held himself back.

No matter how much he wanted Maddy, and she wanted him, when the time came, he would have to leave her. He would have to learn to accept that loss as he had so many other things in his past. Yet, could he?

It was different this time. This was a woman whose heart was now intertwined with his!

Maddy felt more than Black Wolf's eyes on her as she tried to go to sleep. She could feel some sort of force between them, as though his arms were reaching out for her, whereas in truth she knew they weren't.

She had only moments before given him a quick glance to see what he was doing, trembling inside when she again found his eyes watching her. His midnight dark eyes seemed to reach into the very center of her being. They mesmerized her whenever her gaze held his for longer than a moment.

"You've got to stop this," she whispered to herself, making sure he could not hear her.

She squeezed her eyes shut and tried to will sleep upon herself, sighing when again all that she could see behind her closed eyes was Black Wolf's handsome face.

When she felt a hand on her arm, her breath was stolen away, for she knew whose hand it was. What were his intentions? Had he come to tell her something trite, such as plans for tomorrow on the river? Or was it something more that was troubling him . . . such as how he wished to hold her?

"*Mee-tah-ween?*" Black Wolf whispered, speaking low so he would not disturb Jaimie's sound sleep.

His voice, the huskiness in it, the touch of his warm hand sliding up her arm to the nape of her neck, slowly turning her to face him, made Maddy's heart go wild inside her.

This was a moment of decision!

If he wished to kiss her, should she allow it? Should she give in to the feelings that were like a hot wind soaring through her at his mere touch?

Swallowing hard, scarcely breathing, she turned over and gazed up into his eyes. When he swept his arms around her and brought her up against him, she closed her eyes in sheer ecstasy.

With abandon she went into his arms, her lips quivering against his as he kissed her long, hard, and deep. There seemed to be a frenzied urgency to his touch and kiss. She twined her arms around his neck and clung to him, her own desperate need making her feel wild.

And then it stopped as quickly as it had begun when he drew quickly away from her and went back to his blanket. He stretched out on it, placing his back to her.

Maddy was stunned by the torrent of her feelings for this man, so in awe of them she could not ask him why he had abandoned the idea of making love to her.

Without their even speaking, she understood why he had drawn away from her. It was the gentleman in him . . . as well as his concern for their being from different worlds.

She touched her lips with her fingertips, still feeling the desperate press of his lips there.

Tears sprang to her eyes to know that he loved her . . . that he loved her so much he would not take advantage of her being alone with him, vulnerable and in love.

With all of her heart she appreciated his decision not to take advantage of her, because he could have.

Wanting him with every fiber of her being, she would have allowed it!

Chapter Eleven

His presence is enchantment!
—Emily Dickinson

Maddy awakened to the light of early morning, feeling refreshed after a good night's sleep. All the paddling she had done the day before had sent her into a quick, deep sleep.

Surprisingly, she hadn't dreamed of Black Wolf, though as she had drifted off to sleep he was the only thing on her mind.

How could she ever forget his arms around her? His kiss?

She would never forget the desire she had felt while in his arms, his lips trembling against hers, his needs surely matching her own.

But she *had* placed it all from her mind, until now.

As the three of them sat at the small kitchen table finishing their breakfast, Maddy could feel the heat of Black Wolf's passion every time he gazed into her eyes.

She felt it while sipping her coffee . . . while sliding a small spoonful of oatmeal into her mouth. She felt it while attempting small talk with Jaimie, realizing how strange her voice sounded this morning because of her awakened sensuality.

Yes, dealing with so many unusual sensations this morning, Maddy was struggling with her feelings for Black Wolf, finding it harder to maintain her calm as each moment passed, for she wanted this man. The need for him was like a slow ache deep within her. These feelings were new to her, yet deliciously wonderful.

"Sis, I'm finished," Jaimie said, pushing her empty bowl to the middle of the table. "I'm going to go and do a little bit of hunting while you medicate Black Wolf's wound. I assure you we'll have some good meat on our supper table tonight."

"What?" Maddy said, having been yanked from her thoughts.

She looked at Jaimie. "Did you say something, Jaimie?" she asked so awkwardly she knew Jaimie must have noticed.

"Sis, are you all right?" Jaimie asked, leaning closer over the table to look at her sister as the sun's glow reached through the window onto Maddy's face. "You look all right, so where was your mind?"

"Where?" Maddy said, feeling a blush rise to her cheeks.

She gave Black Wolf a quick glance, flinching when she saw a quiet amusement in his eyes.

Surely he had guessed that her deep thoughts were about him.

She rose quickly from the chair and began gathering the dirty dishes from the table, stacking them and carrying them to a small table where she already had dishwater warm and ready.

"I was worrying about the river," she said, giving Jaimie a nervous smile over her shoulder. "That's all."

"The river has receded quite a bit more today," Black Wolf said, scooting his chair back and rising from it.

He was relieved that he no longer became dizzy when he got to his feet. But he still felt pressure around the wound, which caused him some pain.

He went to the window and stared at the rushing water. "But the river still might be a bit too hazardous to travel as far as we need to go," he said warily.

"I know how anxious you are to search for your people," Maddy said, going to stand beside him.

Standing this close to him threatened Maddy's sanity, for she loved him so much it frightened her. Her insides melted as she realized how clean Black Wolf smelled this morning, fresh like the water from a stream where he told her he had bathed earlier while she was sleeping.

Even the buckskin of his breechcloth was clean and soft-looking from the washing.

And Black Wolf's hair, where the blood had been washed from it, was clean and sparkling. In the streamers of sunlight coming through the window, the color of his hair resembled the color of a raven's wing. It was hard to distinguish the black from the blue as those colors blended together, shiny and sleek.

And then there was his sculpted, copper face, the lines so exact, so perfect, making him the most exquisitely handsome man Maddy had ever seen.

Whenever she was this close to him, she could not help remembering the strength of his muscled arms, yet the gentleness with which he had held her.

"Yes, my heart cries for my people," Black Wolf said, his voice catching with emotion. "I can wait only one more day and night and then I must take to the river again and search for them."

"I'm glad you aren't insisting on going today," Maddy said, returning to her dishwashing and gently placing a dish into the sudsy dishwater. "I just don't think it's safe enough."

"Sis, I'm ready to leave," Jaimie said, stepping up beside her with a rifle clutched in her right hand. "And don't start lecturing me about it being dangerous for me to go hunting alone." She glanced at Black Wolf. "Tell Maddy that I'm able to fend for myself, Black Wolf. You know I am, don't you?"

"It is not my place to interfere in your family

129

affairs," Black Wolf said, going to slide a log into the flames of the fireplace.

"You could come with me," Jaimie said, scarcely breathing as she awaited Black Wolf's reply.

"No, he *can't*," Maddy interjected.

She went to Jaimie and ran her fingers gently through her sister's short-cropped hair. "And I truly don't think you should go, either. I've enough food left to last us several days. I only took advantage of Santa's bag of oatmeal this morning because he has so much." She laughed softly. "That man must exist on oatmeal alone. I've never seen so many bags in one place in my life."

"I want to go," Jaimie said, adamantly.

"Jaimie, shame on you," Maddy replied, going to place her hands on her sister's shoulders. "Now behave. Do you hear? Behave. This isn't the time to become stubborn on me."

"But, Sis, you never before refused to let me go hunting," Jaimie murmured, tears shining in her eyes. "Why should you now? I can take care of myself and you know it."

"But if you do go, you *will* go alone," Maddy said, easing her hands from her sister. She glanced over at Black Wolf, knowing that he needed one more day of rest before heading out onto the river.

She took Jaimie's free hand and walked her to the door. "Black Wolf must stay behind," she said softly. "I'm going to doctor his wound."

"I promise not to be gone too long," Jaimie said, her eyes wide with excitement over having won one more battle with her sister. She lifted her rifle for Black Wolf to see. "I'll bring home a fat rabbit for our supper, Black Wolf!"

Black Wolf smiled and nodded, yet felt inadequate at this moment that a child should be going to hunt for food for the dinner table instead of himself.

Yet Maddy was right. He did need more rest. And he welcomed her soothing medication on his head wound. It was again throbbing.

Maddy stood at the door and watched Jaimie until she became lost to her sight in the forest of trees that led away from the river.

Then, sighing, she went back to washing dishes until everything was back in its place.

For a moment she gazed from the window again, wondering about Santa and where he might be. She wouldn't ever forget how badly injured he had been from that damnable trap . . .

The blood drained quickly from her face. "A trap . . ." she whispered, suddenly thinking of Jaimie out in this section of the woods where traps were known to be set by trappers!

Panic-stricken, she turned her wide, wild eyes to Black Wolf. "What if Jaimie doesn't see the traps that are used in this area to catch animals?" she gasped out.

"She is as aware of those traps as you are because she will remember how your friend was injured in one," Black Wolf said.

He went to her and framed her pale face between his large, gentle hands. "*I* remember the traps, and you only told me once about them," he said. "Do you not think that Jaimie will remember them?"

"I hope so," Maddy murmured, swallowing hard as she became entranced by his midnight dark eyes as he gazed at length into hers. "I . . . certainly . . . hope so."

"If you cannot relax with her out there among the traps, one of us can go and bring Jaimie back to the cabin," he said, his voice sounding strangely husky to Maddy. "Or do we stay behind and trust that she is astute enough to know what is best for herself?"

"What do you truly think?" Maddy asked, enjoying having someone else to guide her decisions about Jaimie. The responsibility had been put into her hands the moment someone had thrust the knife into her father's abdomen.

So often she grew weary of making all the decisions . . . decisions that might either take or save her sister's young life.

"It is not my decision to make," Black Wolf said thickly.

"But if it were, what would you do?" Maddy persisted. His hands on her cheeks, so wonderfully gentle, made her feel dizzy.

"I still will not say, because she is not my sister," Black Wolf said, his heart pounding.

He wanted her as he had never wanted anything in his life. His body ached for her. His loins were on fire with a need that threatened to engulf him!

He slowly lowered his lips toward hers, then drew quickly away when they both heard Jaimie's blood-curdling scream from the depths of the forest.

"Oh, no!" Maddy cried, jerking away from Black Wolf. Terror shot through her. "Oh, no! Jaimie!"

She ran to the door and flung it open, then rushed outside with Black Wolf close beside her as they ran toward the forest.

Guilt overwhelmed Maddy to think that she had been negligent in her duties toward her sister while in the arms of the man she adored, hungering for his kisses while she should have been going after Jaimie.

Now, because she had been lax in her duties for that one moment, Jaimie might have gotten caught in a trap.

She might be disfigured forever because of it, or worse yet, she might die from it!

Breathless, fighting off low-hanging branches and stumbling over the many fallen, decaying limbs on the ground, Maddy hurried onward, wondering why Jaimie hadn't cried out again.

Oh, Lord, she thought with despair. That could mean that Jaimie was unconscious.

Or . . . dead . . . !

When Maddy saw Jaimie through a break in

the trees, and saw that she was not injured, but was standing over the body of a man, relief flooded her. Jaimie had not come to any harm.

But when she got close enough and she saw who was lying there, she stopped short and turned her eyes away. She vaguely realized that Black Wolf was holding her as she bent over and threw up the breakfast that she had eaten only a short while ago.

"Santa . . ." she whispered when her stomach was empty. "Oh, Lord . . . it's . . . Santa."

Black Wolf drew her up and into his arms and held her against him as he looked over her shoulder at Jaimie, who was walking dispiritedly toward them, her eyes filled with tears.

"It's *Santa*," Jaimie sobbed as she came and stood beside Maddy and Black Wolf.

Black Wolf placed his large hand on Jaimie's head and brought her against him. She hugged him desperately, her whole body racked with sobs.

Maddy eased from Black Wolf's comforting arms and bent down to draw Jaimie into her embrace. "There, there," she murmured, caressing Jaimie's back. "Cry it out, Jaimie. Go ahead and cry it out."

"I . . . found . . . him lying there so cold . . . so . . ." Jaimie sobbed out, unable to finish telling how she had found Santa's nude body, decayed and disfigured, or how ants and flies covered him, feeding on his flesh.

Black Wolf left them long enough to go and

kneel down beside Santa's naked body. His gaze looked past the rotted flesh of the man and the ravenous insects devouring it and saw a knife wound in his abdomen.

In his mind's eye, he recalled how he had found his father. He had also been stripped of his clothes and lay beneath tall oak trees with the same sort of wound.

But Black Wolf had found him the same day he had been killed, so his body had not suffered the same insults as this man's.

He went back to Maddy and Jaimie. He knelt down beside Maddy. Their eyes met. "Like my father and your father, this man was killed with a knife in his belly," Black Wolf said thickly. "I have to ask you, Maddy. Were your father's clothes removed? Did the one who killed him remove his clothes?"

"Yes," Maddy said, almost choking on the word as she recalled wondering why anyone would need the clothes of the man he had slain. Unless he was in desperate need of anything he could collect from those he killed.

"Then I now know that there is a killer running loose in these forests of Illinois who kills, then steals from the dead, no matter that what my father wore was only a brief breechcloth," he said bitterly.

"Are you saying that whoever killed Santa might have also killed your father and mine?" Maddy asked, eyes wide.

"It does seem that way," Black Wolf said, nodding.

"Poor Santa," Maddy said, tears flooding her eyes again. "He never harmed anyone. He lived alone. He was so decent . . . so kind. And this is how his life ends? By the hands of some crazed lunatic?"

"We must leave this area today, not tomorrow," Black Wolf said, his voice drawn.

"But are you able to?" Maddy asked as Jaimie eased from her arms, shuddering when she glanced over at Santa. "And what about the river? It's still so swollen."

"I am able to," Black Wolf said. "And we will challenge the river with the best of our abilities."

Maddy's insides stiffened when she gazed at Santa. "I must first give him a proper burial," she murmured. "He deserves nothing less than . . . a . . . proper Christian burial and words spoken over him from the Bible."

Black Wolf sighed heavily. "He is in no condition to be moved unless wrapped first," he said, kneading his chin thoughtfully. "We must return to his cabin and get several blankets."

"Also a shovel for digging," Jaimie said, finally composed after the initial shock of what she had experienced wore off. "I can go and get them."

Maddy reached over and grabbed Jaimie. She held onto her for dear life. "No," she said, swallowing hard. "I'm not letting you out of my sight."

"We can all go together," Black Wolf said, taking Maddy's hand from Jaimie's arm. He put himself between them and took each of their hands. "Come. We will do what must be done, then leave immediately."

"Suddenly the world I always knew before my father and mother died has been turned into a nightmare," Maddy said, fighting back the tears that threatened to spill from her eyes again. "Will it ever end?"

"For so long my people's plight seemed as yours now seems . . . endless," Black Wolf said softly as the cabin came into view through the trees. "I learned long ago to focus on the word 'hope,' and in time things did seem much better. It will be the same for you and your sister, *Mee-tah-ween*. Concentrate on the word 'hope' and it will come to pass for you."

"That you can feel hope after all that has happened to you and your people speaks well for your character," Maddy murmured, their eyes locking as they looked at one another. "I admire you so, Black Wolf."

She wanted to cry out how much she loved and adored him, but with Jaimie there, she knew that it was best to wait until she was alone again with Black Wolf.

When they were, she would initiate lovemaking, for she knew from having seen so much death these past years that one must take advantage of life while living it.

And she wanted Black Wolf with her every heartbeat!

After arriving at the cabin and gathering blankets to wrap around Santa's body, and a shovel for digging his grave, they all went back and saw to his burial.

Tears flowed down Maddy's cheeks as she knelt over the fresh grave and said a soft prayer, reciting verses from the Bible that she had memorized as a child in Sunday school class.

Soon they had the boat packed again and were traveling down the middle of the Ohio River.

Maddy didn't tell Jaimie or Black Wolf, but she was more worried about Farris Boyd possibly seeing her in the river with Black Wolf than a murderer running loose in the area. Farris had surely gone back to the cave by now and found her and Jaimie gone.

She hoped that he hadn't destroyed the personal belongings that she had been forced to leave behind. She had planned to return for them once she established another home.

Black Wolf's mind was also on Farris Boyd. He was thinking about the possibility that he was the one killing innocent people along the banks of the Ohio!

For certain Farris would have had a reason for killing Maddy's father, and also Black Wolf's own.

But what could his connection be to the man who was called Santa?

As Black Wolf's eyes slowly raked over the banks of the Illinois side of the river, he vowed not to allow that man to harm Maddy or Jaimie.

If he touched either one of them, Farris would be the recipient of a knife wound in *his* belly. Black Wolf would take delight in killing the murderous, lying white man. His death should have come long ago. He hadn't deserved to live one day longer than Black Wolf's cousin Crazy Horse!

Chapter Twelve

Out of the day and night
A joy has taken flight—
Move my faint heart with grief, but with
    delight,
No more, O nevermore!
                    —Percy Bysshe Shelley

Maddy worried about Black Wolf rowing the boat, afraid that he was trying to do too much after having been so ill from his head wound. She sat behind him, watching his arms drawing the paddle rhythmically through the water.

Maddy and Jaimie joined him in scanning the shore with their searching eyes for signs of his people.

So far, nothing.

Maddy saw Black Wolf's gaze shift slowly to the left and knew that he was gazing at the very spot where his village had been as recently as yesterday. She could read the deep despair in his eyes. She could almost feel it inside her heart.

She wished to go and sit next to him, to say words of comfort to him, but she sensed that he needed time to work out his feelings, alone.

She reached over and took Jaimie's hand, drawing her sister's questioning eyes to her.

"I'm so glad we have each other," Maddy whispered. She slid an arm around her sister's waist and drew her closer.

"Me too," Jaimie whispered back. She was also watching Black Wolf, wondering what he was thinking.

Gazing to his left, Black Wolf slowly rowed past the place where his village had been located, where his people had learned to relax and enjoy life again after having been forced from their homeland.

Now his people would have to start over again. He prayed that they were still together as one group. If they were scattered they would be completely at the mercy of white men.

He wondered how many times his people could stand up under the continued pressure of disappointments, and indifference from white people, who saw them as scavengers.

Black Wolf vowed that he would not stop until he found all of his people and gathered them together as one unit again.

He was afraid, though, that he would have to start all over again in making them believe in such a thing as hope . . . and in their future.

He felt deep despair, himself, over having lost everything again. He was afraid that he might join his people in doubting that life could ever be good to them once more.

But remembering the woman who sat behind him, picturing in his mind's eye her sweet smile, recalling her wondrous, soft laughter, he found much to live for.

In *her* he would find a shred of hope and cling to it. Because of her, he had the courage to go on.

He *would* find his people and pass this courage on to them! They would sing again around great fires in the night. They would feast after a successful hunt. They would rebuild their homes and fill them with love and laughter.

But now, as he once again saw the void in the water where his village had been before the river came roaring down across their land, he felt an emptiness inside him that he found hard to fight.

The water had receded somewhat, making visible more of the trees that had shaded their lodges. Mud and debris clung to the powerful limbs of those majestic trees, a reminder of how unmerciful Mother Nature could be.

She gave so much to his people, yet she also took away!

Maddy could see how despondent Black Wolf was as he gazed over his shoulder at the spot where his village had stood. She felt helpless to relieve him of his burden. She was a mere woman . . . a white woman, at that. It was his people that he needed at this time . . . to know they were all right. As their leader, he wished to guide them to a safe haven away from the ravages of the river.

She wondered, at this moment, if she had fooled herself into believing that she might fit into that world with Black Wolf and his people. When he did find them—and find them he would, for his devotion to them was fierce— surely she would come second, perhaps even last, in his mind and heart.

For now, she served a purpose. But would she still have a purpose in his life when he became involved in setting things right for his people again? She doubted it.

She solemnly watched as he rowed onward, taking them past her and Jaimie's cabin. Water stood halfway up the walls and debris clung to the roof, evidence that it had been covered by water, if only for a short while.

It was time now for her to brood and feel empty inside, for when her family had celebrated the building of this home, they had seen such a wonderful vision for their future.

Maddy's mother had been pregnant with her third child.

Her father had come ahead of them by several weeks and had planted seeds for crops that were already pushing their green sprouts through the black, fertile soil when Maddy, Jaimie, and her mother had arrived there.

They had laughed and found it fun to camp outside beneath the stars until the cabin was finished.

Now all but the memory of those hopeful times was gone. All that remained of their dreams of the future were the two sisters whose dreams were now changed forever.

After having met Black Wolf, Maddy had allowed herself to believe that her dreams might one day be his.

As for Jaimie, everywhere Maddy would go, and whatever she would do, her beloved sister would accompany her . . . until she grew old enough to find a man who would fill her heart with the same sort of feelings that Maddy had for Black Wolf.

Maddy looked away from the shore when Black Wolf continued drawing the paddle through the water, taking them farther and farther downriver toward River Town. She knew that she had to get hold of herself and think of their present circumstances.

Realizing that River Town, or what was left of it, was just around the bend in the river, Maddy tensed. If those who had survived the flood there saw her and Jaimie with an Indian in the boat, they might think he had abducted them. She knew that most whites in this area did not trust any man with red skin. They even feared the Shawnee, whose palisaded village was downriver a short distance from River Town and had never caused any trouble for the whites in the area.

Black Wolf's people, who had isolated themselves on an island, rarely left the island to come into River Town except when they needed supplies.

She swallowed hard and clung to Jaimie as they rounded the bend and saw what was left of the small town. The river was still lapping at the roofs of the buildings that had been built along the shores of the Ohio. Those few that sat farther back had water up to their windowsills.

Luckily, because of the commotion at the riverfront, with small boats moving frantically from place to place and people shouting at one another from boat to boat, no one noticed them go by.

Sighing with relief that they had succeeded in getting past River Town without being noticed, especially by Farris Boyd, Maddy relaxed somewhat as Black Wolf kept rowing down the middle of the river.

"How much longer are we going to be in this boat?" Jaimie whined, snuggling closer to Maddy. "Maddy, I'm so tired. I'm so hungry."

"It's up to Black Wolf," Maddy murmured. She reached for a blanket on the floor of the boat and gently wrapped it around Jaimie's shoulders. "Just rest against me, Jaimie. Go to sleep. I'll wake you up when we stop."

"I wonder if he'll ever find his people," Jaimie murmured, gazing up at Maddy with wistful eyes.

"Yes, in time he will," Maddy said, amazed at how steadfastly Black Wolf kept rowing, when only yesterday he was so lightheaded and dizzy he could scarcely keep steady when he walked. "I just don't know where . . . or when."

"I wish he'd find them today," Jaimie said, closing her eyes and yawning. "I wish I could help him find them."

"Me too, sweetie," Maddy said, inhaling a quivering breath. "Me too."

Maddy's eyes widened when she got her first glimpse of the palisaded walls of the Shawnee camp a short distance ahead. She could tell that the river had not affected it. The Shawnee had been knowledgeable enough of the Ohio River to realize that it could not be trusted and had built their village far above the flood line.

She studied the village as they drew closer. The walls rose high around it on all four sides, yet the crops had been planted outside the walls. Row after row of corn sprouts were coming up through the black, tilled soil.

She could see beans twining up sticks that had been placed in the ground in the shape of tepee lodge poles.

Green vines of pumpkins were weaving along the ground, and various other green sprouts that Maddy did not recognize were also shooting up through the fresh earth.

Closer to the wall was a large corral filled with an assortment of horses. She could see a warrior standing guard at the far side, keeping the herd safe from horse thieves.

And now, as they drew closer to the village, Maddy saw that the wide gate was open. Children ran to and from it, dogs yapping at their heels. Smoke rolled heavenward from cook fires inside the fence. The smell of food wafting down toward the river in the breeze stirred Maddy's stomach to growling, a reminder that they had eaten only one meal today. They had not planned to make such a quick exit from Santa's cabin.

"Santa," Maddy whispered, her heart sinking as she remembered how he had died. She wondered how long he had been there on the cold ground at the mercy of the insects.

"We will stop at the Shawnee village," Black Wolf said, giving Maddy a quick look over his shoulder. "My father and I have been at the village. We have held counsel with the Shawnee. They are a kind people. They will welcome us. Perhaps they will offer some assistance in finding my people. Perhaps they will ask us to spend the night. My head . . . I am not sure how much longer I can hold it up. The pain has returned."

Maddy started to go to him and check his wound, to see if it had broken open from the exertion of paddling the boat for so long.

But she stopped when someone shouted Black Wolf's name from the shore. She saw in Black Wolf's expression—the excitement in his eyes—that he knew the one who was calling for him.

"It is Lone Beaver!" Black Wolf cried, guiding the boat toward shore.

"You know the man?" Maddy asked, seeing an Indian running toward the river, waving, his smile broad and filled with excitement. "Is he Shawnee?"

147

"No, he is not Shawnee," Black Wolf said, laughing. "He is Sioux! Lone Beaver is my best friend. The Shawnee have once again reached out to the Sioux in friendship. Surely the rest of my people are at the Shawnee village seeking refuge from the ravages of the river."

His smile faded as he reminded himself that he been separated from his people. Couldn't the same have happened to Lone Beaver? What if Black Wolf's search still was not over? How much longer could he continue onward before he dropped from exhaustion and pain?

When he got as close as he could in the boat, he jumped over the side into waist-high water.

Lone Beaver ran into the water and helped Black Wolf drag the boat to dry land. Then they fell into each other's arms, hugging and speaking in the Sioux tongue, saying things Maddy could not understand as they splashed onto dry land.

The camaraderie Maddy saw between these two Indians made her feel warm and good inside, for she knew the joy that Black Wolf must be feeling. She could feel it inside her own heart, as though her joy was an extension of his.

As Maddy and Jaimie started to leave the boat, Maddy grabbed Jaimie's arm and stopped her when she saw a crowd of people coming from the Shawnee village. She knew by their emotional reaction to seeing Black Wolf that they were his people . . . that he was finally being reunited with his loved ones.

They flocked around him. They shared hugs and laughter, rejoicing to know that their leader was alive.

Maddy discovered through hearing some of them speaking English that none of his people had died. They were as one again, the promise of tomorrow bright in their eyes just knowing that Black Wolf was there to lead them!

Maddy continued to sit with Jaimie, watching, slowly realizing that she and Jaimie were out of place here, especially when the crowd began moving toward the gate in the huge fence with Black Wolf amidst them.

It stung her heart, as though hornets were inside her, to see how Black Wolf had so quickly forgotten her. He was walking away from her without even one glance back at her.

She tried not to feel jealous of his people. Perhaps this was the way it should be. Although it broke her heart to think of leaving Black Wolf, Maddy knew that it was best for both her and Black Wolf. She would only bring danger into the lives of Black Wolf and his people.

Trying not to be hurt so deeply that Black Wolf had forgotten her the very moment he found his people, Maddy climbed from the boat.

"Come on, Jaimie," she said, already dragging the boat back toward the river. "Help me. Let's get this thing in the water. Black Wolf doesn't need us any longer."

"What?" Jaimie said, her eyes raised in disbelief that Maddy could leave Black Wolf so easily, and without even telling him goodbye.

Jaimie had seen how Black Wolf had momentarily put Maddy from his mind. But she knew that it was due to his excitement at having found his people.

She expected him to turn around at any moment and tell Maddy to come and join him during his time of rejoicing.

"Help me get this thing in the water, Jaimie, and no back talk," Maddy grumbled, the muscles in her arms aching as she continued to shove the boat with all her might.

She wanted to make a quick exit. The sooner she got away from Black Wolf, the sooner she might be able to start forgetting him!

When she suddenly heard Black Wolf shouting her name, Maddy stiffened. Her pulse raced at the knowledge that she had been wrong to think he could forget her so easily. She longed to go to him and stay with him.

But she had made her decision.

She knew that it was best to go on and forget Black Wolf.

He had his people. He didn't need her in the way of what lay ahead of them. The Sioux had so much to do to set their lives on the right path again!

"Hurry, Jaimie!" Maddy cried, giving one last shove that finally sent the boat into the river. "Get in, Jaimie!"

Maddy sat down and grabbed the paddle, and as Jaimie scurried to sit down behind her, she already had the boat splashing through the waves as it headed for the middle of the river.

Maddy winced and pinched her eyes tightly closed when Black Wolf stood at the riverbank, crying her name over and over again.

Her heartbeats slammed against her chest. Tears flowed from her eyes.

Her fingers ached as she clutched the paddle and drew it over and over again through the water.

"Why, Maddy?" Jaimie cried. "Why are you ignoring Black Wolf? Why would you do this?"

"Because that's how it must be, Jaimie," Maddy said, her voice breaking. "Now just be quiet. We've got our own lives to set in order."

"But why must we do it without Black Wolf?" Jaimie asked with a sob.

Maddy didn't make any response to her sister's question, for she wasn't quite sure she had an answer. All of the reasons why she had shoved the boat back into the river did not seem to make sense now.

The pain of regret was so overwhelming that she grabbed at her chest and gasped. "I've lost him," she whispered, paling at the realization of what she had done.

Chapter Thirteen

Love, faithful love, recalled thee to my
    mind—
But how could I forget thee?
    —William Wordsworth

Tormented by the memory of Black Wolf shouting her name over and over again, Maddy continued paddling away from the Shawnee village. She still couldn't believe that she had left Black Wolf in such a callous way, yet if she hadn't, she knew that parting with him would have been impossible. After seeing him with his people, and realizing that she would only be a distraction when he had so much to do to make things right for his people, how could she have stayed?

And she would keep reminding herself of how he had momentarily forgotten her as he mingled with his people. Even that memory made her feel forlorn now, not because he had seemed to lose interest in her as soon as he was among his people, but because she had allowed those feelings of rejection to make her jealous.

But still she knew that she was right to go on

her way without him. Being with him, knowing such a man for at least a short while, and believing that he did truly love her, would have to sustain her.

Of one thing she was certain. Having lost the man she would love forever, she vowed that she would not lose Jaimie. The land that her father had bought with hard cash upon their arrival in Illinois still belonged in her family. She would not leave it because of such a man as Farris Boyd. She wouldn't let him frighten her away from land her father had poured his heart into.

She would not build on the exact spot of the original home. Their new cabin would be on higher land, away from the flood line. She and Jaimie would build something wonderful, for it would be Maddy's home forever; she now knew that she would never marry. She could never love anyone as she loved Black Wolf, and she would not marry any man unless she loved him.

"Maddy, where are we going?" Jaimie asked, breaking through Maddy's troubled thoughts. "I . . . I . . . thought we were going to stay with Black Wolf. It could have been so intriguing living with Indians."

"One does not live a certain way just because it is *intriguing*," Maddy said, giving Jaimie a glance over her shoulder. Jaimie was sitting behind her, huddled beneath a blanket that she held clutched around her shoulders. "And I don't want to discuss Black Wolf. We've much to do, Jaimie, to set our lives back in order. And we will do it without anyone's help. I've learned through this experience that you must grab on to and keep what is rightfully yours. Pa's land? It is now *ours*. We will rebuild and replant and make Pa smile as he looks down on us from heaven."

"But . . . what . . . about Farris Boyd?" Jaimie asked guardedly. "Maddy, you know how determined he is to have you."

"Well, we'll just have to show him who's boss, won't we?" Maddy said, stubbornly setting her jaw.

"He's a scheming, evil man," Jaimie said. "Crossing him is perhaps worse than crossing the devil."

"Yes, I know I . . . *we* . . . have a fight on our hands where he is concerned, but, Jaimie, we will win," Maddy said, rowing on past the remains of River Town. She was dreading returning to the cave although she was trying hard to look brave and courageous in the eyes of her little sister.

She knew for certain that they had much to fear from Farris, especially when he realized that she had lied to him when she had told him that she would accept his courtship.

In truth, she would die before going anywhere with him unless it was at gunpoint. She would have to just face him with the truth and stand up to any threat he might make.

Surely that would prove to him that her word was final.

"So you're going back to the cave?" Jaimie asked, looking at the buildings in River Town. The water had receded some more, making it possible now for people to go inside the muddy remains of the establishments on higher ground.

"Yes, we're going back to the cave," Maddy said. "We'll stay there while we build our cabin a short distance away."

"Closer to Ma and Pa's and the baby's graves?"

"Yes, close enough that we will feel their presence each night as we say our bedtime prayers," Maddy said, her voice breaking.

Her thoughts returned to Black Wolf, knowing that he and his people would not stay at the Shawnee village for long. Black Wolf would be anxious to find a new home for his people where they could erect their permanent lodges again. She wasn't sure if it would be on the Illinois side of the river, or the Kentucky side. No matter which, she would have to fight against wanting to go and find him once she had a cabin built for herself and Jaimie and would have time to dwell on missing Black Wolf.

She wondered if he might search her out once he had things right in his world again, or would he take her rejection of him as humiliatingly final?

"Sis, there's our cabin," Jaimie cried, bringing Maddy out of her reverie. "Look, Maddy! The river has receded enough now so that we can go into the cabin if we wish. Let's, Maddy. Oh, please, let's."

"Everything we left in there is ruined, Jaimie," Maddy said sadly as she gazed at the cabin. Water was lapping at the door. Mud and debris were clinging to it. "Let's not punish ourselves by looking at it. Let's go on to the cave and begin making plans for our new home."

"Whatever you think is best," Jaimie said, sighing resolutely.

There was a quiet pause between them as Maddy turned her boat and began rowing toward shore. Then Jaimie broke the silence.

"Maddy, what if Farris is at the cave waiting for us?" she asked, her voice drawn.

"Surely he has better things to do than bother us," Maddy said. "You saw River Town, Jaimie. He's the sheriff. He has responsibilities to the town that any community leader would have. I imagine he is there helping those who are in need."

"Ha," Jaimie said sarcastically. "Surely you don't believe that, Maddy. Farris? An angel of mercy?"

"I'd never call him an angel of anything," Maddy said, laughing softly. "But let's think positively, Jaimie, and picture him at River Town, so busy that we are the last people on his mind."

When Maddy came close enough to the shore, she jumped into the river, flinching when she felt her feet sink to her ankles in mud. She fought the suction of the mud until she finally got the boat secured on dry land, then helped Jaimie out.

"Oh, Sis, look at your shoes," Jaimie said, visibly shuddering.

"Yes, I know," Maddy said, sighing. She sat down on the riverbank and removed her shoes.

As Jaimie unloaded the boat, Maddy cleaned her shoes, removed her sockings and washed them out in the river, then splashed her feet around in the water until they were clean.

Not wanting to walk around in squishy shoes and socks, she placed them in a box and scrambled through her belongings until she found a pair of leather boots her father had brought home for her one day from River Town.

She struggled into the boots, then looked up the hill where she had left her horses and cow. She shuddered when she found they were no longer there.

"Jaimie, we tethered our animals well enough, didn't we?" she said, drawing Jaimie's attention to the missing animals.

"Yes, I, myself, tied the knots," Jaimie said as she stared at where she had last seen their horses and cow. "Oh, Lord, Maddy, someone stole them."

Maddy sighed and filled her arms with a box of belongings. "Yes, someone profited from our loss," she said, walking up the hill toward the cave. "I guess I should have expected it."

"We should've left them in the cave," Jaimie

said, tears spilling from her eyes over having lost the animals, especially the horses.

"No, we did the right thing by placing them outside in the fresh air with grass to feed on," Maddy said, huffing and puffing as the hill became steeper. "Once we're settled in, Jaimie, we'll purchase another horse and cow."

"But we needed the horses to trade for supplies to build a new house," Jaimie fussed, more angry now over the loss than sad.

"Yes, I know," Maddy said, sighing. "But we must learn to accept things as we find them."

Her thoughts went to Santa and how he had been murdered and left for the insects and animals to feed upon.

She felt lucky that she and Jaimie were alive. In a heartbeat even that could change.

She glanced over at Jaimie. Although precocious at times, she was such a precious, endearing child. Maddy would make sure her sister got a full chance at life. She would let nothing harm her!

"We're finally there," Jaimie said, stepping up to the cave entrance. "Maddy, I'll set these things down and go back to the boat for more."

"No, wait a minute," Maddy said, eyeing the cave entrance warily. "Let's check things out first, then together we will go back to the boat for our other things. We must not be separated, Jaimie, not even for one minute. Not until things in the area become normal again."

"Will they ever?" Jaimie said dispiritedly, lowering the box she had carried to the ground. "There's a murderer running around killing innocent people. The river has changed so many people's lives. Oh, Lord, Maddy, there are so many things that have happened to change ours."

She hung her head, then welcomed Maddy's arms around her.

"Jaimie, oh, dear, sweet Jaimie," Maddy murmured. "Life does have a way of testing humans. It just seems that right now the tests are never-ending."

"I want Ma and Pa," Jaimie said, bursting suddenly into deep, harsh sobs as she clung to Maddy.

This surprised Maddy, for Jaimie, up to now, had always seemed the stronger of them. Maddy was the one who always seemed to be taking comfort from Jaimie!

But now, with the changes in their lives came changes in her little sister that Maddy welcomed. She had begun to worry that Jaimie's heart was becoming too toughened by the continuing challenges in their lives. Now Maddy knew that Jaimie was still a vulnerable ten-year-old girl.

"There, there," Maddy murmured, stroking her sister's back. "Things will be all right. I'll make them all right, Jaimie. Now let's go inside the cave and get a warm fire started. We'll sort through our things and find the popping corn. Tonight we'll eat popped corn and tell stories."

"That sounds so good," Jaimie said, sniffling as she eased from Maddy's arms. "It'll be like old times, won't it, Sis? When we sat by the fire in our home and ate popcorn and told stories?"

"Yes, like old times," Maddy said, taking Jaimie's hand. "Now come on. Let's get that fire started."

"Sis, I sure do love you," Jaimie said, smiling up at Maddy as they walked into the cave together.

"Honey, I love you, too," Maddy said, squeezing Jaimie's hand affectionately. "And we're going to make it just fine, sweetie. I promise you that."

"I know," Jaimie said, then stopped suddenly and went pale when she and Maddy simultaneously saw a match ignite inside the cave. They watched as the flame was set to the wick of one of their kerosene lamps, giving off enough light for them to see Farris Boyd standing there, a rifle aimed directly at them.

"Scat, Jaimie," Farris growled out, his eyes locked on Maddy's pale, fearful face. "You get on outta here. And don't come back if you know what's good for you and your sister. If I ever set eyes on you again, I'll not hesitate to shoot you, and even Maddy, if I'm forced to."

"Jaimie, do . . . as . . . he says," Maddy said stiffly, slowly releasing Jaimie's hand. "Leave. I'll be all right."

"But, Maddy—" Jaimie cried, her eyes wild.

"Jaimie, do as you are told," Maddy said flatly. "*Leave.*"

"I'll go get help," Jaimie cried, slowly backing away.

"You heard what I said," Farris growled. He then laughed sarcastically. "And even if you did go for help, no one would listen. Especially not to a dumb kid's complaints when they've got problems of their own. The river has taken most everything from everyone."

"Maddy, oh, Maddy . . ." Jaimie cried, frantic.

Maddy bent suddenly and swept Jaimie into her arms. "Just remember that I love you," she murmured, then leaned closer to Jaimie's ear. "Go to Black Wolf. He'll find a way to help us."

"Stop that!" Farris shouted. "Get away from her, Maddy! Get out of here, Jaimie, or I'll shoot you."

Sobbing, Jaimie rushed from the cave. She stumbled and half rolled down the hill toward the river, then got back to her feet and went and boarded the boat. Her heart pounding, she headed downriver for the Shawnee village.

Chapter Fourteen

From little cares; to find with easy quest,
A fragrant wild, with nature's beauty drest,
And there into delight my soul deceives.
                                    —John Keats

"You're not going to get away with this," Maddy
said, squaring her shoulders and glaring at Farris as he took slow steps toward her.

"What do you mean by *that*?" Farris said,
chuckling. "You don't know what you're talkin'
about. You the same as promised to marry me,
didn't you? I'm only seeing that you keep your
word."

Regretting her lie to Farris more and more,
Maddy left the cave at gunpoint. "Where are you
taking me?" she asked, looking deperately down
at the river, sighing with relief when she saw
that the boat was not there.

That had to mean that Jaimie was safely gone.
She hoped that Jaimie could make it to the
Shawnee village and that Black Wolf would
come to her rescue.

"I'm taking you to that beautiful home I promised you," Farris said, laughing.

He grabbed Maddy by an arm and directed her toward the dense forest, where she soon saw not only his horse but also hers. Even the cow was there.

He was the thief who'd stolen them!

"I should've known," she said sarcastically, her breath momentarily knocked out of her when he slammed her against the hard body of the strawberry roan.

"Get on that horse," he growled out, his eyes narrowed angrily.

"I . . . am . . . not skilled . . . at riding," Maddy panted, gasping for breath.

"Get on anyhow," he shouted, boosting her roughly onto the horse, bareback.

He shoved the reins into her hands, then went and mounted his own white stallion.

Truly frightened of horses, Maddy clung to the reins and tried not to slide from the roan's back as she was forced to ride beside Farris through the forest.

Tears fell from her eyes as she tried not to envision this ugly, terrible man forcing himself on her sexually before she was rescued!

Chapter Fifteen

As thus with thee in prayer in my sore need,
Oh! Lift me as a wave, a leaf, a cloud!
I fall upon the thorns of life!
I bleed!

        —Percy Bysshe Shelley

Her mouth dry, her pulse racing, her small arms aching from having paddled the boat without resting until she had beached it near the Shawnee camp, Jaimie now ran toward the palisaded village. Her arms flailing in the air as she waved anxiously to the Indians outside the huge fence, she began screaming Black Wolf's name.

When he appeared suddenly at the gate and ran toward her, she flung herself into his arms.

"Maddy!" she cried. "Oh, Black Wolf, you've got to help Maddy!"

Seeing Jaimie's desperation, and knowing that Maddy was in some sort of trouble, Black Wolf knew a terrible fear. He reached down and placed his hands on Jaimie's shoulders and gently held her away from him.

"*Tahn-kah*, younger sister Jaimie, you must

tell me where she is," he said thickly, his heart thumping inside his chest. His eyes locked with Jaimie's as she gazed up at him. "Tell me what has happened to Maddy."

"She . . . she . . ." Jaimie said, stammering over the awful words. "Oh, Black Wolf, Farris Boyd has her!" Her sobs made the words come out in jerks. "He . . . made . . . me leave. Farris was holding a rifle on Maddy. Who is to say what his plans are for her?"

"*Tahn-kah*, where are they?" Black Wolf demanded, his eyes narrowing as anger engulfed him.

"At the cave," Jaimie said. She wiped tears from her face with the hem of her shirt. "When we arrived at the cave he was already there waiting for us. He was waiting with his rifle."

Several armed warriors, both Sioux and Shawnee, rushed from the fort and circled around Black Wolf and Jaimie.

Lone Beaver moved to Black Wolf's side, a rifle clutched in his right hand. "What has happened?" he asked, gazing from Jaimie to Black Wolf. "Why is the young brave crying? What news has he brought to you?"

"I'm not a boy," Jaimie blurted out. "I'm a *girl*. And . . . my . . . sister Maddy is in trouble. She needs Black Wolf's help."

Black Wolf knelt down and drew Jaimie into his arms. He held her and comforted her as he explained to his warriors what had happened to Maddy and what he was going to do about it.

"You are certain you do not want to take warriors to rescue her, instead of just going yourself with the child?" Lone Beaver asked. "Many warriors can achieve much more than one." He glanced at Black Wolf's wound. "And are you well enough to go on such a rescue?"

"My body is healed enough for me to do anything I wish to do," Black Wolf said, his jaw tight. "And finding the man and making him pay for his evil deeds is something I need to do alone. It is something I should have done long ago."

"Why do you say this is something you needed to do long ago when it is only recently that you have met the woman?" Lone Beaver asked, arching an eyebrow.

"The man who holds her hostage, Lone Beaver, is a man whose name is familiar to all Sioux," Black Wolf said. "Farris Boyd. Do you not now see why I must seek vengeance on this man once and for all? Do you see why I never should have rested until I saw that he was dead and his mouth was sealed forever, unable to brag about having killed my cousin Crazy Horse?"

"*Hetchetu-aloh*, it is so indeed. I see, and I wish you well," Lone Beaver said wearily, then squared his shoulders and held his rifle out for Black Wolf. "Since I cannot go with you to see this man's end, it would please me if you would down the man with a bullet from my rifle. That way, at least, I will have a part in his demise."

Black Wolf rose to his full height. His eyes filled with pride, he took the rifle. "Yes, my best friend, I will use your rifle," he said thickly.

He glanced over at his horse, which had been placed with the rest of the Sioux horses that had been saved from the island. They were scattered among the Shawnee mounts grazing in the corral.

He then nodded at one of his people's young braves who had wormed his way through the circle of Sioux warriors to stare questioningly at Jaimie.

"Eagle Wing, go and get my horse and bring yours for Jaimie to use," Black Wolf said, placing a firm hand on the young brave's bare, slim shoulder.

Eagle Wing smiled broadly up at Black Wolf. "I will proudly do this for you," he said. Then as the warriors parted to make room for him to leave, he ran to the horses and got them for Black Wolf.

Black Wolf turned to Jaimie. "*Tahn-kah*, you can ride, can't you?" he asked, assuming that this child who seemed skilled in all masculine pursuits could also ride.

"Yes, I can ride," Jaimie said. "Pa taught me how when we still lived in Kentucky. I love horses, Black Wolf, and when Maddy and I left you a short while ago and went to get our horses . . . we . . . discovered that ours had been stolen."

"Do not fret so," Black Wolf said, placing a

167

gentle hand on her cheek. "Later, after we have Maddy safe and my people are in their rebuilt homes, I will let you choose which horse among mine you wish to have as yours."

"Really?" Jaimie gasped, her eyes widening. "You would do this even though Maddy and I left you without saying goodbye?"

"I am sure Maddy had reasons for leaving that she can explain to me," Black Wolf said. "And after I rescue her, I am sure she will see how wrong it was for her to leave the safety I offer her. She will come with me now, will she not, Jaimie, once you and I find her?"

"I cannot speak for her," Jaimie said, swallowing hard. She desperately grabbed Black Wolf's hand. "Oh, please don't let my saying that keep you from going to help her. She does need you, Black Wolf." She swallowed again. "So do I."

"Nothing would stop me from going to save her," Black Wolf said, nodding a thank you to Eagle Wing as the young brave handed him the reins of Black Wolf's horse, and then gave the reins of his own horse to Jaimie.

"Thank you, oh, thank you," Jaimie said, tears threatening to spill from her eyes again. But a determination to save her sister kept them from falling. Besides, the young brave was watching her, and she refused to act like a baby.

As curious about the young brave as he seemed to be about her, she had studied him while Black Wolf and Lone Beaver were talking. He seemed maybe two years older than herself.

Although he was thin and wiry, the muscles in his arms and legs had already developed.

Like Black Wolf, he wore a breechclout and moccasins, leaving his chest bare. His skin was hairless and smooth, the color of copper. Jaimie found herself feeling strangely drawn to him, but in a different way from how she had been drawn to Black Wolf. She was attracted to this young boy, whose dark eyes seemed to speak to her soul.

Now Eagle Wing stared at her, their hands having brushed as the reins had been passed from his to hers. "Thank you for allowing me to use your horse," Jaimie said, blushing when Eagle Wing smiled his friendly smile again.

"He is a good horse," Eagle Wing said, stroking the horse's thick white mane. "He will take you where you need to go today and bring you back safely again to our people."

"Thank you," Jaimie said softly. "I appreciate your trusting me with your horse."

"It is time now to go," Black Wolf said, swinging himself into his saddle.

Jaimie's heart melted when Eagle Wing helped her up into his saddle. For the first time in her life she knew how it felt to have an infatuation for someone of the opposite sex.

Again she blushed when her eyes met Eagle Wing's, then she yanked on the reins, swung the horse around, and rode off with Black Wolf.

Finally, when the cave was in sight, she drew

169

her horse to a halt beside Black Wolf's and dismounted.

"We will leave our mounts here," Black Wolf whispered, already tying his reins to the low limb of a maple tree.

Jaimie frowned. She gazed at the cropped grass, and at the small stream, then looked at Black Wolf uneasily. "This is where Maddy and I left our horses before," she whispered. "What if someone steals these?"

"Whoever stole your horses is surely far away now and is no longer a threat," Black Wolf said, placing a comforting hand on Jaimie's shoulder. "Now tie in your reins with mine. We must hurry, *Tahn-kah*. Maddy has been with the evil man for too long already."

"Yes, I know," Jaimie murmured, tying the reins. She gave Black Wolf a glance. "I hope . . . we . . . are in time."

"If that man has wrongly touched her, his death will be slow and painful," Black Wolf growled out. When a pain shot through his head wound, he winced and grabbed for his brow.

Jaimie noticed his discomfort. "Are you going to be all right?" she asked. She looked at the wound and noticed that the scab had broken open. Blood oozed from it through his black hair.

"Do not worry about Black Wolf," Black Wolf said thickly. "Your sister is our only concern at this moment." He nodded toward the cave. "Let us go now, *Tahn-kah*. But stay out of the line of fire. The man who is holding your sister captive is capable of anything. He would not hesitate to shoot you, even though you are a child whose whole life lies ahead of you."

"Yes, I know the true villain he is," Jaimie said, shivering at the thought of Maddy being with him.

Stealthily, they moved together toward the cave.

Just as they reached the entrance, Black Wolf reached a hand out for Jaimie, stopping her. "*Tahn-kah*, you stay here," he whispered. "I will go inside."

"I want to go with you," Jaimie whispered back, her eyes pleading with Black Wolf.

"Do you not remember what I said about staying out of the line of fire?" Black Wolf said, frowning at Jaimie. "You stay here, *Tahn-kah*. Do not follow me unless I speak your name!"

"All right, whatever you say," Jaimie said, sighing heavily.

She stepped aside and watched Black Wolf go into the cave, her heart pounding as she waited for gunfire to break out.

When she heard nothing, she wasn't sure if she should feel hopeful, or afraid. There was no telling how to feel when she had no idea what was going on inside the cave.

She started to go inside, but forced herself to stop, remembering that Black Wolf had told her not to come unless he called for her.

"What is he doing?" Jaimie whispered to herself, kicking at a rock.

Black Wolf came from the cave, his brow furrowed with a worried frown.

"Well?" Jaimie asked. She looked past Black Wolf, then looked up at him again with pleading eyes. "Where is my sister, Black Wolf? Wasn't she there?"

"She and the evil man are gone," Black Wolf said, nervously kneading his brow with his free hand.

He looked down at the cabin. Then he looked slowly from side to side. His spine stiffened when he saw fresh footprints on the ground, and then hoofprints made by three horses, and some other animal Black Wolf was not familiar with.

Jaimie followed Black Wolf's steady stare. "What are you looking at?" she asked, then saw the prints on the muddy ground.

She could tell that three horses had been there, and also. . . .

"Our cow!" she cried, looking quickly at Black Wolf. "Black Wolf, do you see the cow's prints? Surely they were made by our cow." Her jaw tightened. "And I bet two of the horses are also ours."

She gasped and looked wide-eyed up at Black Wolf. "He stole them," she said excitedly. "Not only did he take Maddy, he also took our horses and cow!"

"The *wihio* is not a very clever man," Black

Wolf said, chuckling. "Does he not know that he can be tracked by these prints?"

"I imagine not," Jaimie said, laughing softly. She grabbed Black Wolf by a hand. "Come on, Black Wolf. Let's get our horses and follow the prints. Oh, Black Wolf, we're going to find Maddy!"

They ran to the horses and mounted them, then began following the tracks that led away from the cave to much higher ground.

"I wonder where he's taking Maddy," Jaimie murmured as she watched the tracks.

Then she let out a loud whoop. "I know!" she cried, drawing Black Wolf's attention. "I know where these tracks will lead us. Farris bragged often of his house and what a mansion it is compared to the rest of the homes in this area. And he said that it was high on a hill, safe from the ravages of the Ohio. Oh, surely, Black Wolf, that's where we'll find them! He wanted Maddy to marry him and live there with him!"

Jaimie went pale. "Lord, no," she gasped out. "What if he gets a preacher and forces her to marry him before we reach them and stop it from happening?"

Black Wolf and Jaimie exchanged silent, worried stares.

Chapter Sixteen

I never hear the word "escape"
Without a quicker blood,
A sudden expectation. . . .

—Emily Dickinson

Maddy stood in awe of the house that Farris had taken her to. It was so lovely it wasn't something that she ever could have imagined. It was most certainly a home that she had never seen before. He had built it way back in the forest, having downed only enough trees to make space for the building.

Surely he had hired many men to build it, for it was even larger than the mansions she had seen on the vast horse farms back in Kentucky.

It had tall pillars at the front, and a broad porch reaching out along the whole front of the house, where she could envision a lovely, full-skirted lady sitting demurely for an afternoon of mint juleps. She had to try hard not to show how the house took her breath away.

"You *are* quite taken with my home, aren't you?" Farris said, taking the horse's reins from

Maddy. He flipped them around a hitching pole, then stood beside Maddy and gazed at the house along with her. "The home is now not only mine, Maddy, but yours. Soon we will be united in a bond of marriage."

His mention of marriage brought Maddy out of her trance.

She sent Farris an angry stare. "I'll never marry you," she ground out, her eyes narrowing. "You're daft if you think you can force me into it. And what preacher would marry us if he knew I was totally against it?"

"You'll not say a word against it in the presence of the preacher or, by God, I'll go and find Jaimie and slit her throat," Farris growled. He grabbed her by an arm and forced her up the steps to the porch. "You know I'd do it, Maddy. I'll stop at nothing to have you. I've already done more than you'll ever imagine to reach this point in our relationship."

"What do you mean?" Maddy asked warily. "What have you done?"

Farris's eyes narrowed and his jaw tightened as he ignored her question.

His hold on her arm hurting her, Maddy tried not to grimace. "So you won't answer me. Well, hear me when I tell you there *is* no relationship," she said bitterly, lifting her chin haughtily. "Why can't you understand that there never will be a . . . relationship between us."

"And so you would turn your nose up at what I offer you, even though you are too stubborn to admit that no one else on this earth could be so generous?" Farris said, still holding her in a tight grip, while with his other hand he opened the door and forced her inside to the spacious foyer, which revealed two magnificent parlors, one on each side.

"Take a long look, Maddy," Farris said, chuckling as he took her into a lavish parlor. "It's yours for the asking. Everything my mother cherished is now yours. Look around you, Maddy. Can't you see my mother in everything that is here?"

That thought gave Maddy cold shivers. It disturbed her to realize that most of the house was furnished with the possessions of a dead woman.

As she slowly scanned the room, she could almost envision a small, elderly lady with gray hair rolled into a tight bun atop her head. Perhaps she would run her lean fingers over the velveteen divan and matching chairs, or pick up a piece of the lovely crystal that was displayed in a hutch on the far wall and hold it against the light at the window so that the rays of sunlight reflected from it in purple and blue rainbows along the floor.

Or the lovely, tiny lady might even be sitting on the beautiful chaise longue beside the French door that led out to a lovely veranda. She could be reading a book, or sipping tea and eating lovely, small, delicate cakes with fancy icing.

Yes, there was so much in this one room that spoke of wealth and grandeur, it made Maddy feel strange standing in the midst of it, for never had she dreamed of owning anything so lovely.

Silvery blue slate surrounded the fireplace. A Scottish plaid woolen rug was stretched out over a portion of the beautiful polished oak floor.

The parlor was a clean, airy space, illuminated by broad windows and filled with fine furniture and important pieces of art that hung on the wall above an oak writing desk.

"A woman comes once a week to clean the house, shine the crystal, and bake an assortment of breads that last me until she returns again the next week," Farris said, his words fading away as he noticed Maddy staring at something else . . . something that belonged solely to him and which his mother never would have approved of.

Now that his mother, Petulia, was dead, he had hung his prized possession where no one could help seeing it.

"The rifle with the bayonet?" Maddy said, her voice drawn as she gazed at the rifle mounted over the mantel of the fireplace. She turned slow eyes to Farris. "Is . . . that . . . the . . . one . . . ?"

"Yes, that bayonet is the very one that killed Chief Crazy Horse," Farris bragged, proudly thrusting out his chest.

"I don't understand how you can feel so good about having killed that proud Indian chief and so many other Indians," Maddy said, turning swiftly to place her back to the gory sight of the rifle and bayonet.

She turned slowly and faced Farris. She looked him directly in the eye. "Did you know that Crazy Horse was only thirty years old when you killed him?" she asked. "He . . . he . . . was in his prime. He had so many years ahead of him."

"The sonofabitch was lucky to die when he died," Farris said with a jerk of his head. "He would've lived the rest of his life behind bars." He reached a slow hand toward Maddy's face. "So you see, my pet? I did the savage a favor."

She slapped his hand away and glared at him. "You are a low-down murdering swine," she hissed out. "And you are wrong to call Indians savages. Those I have known are much more civilized than you."

"And so she has spirit, does she?" Farris said, his eyes gleaming as he chuckled. "I like that in you, Maddy. It'll make our time together, especially in bed, even more interesting."

Knowing that Farris might soon try forcing himself on her sexually, Maddy thought desperately of a way to make that impossible.

She turned on a heel and gazed up at the bayonet, then turned coy eyes back to Farris. "Yes, I *will* make lovemaking interesting," she said in a flirting way. "But, Farris, I can't go to bed with you with that . . . that . . . thing hanging there. I can't help envisioning the Indian's blood on the bayonet. It . . . gives me the shivers to think about it."

She took a slow, lazy step toward him and

teasingly, daringly, reached a hand to him. Slowly she ran a finger over his upper lip. "Darling Farris, will you please remove that thing from the house?" she murmured. "Although I know you don't want to hear me say it, I loathe it as much as your mother surely despised it. No woman wants a firearm with a bayonet as the focal point of her home. Especially not me." She gazed around the room. "It ruins the very essence of the room, don't you think?"

"Are you saying that the rifle and bayonet are the only things standing between you and me and our being together?" Farris asked thickly.

"Yes, I would say that," Maddy said softly. "Could you place it, let's see now . . . perhaps in . . . the cellar?"

"Yes, I have a cellar," Farris said, eyeing her questioningly. "How would you know?"

"Most homes, even those less grand than this one, have a cellar, don't they?" Maddy said, proud of having correctly guessed that there was a cellar in this house.

Where there was a cellar there was a trap door that closed over it. If she could just get him to go down there without her . . . !

"Yes, I made sure I had a cellar in my home," Farris said, already going and reaching up to remove the rifle from the wall. "In it is stored a good supply of food canned by the women of the community. Upon my first arrival in River Town, the women from the Baptist church came calling one day with a whole wagonload of various canned products from their gardens."

He held the rifle in his arms, resting it across them as he turned and smiled at Maddy. "That's one advantage to being a bachelor in the community," he said, chuckling low. "The women tend to dote on you."

"I know. That was right after you had your house completed," Maddy said, trying to keep her dislike out of her voice.

"Yes, it was," Farris said guardedly. "How did you know? Were you asked to contribute?"

"Yes," Maddy said, almost choking on the word, recalling the jars of canned tomatoes that she had given to the ladies who had planned this generous offering to their community's newest bachelor.

It was afterward that everyone grew to know the true man Farris was . . . a braggart and bully.

After the women had discovered him for what he was, they avoided him as though he were carrying the plague.

"Oh?" Farris said, raising his eyebrows. "And what, may I ask, did you lend to the cause? We can have it for supper tonight."

"Stewed tomatoes," Maddy forced out, hating for him to know that he had fooled her back then.

"Tomatoes?" Farris said, smiling broadly. "From your very own garden?"

"Yes, from my very own garden," Maddy sighed, wishing he would go to the cellar so that she could seal him down there as though it were his grave.

"I'll go and get the tomatoes as I take the rifle down there," Farris said, a skip in his step as he walked from the parlor. For the moment he'd forgotten that he usually limped. "Come on with me, Maddy. Let me show you just how much food I have in the cellar. I'm sure you can find enough food to make us delicious meals for many days. Thank God I have such a good supply. All of the food in River Town has been destroyed."

Afraid that he would insist on her going down to the cellar with him, Maddy walked halfheartedly beside him.

She *had* to find a way to get him down there before her!

Once he took only a few steps down the stairs, she could drop the door on him and lock it. She could make a fast escape!

She would surely meet Jaimie and Black Wolf halfway as she rowed her way down the river toward the Shawnee village. The delight that she would see in their eyes would be something. The delight in her own heart to see them would be wonderful!

As she walked with Farris down a long corridor lined on each side with portraits of what she thought were Farris's relatives, Maddy felt as though the eyes in the paintings were following her.

It made her skin crawl, for she couldn't imagine anyone related to Farris being any other way than exactly like him. Cruel. Heartless. Despicable.

She was glad when they finally reached the back of the house, where she stepped into the kitchen. Bright sunshine streamed in through long, wide windows, casting its golden light on a room such as she had never seen before. Instead of hand-hewn tables and chairs and work tables positioned here and there around the room, she saw grand oak cabinets reaching from floor to ceiling, and a counter on which she saw lovely crockery and cooking utensils. Close by that was a cooking stove fitted with shiny copper.

This room alone could persuade a woman to marry a man, unless that man was Farris Boyd. Nothing but an escape from him was all that any woman would want.

Especially Maddy.

She forced herself not to stare at the wonders of this room, but instead focused on the trap door that Farris had bent to open.

"Ladies first," Farris then said, as he laid the door back to rest against the floor. He gestured toward the steps that led to the dark void below.

When he saw her hesitate, he laughed. "If the darkness is what you're afraid of, I'll light a lantern as soon as we reach the foot of the steps," he said mockingly.

"It's not so much the darkness as it is what might be down there besides canned food,"

Maddy said, forcing herself to look afraid as she took slow steps away from the opened space in the floor.

She made sure not to go too far, though. She didn't want to miss the opportunity of slamming the door shut the moment he went far enough down the steps so that his head would clear the door as it closed.

"What do you think is down there?" Farris asked, idly scratching his brow with his free hand, the rifle resting aimlessly in the crook of his left arm.

The sunlight reflected on the bayonet of the rifle into Maddy's eyes, reminding her of how much she had to make her fear look sincere. It sickened her to know where this bayonet had been, how many lives it had claimed, and how it had been marveled at by so many men as Farris bragged about his conquests with it.

"*Snakes,*" Maddy blurted out, making herself visibly shudder. "Farris, the river has surely forced snakes higher to dry land. What if one or more have found their way into this cellar? Lord, Farris, not so long ago I found a snake in the cellar of *my* home. It . . . was . . . a water moccasin. Had I not seen it in time, I . . . wouldn't . . . be here now."

Ah, but wasn't she getting skilled at lying? she thought smugly to herself. There was no cellar in her home, and certainly no water moccasins!

Farris studied her intently. "I see that you are truly afraid," he said. "Well then, Maddy dear, you don't have to go to the cellar with me. I'll take the rifle down there. I'll check things out and if there are no snakes, perhaps later, when we get hungry, we'll go down again together, and you can choose what you wish to cook from the supplies on hand."

"Oh, thank you," Maddy said, sighing heavily. "I truly appreciate your understanding my fear, Farris. Truly I do."

"I'll be only a moment," Farris said, stepping down onto the top step.

Breathlessly, Maddy waited for him to go farther, her eyes moving from the door of the cellar to Farris's bald head.

When he finally took the one step that brought his head lower than the level of the floor, Maddy rushed to the door, lifted it quickly, and slammed it closed.

She fell to her knees, and her heart pounded like distant thunder within her chest while Farris cursed her. Hurriedly she bolted the door, sealing him down below.

Her knees trembling and weak, Maddy pushed herself up from the floor.

Her pulse still racing, her cheeks hot from her nervousness, she stared at the closed, bolted door, then smiled triumphantly as she listened to Farris's ranting and raving.

Her smile faded when she heard him using something to pound against the door.

She covered a gasp behind her hands when she saw the hinges that held the bolt in place quivering every time Farris crashed against the underside of the door.

"No," she whispered, her throat growing dry. "Lord, *no*."

"I'm going to get you, you bitch!" Farris screamed at her. "You're going to wish you never heard of Farris Boyd! You lying wench! I'm going to wring your neck when I get out of here! Do you hear? Wring . . . your . . . neck! No one, especially a *woman*, gets away with making a fool of Farris Boyd! I'm a war hero! Do you hear? A damn war hero!"

"Hero?" Maddy shouted back at him, that idiotic boast making it impossible for her to keep quiet. "No one capable of killing as many innocent Indians as you is a hero! I see you as a low-down coward!"

"You're going to pay, bitch!" Farris cried, still pounding the bottom of the door. "You're the same as dead!"

Knowing that Farris would not stop now until he saw her dead, Maddy knew she must get far away from this place, just in case he did manage to get himself free. The more the man hit the door, the more the hinges, and now even the nails, were coming loose.

Maddy looked desperately around the room for something to shove onto the door.

She saw a tall crock of pickles, and knew just how heavy it was, because she had struggled to transport a similar crock of pickles from the general store in River Town only a few days before. She smiled and put every muscle in her body into shoving the heavy container over on top of the door.

"*Now* try to get free," she whispered, brushing her hands clean on the skirt of her dress. "You won't, Farris. You're in there until someone is merciful enough to release you."

She lifted the skirt of her dress and rushed from the house. Breathless, she mounted the horse that was nearer to her, which happened to be Farris's prized white stallion, and rode it down to the river's edge.

Then, after tying the reins to a low tree limb, she began running up and down the river, her eyes searching, until she finally found a boat drifting close enough in the water for her to reach.

Her heart pounding, she climbed into the boat and began rowing downriver toward the Shawnee village.

She kept watching for another boat, one that would be headed upriver toward her, the boat that would be bringing Jaimie and Black Wolf to her rescue!

She was proud to be able to show them that she had managed to escape all by herself. Too often people thought her as frail as a dove. She was quickly proving them all wrong.

"Where are they?" Maddy whispered, puzzled over not having yet seen Jaimie and Black Wolf.

By now Jaimie should have reached the Indian village. They should even now be in the river headed her way!

"Unless Black Wolf no longer cares . . ." she whispered, paling at the thought.

Chapter Seventeen

The soul unto itself
Is an imperial friend—
Or the most agonizing spy
An enemy could send.

                    —Emily Dickinson

His arm aching from having slammed the sledgehammer for so long against the trap door, Farris dropped the hammer to the floor. Groaning, he grabbed his right arm as the muscles spasmed.

After the spasm passed he searched around the dark, dank cellar for his lantern.

He cringed when he felt his hands reaching through thick cobwebs, then jumped with alarm when he felt something crawling up inside the sleeve of his shirt.

"God, no," he cried as he worked frantically to take his coat off so that he could then remove his shirt to get at whatever was crawling on him.

Having just made his way through thick cobwebs, he was afraid that it was a spider. That thought sent spirals of dread up and down his spine, for the one thing he hated more than Indians was spiders!

As a child he had had terrible nightmares of huge, hairy spiders. One night he dreamed he was surrounded by many huge, black and hairy, large-eyed tarantulas. When he awakened, he found a spider crawling on his leg beneath the blanket.

He had screamed over and over again until his mother came into the room and killed the spider before it bit him.

Recently the nightmares had begun again. . . .

Just when Farris dropped his coat to the floor, he screamed as a hot, sharp pain shot through his arm. Frantically, he swatted at whatever had bitten him.

"Oh, Lord, it's lodged inside my sleeve!" he cried, swatting at his shirt again in an attempt to kill whatever was beneath it.

He cringed when he realized that he had finally smashed the insect flat against his skin. But then he screamed again when he realized that whatever it was had managed to bite him again just before dying.

"God . . . God . . . !" he cried when his arm began to feel as though it were on fire.

He managed to tear off his shirt just as a nauseous feeling overwhelmed him, and then a terrible dizziness. He fought to remain conscious, but lost the battle as he sank into a dark void, his body slumping slowly to the earthen floor.

Chapter Eighteen

Fiend, I defy thee! with a calm, fixed mind.
All that thou canst inflict, I bid thee do.
                              —Percy Bysshe Shelley

"Look, Black Wolf! Over there!" Jaimie cried as
she pointed at a break in the trees a short distance away where she was able to see a huge,
pillared home. "I bet that's where Farris lives. He
described a magnificent place like this when he
boasted about his home. I've seen nothing else
in the area so opulent. Let's go and see if this is
it!"

"*Tahn-kah*, we must go the rest of the way on
foot," Black Wolf said, drawing his steed to a
halt. "If this is Farris Boyd's house, we do not
want to alert him that we have found him."

Jaimie dismounted as Black Wolf swung himself out of his saddle.

They tethered their steeds to a tree, then
moved stealthily through the woods. Black Wolf
tightly clutched his rifle.

When they got directly behind the house,
where a stable and a barn stood nearby, Jaimie

widened her eyes with excitement, for she saw not only her two beloved horses but also her cow.

She sidled closer to Black Wolf. "If this isn't Farris's house, at least we've found our horse and cow thief," she whispered, anxious to go and reclaim the animals.

Black Wolf had scarcely heard what Jaimie said about the horses and cow, for his eyes were on the house. He watched for movement at the windows.

When he saw none, he nodded at Jaimie. "It is safe to go on to the house," he whispered. "Shh, listen. Follow behind me. Keep watch for any movements anywhere!"

Jaimie nodded. Her heart beat rapidly at the thought that she might be reunited with her sister soon. She loved Maddy so dearly. If anything had happened to her . . .

She walked beside Black Wolf up the back steps and circled around with him to a long window.

She pressed her back stiffly against the house as Black Wolf inched closer to the window and looked inside.

"Still nothing," he said, giving Jaimie a quick glance. "Come. We are going inside now."

Her pulse racing, her throat dry, Jaimie stood aside as Black Wolf opened the back door, then crept inside the kitchen with him.

The first thing she noticed was the huge crock of pickles on the trap door that she knew should lead to the cellar. She stopped and stared at it, then looked quickly up at Black Wolf.

"This is out of place here," she said in a loud whisper. "There is no logical reason why that crock of pickles should be in the middle of the floor on the cellar door. It would be in the way of whoever cooked in this kitchen."

She stared at the cellar door again. "I wonder if it might have been placed there to keep someone in the cellar," she asked, her pulse racing.

Black Wolf stopped, whirled around and stared at the crock, then went to it and with one shove removed it from the door.

He looked over at Jaimie, then handed her the rifle. "*Tahn-kah*, hold this and be ready to use it should something be awry in the cellar," he whispered.

Her eyes anxious, Jaimie took the rifle, then scarcely breathed as she watched Black Wolf flip the lock aside, then slowly lift the heavy, wooden door.

When the door was completely open and resting back against the floor, and no one pounced out at them, Jaimie's hopes sank. Perhaps this had nothing to do with Maddy, after all.

As Black Wolf started down the stairs, Jaimie rested the rifle against the leg of a chair. She would waste no more time with this damnable cellar. She would search the rest of the house for signs of Maddy. If this was Farris's house, it seemed as though he and Maddy might have been there and left.

"But where would he take her?" she whispered

as she stepped into the corridor, where her gaze was caught by the huge portraits of people hanging in gilt frames along the wall. When she saw that one of the portraits somewhat resembled Farris, she stopped and stared.

Black Wolf felt around in the cellar for a lantern, feeling nothing but thick cobwebs hanging everywhere.

When he took another step, he stumbled over something and almost fell. After straightening and steadying himself, he felt around with his moccasined foot and grew cold when he realized that he had stumbled over a body.

When Maddy's sweet face flashed into his mind's eye, stark terror swept through him to think this might be her body on the floor.

She might have tried to fight off Farris Boyd.

He might have tired of her and left her there.

She might have fainted from lack of air!

Bending to one knee, Black Wolf reached out a trembling hand and ran it over the form he still could not make out in the dark. When he discovered a bald head, he sighed with relief, for he knew the unconscious person lying there was a man.

He was happy to know it wasn't Maddy, but now he wondered who it *was*. Black Wolf shouted for Jaimie to find and bring him a lantern.

When Jaimie heard Black Wolf calling for a lantern, she tore her gaze away from the painting and found a beautifully designed lantern on a table just inside the sitting room. She grabbed matches from a tiny vase. She lifted the chimney from the lantern, lit the wick, then ran to the kitchen and fell to her knees beside the cellar opening.

"Here, Black Wolf," she said, leaning down as far as she could to hand Black Wolf the lantern as he reached up for it. "What did you find? Anything?"

"A man is unconscious on the cellar floor," Black Wolf said.

"*Who*, Black Wolf?" Jaimie asked, too curious not to go on down and see for herself.

She scampered down the wooden steps, then stopped and gasped out Farris's name, gaping at Farris Boyd as Black Wolf held the lantern above his body, slowly moving it over him so that he and Jaimie could get a better look. Strange how his coat and shirt had been removed, and . . .

Jaimie gasped when she saw that Farris's left arm was twice its usual size. Around an oozing bite of some sort, the skin was a blotchy, beet red.

Black Wolf also saw the arm, then lowered the lantern close to the floor and studied something else. "This is what bit Farris," he said. "See, *Tahn-kah*? Do you see the remains of a spider?"

Jaimie leaned closer and saw what remained of the spider, shivering as she pictured how large it had been before being squashed. Two legs that had broken away from the spider lay only a few inches from the body. They were large, hairy, and grotesque.

"It's gruesome," Jaimie said, looking quickly away. She shivered again. "I hate spiders."

"This spider is one I am not familiar with," Black Wolf said, picking up a small stick and pushing the spider around as he studied it. "But it surely is a poisonous one to have caused Farris Boyd's arm to react so to the bite."

Jaimie studied Farris's still face as his cheek lay against the cold cellar floor. "He's unconscious, Black Wolf. Perhaps he's dying."

She looked quickly up the steps, toward the kitchen. "I wonder where Maddy is," she said worriedly.

She recalled the crock of pickles and smiled. "That's why the crock was placed on the door," she blurted out. "Maddy was surely the one who put it there to keep Farris from escaping from the cellar!"

Black Wolf was only half aware of what Jaimie was saying. As he continued to move the lantern around, to inspect things, he had found something else that he had not counted on: the gun, with its bayonet on one end bringing gruesome memories of how the white pony soldiers had used such bayonets to kill innocent Sioux . . . men, women, and children.

He recalled the tales of this white man who bragged that it was his bayonet that had killed Black Wolf's cousin Chief Crazy Horse! This gun with its ugly bayonet lying beside Farris was the weapon the evil man bragged about!

Black Wolf set the lantern aside and, growling, took the bayonet from the gun and snapped it in half, then threw it down on the floor beside Farris.

Jaimie stared at the broken bayonet, then gazed into Black Wolf's eyes. She had never seen such tumultuous emotion in her life as she now saw on this man's face as he stared with contempt at Farris Boyd.

She then recalled Farris Boyd bragging so often, so callously, about having slain the Sioux Chief Crazy Horse with his bayonet. She paled as she looked down and stared at the broken bayonet, having watched the rage with which Black Wolf had snapped it in two.

"Is that the one he used on Crazy Horse?" Jaimie blurted out, then wished she hadn't asked when Black Wolf gave her a quick, reproachful glance.

She thought fast, hoping to say something that might help ease Black Wolf's feelings, for she now knew that he had understood all too well about the bayonet.

"Black Wolf, finding Farris here like this must surely mean that Maddy is all right," she rushed out. "She's probably the one who put the crock of pickles on the door of the cellar to imprison Farris in it."

She again stared at the bite on Farris's arm.

"She never imagined, I'm certain, what might happen to the man," she murmured.

"It is good to know that Maddy is not at the mercy of this madman any longer. I am sure that when we leave here, we will find her," Black Wolf said, feeling keen relief that his woman was safe.

"I imagine Maddy is on her way to the Shawnee village," Jaimie said, sighing. Tears sprang to her eyes as she stared at the unconscious man. "You just don't know how relieved I am to know she is no longer at the mercy of this . . . this . . . vile man."

Black Wolf reached a hand over and placed it on Jaimie's shoulder. "She sent you for me, and now you believe she is probably on her way to the Shawnee village to be with me, yet she left me before without telling me why," he said, his voice drawn. "What sent her away from me? She had spoken of wanting a future with me and my people. What changed her mind?"

"That is something you should ask *her*," Jaimie murmured, swallowing hard.

"And that I shall, soon," Black Wolf said, his jaw tight. He glared at Farris, who was still unconscious.

Jaimie also looked at the bald-headed man lying there so lifelessly. "What are you going to do about him?" she asked. She looked at Farris's red and swollen arm, then gazed over at Black Wolf. "Surely the bite was a lethal one. If left untended, I imagine Farris will die."

197

"Let him die," Black Wolf said, his voice filled with loathing. "He won't be able to harm anyone else, and finally his bragging about having killed Chief Crazy Horse will be silenced!"

He blew out the lantern, set it aside, then lifted his rifle and rose to his full height. "Come, *Tahn-kah*, let us go and find your sister," he said. He nodded toward the steps that led from the cellar. "You first. I will follow."

Jaimie scurried up the steps, then waited for Black Wolf to follow her.

And once they were both in the kitchen, and Black Wolf had closed the door to the cellar again, Jaimie glanced at the crock of pickles. She wondered if it should be placed over the door again. If Farris came to, would he have the strength to escape the cellar?

In her mind's eye she saw his swollen arm, the yellowish pus oozing from the center of the bite. She shrugged. No, she didn't think that man was going anywhere. He certainly wasn't capable of harming Maddy any longer.

And soon Black Wolf would be with Maddy again and Jaimie knew that he would make certain that her sister did not leave him a second time.

Jaimie could see the determination in his step as they left the mansion and hurried toward the tethered horses.

"My horses!" Jaimie said, stopping suddenly. "I must go and get my animals!"

"The animals come second to Maddy," Black

Wolf said, turning to place a firm hand on Jaimie's shoulder. "They would slow us down. We must go now and make sure your sister is safe."

Jaimie smiled weakly up at Black Wolf, then glanced through the trees toward where her horses still stood, feasting on thick, green grass beneath a tall maple tree.

She gazed up at Black Wolf and nodded, then went with him to the horses they had left tethered at the fringe of the forest.

They mounted the steeds and rode off. Then Jaimie looked quickly over at Black Wolf. "What if Maddy isn't at the Shawnee village?" she asked. "What if something happened to her on the way?"

Black Wolf gave her a wavering glance. "She . . . will . . . be there, safe," he said, knowing it might not be true. There were many men just like Farris running loose who would welcome a beautiful woman like Maddy as their traveling companion.

"But what if . . . ?" Jaimie gulped out, stopping when Black Wolf gave her a dark frown.

She swallowed hard and turned her eyes straight ahead. She said a silent prayer that she was wrong to have this strange foreboding inside her heart every time she thought of her sister. She should be rejoicing, instead, that Farris was no longer a threat to their lives!

But still, it plagued her, this deep, gnawing uneasiness. . . .

199

Chapter Nineteen

Innocent is the heart's devotion
With which I worship thine.
—Percy Bysshe Shelley

Just as Maddy turned a bend in the river and was able to see the Shawnee village, she again recalled how she had left Black Wolf so abruptly. She could still hear him calling her name as she rowed away from him.

Yet then, as now, she could not help thinking it was best not to plan a future with Black Wolf. Not unless he convinced her that she was wrong to feel that way.

She gave a quick look over her shoulder, searching the wide breadth of the water behind her. She was now more puzzled than before as to why she hadn't met Black Wolf and Jaimie on the river.

"Where could they be?" she whispered, then turned her head back in the direction of the Shawnee village when she heard someone shout her name from the embankment.

"Black Wolf?" she whispered, her heart beating wildly. But her hopes sank at the sight of someone else standing there. It was an Indian warrior. But it wasn't Black Wolf. It was his best friend, Lone Beaver.

As she made a slow turn with the boat and headed toward shore, she watched as others came from the Shawnee's palisaded village, joining Lone Beaver to watch her approach.

Her eyes searched for Black Wolf, then Jaimie, thinking they had not left yet to rescue her. She saw neither. That had to mean they were both gone.

But where? she wondered desperately. What if something had happened to Black Wolf and Jaimie?

She was glad when Lone Beaver entered the water and waded out to her. He grabbed the side of the boat, dragging it onto the embankment and beaching it.

"Lone Beaver, where's Black Wolf?" Maddy asked as he placed his powerful hands at her waist and lifted her from the boat.

She expected him to set her down in the water so that she could go the rest of the way by herself. She was surprised when he carried her gently, as though she were a precious flower, to dry land and then placed her on her feet.

But it unnerved her when Lone Beaver took his time answering her. He was distracted by a long-legged young brave who tugged on his breechclout, asking him something in the Sioux tongue.

Maddy impatiently ran her fingers through her long, golden hair, frustration building inside her. She needed to know where Black Wolf and Jaimie were. She looked past Lone Beaver at the group of Indians who continued to gape at her.

Feeling as though she were on display, as though she were an oddity, Maddy swallowed hard and smiled awkwardly.

The sound of Lone Beaver speaking to her brought her eyes back to him.

"Your sister came and told Black Wolf about your abduction," he said, his gaze taking in the soft, beautiful features of her face. "They left together."

"But I didn't see them on the river," Maddy said.

"They did not leave by water," Lone Beaver said, looking over his shoulder toward the forest, where he had last seen his friend riding away on a horse, the young girl with him.

He gazed at Maddy again. "They travel on horses today," he said softly.

"That explains it," Maddy said, sighing. "That's why I didn't see them. I was so worried that something might have happened to them."

"When they left here they were all right," Lone Beaver said.

"Then surely they will return soon, once they see that I escaped from Farris Boyd," Maddy said, seeing how that man's name brought Lone Beaver's eyes back to her, with hatred gleaming in their depths.

He placed a gentle hand on Maddy's shoulder and looked her over. "The evil white man did not harm you?" he asked solemnly.

"No," Maddy said softly. "He didn't harm me."

She was touched deeply by Lone Beaver's sincere concern. Surely Black Wolf had told Lone Beaver about her. From the way Lone Beaver was treating her, surely Black Wolf had not spoken words of bitterness.

And the fact that Black Wolf had gone to save her from Farris Boyd proved that the way she had left him without as much as a goodbye had not made him hate her.

"How did you escape?" Lone Beaver asked, genuinely interested. "I know of this man, Farris Boyd. He is a man of no conscience . . . of no heart. Once he had you alone, I would have thought he would have defiled you."

The word "defiled" sent a heated blush to Maddy's cheeks. To have this warrior speak so openly of such things in front of so many people was embarrassing to Maddy, yet his openness was somehow refreshing.

"I'm certain he had that on his mind," Maddy said, smiling shyly. "But I managed to stop him before he had the chance."

"You, a white woman, so frail and tiny, stopped the evil Farris Boyd?" Lone Beaver said, lifting an eyebrow.

"It was something that did not require physical effort, unless you count my having to shove that heavy crock of pickles over the trap door of the cellar," Maddy said, her eyes twinkling as she thought of the way she had outwitted Farris Boyd.

"Crock . . . of . . . pickles?" Lone Beaver said, arching an eyebrow. "What is a crock of pickles?"

Maddy saw the puzzlement building in Lone Beaver's eyes. She tried to explain how pickles were prepared and stored in vinegar in large crocks and sold at the general store to those who did not grow or prepare their own cucumbers for pickles.

"I trapped that filthy man down in the cellar," Maddy said, feeling smug in knowing that Farris might even now be clawing at the door, desperate in his imprisonment, which served him right for having enjoyed placing innocent Indians in prison during the Civil War.

Then a thought came to her that made her stiffen. Her smile faded. Her smugness changed to worry.

What if, after Jaimie and Black Wolf arrived at Farris's mansion, they saw the crock of pickles on the trap door and moved it? It made her sick to think that Jaimie might open the trap door and become so startled at seeing Farris there that she would freeze long enough for him to grab her and yank her into the cellar and lock her in.

Or he might use Jaimie as a hostage and escape on a horse, with Jaimie at his mercy now instead of Maddy. Or he might grab his rifle and shoot Jaimie and Black Wolf before they had the chance to disarm him.

"I feel ill suddenly," Maddy said, holding her face in her hands. "Oh, Lord, I hope Black Wolf and Jaimie are all right."

"You think they are not?" Lone Beaver said, grabbing her shoulders. "Speak to me of your fears. What are they?"

His fingers tightened on her shoulders, and Maddy looked quickly up at Lone Beaver. She hurriedly told him about the possible reasons why Black Wolf and Jaimie hadn't returned yet.

"Oh, surely I am wrong," she cried as she saw how her concerns affected Lone Beaver.

As he dropped his hands and took a shaky step away from her, she could see alarm in his eyes.

Lone Beaver turned and began issuing brisk orders to his warriors.

Some were to go up and down the river in their canoes searching for Black Wolf and Jaimie. Others were to fan out in all directions in the forest in an extensive search.

Maddy watched them all go to the village, then come out again armed with various weapons, some with bows and arrows, others with rifles, and others with long, vicious-looking lances. She stood cold as stone as they all went their separate ways, Lone Beaver on the lead horse as he led a group of warriors into the forest.

The touch of a hand on hers drew Maddy's attention. She discovered the young brave who had distracted Lone Beaver earlier. He was smiling warmly up at her.

"Come with me," Eagle Wing said, softly tugging on her hand.

Just as she started walking beside the young brave, a lovely middle-aged woman joined them, walking on Maddy's other side.

"My son is intrigued not only by you, but also your little sister," Moon Beam said, smiling at Maddy. "His questions about your sister are endless, for he has never seen a girl wearing such clothes as your sister wears. Nor has he ever seen hair shorn short like your sister's."

"Yes, my sister is different," Maddy said, glad to have someone to talk to, to help her get past these next moments, when she might find out that something had happened to the two people in the world that she loved the most. "There is no one else like my Jaimie. She might wear boy's clothes, but she is as sweet as sugar candy."

"Sugar candy?" Moon Beam asked, looking curiously at Maddy.

"It is something that tastes like the maple sugar that your people collect in large buckets in the spring," Maddy explained. "It's sweet and wonderful."

When she heard the sound of approaching horses behind her, Maddy's heart skipped a beat. Then she spun around and saw Black Wolf and Jaimie approaching on their horses with Lone Beaver and the other warriors, and a wonderful feeling of relief flooded through her.

She lifted the skirt of her dress and broke into a mad run toward them. At that moment, her eyes and Black Wolf's met and held, and in his eyes she saw such love and adoration, she knew that she could never live without him!

"Black Wolf!" she cried, a sob of pure joy lodging in her throat.

Chapter Twenty

The eyes glaze once, and that is death.
Impossible to feign
The beads upon the forehead
By homely anguish strung.
                    —Emily Dickinson

Farris awakened to sounds in the house overhead. He heard the creaking of the floorboards and voices. He strained to hear the voices, not recognizing them. There seemed to be a child, a man, and a woman there.

"Maddy?" he whispered, his thoughts fuzzy. "Jaimie?"

But who would the man be?

When the voices grew closer, he knew they were those of people he didn't know. Strangers were in his house!

He flinched when he heard the pattering of a dog's feet just overhead.

He tried to get up, but fell back to the floor, hindered by a fever and an arm and hand swollen twice their size. Moaning, Farris lay on the floor of the cellar, trying to recollect just how he

A Special Offer For
Leisure Romance Readers Only!

Get
FOUR
FREE
Romance
Novels
A $21.96 Value!

Travel to exotic worlds filled with passion
and adventure —without leaving your home!
Plus, you'll save $5.00 every time you buy!

Thrill to the most sensual, adventure-filled Historical Romances on the market today...

FROM ▐ *LEISURE BOOKS*

As a home subscriber to Leisure Romance Book Club, you'll enjoy the best in today's BRAND-NEW Historical Romance fiction. For over twenty-five years, Leisure Books has brought you the award-winning, high-quality authors you know and love to read. Each Leisure Historical Romance will sweep you away to a world of high adventure...and intimate romance. Discover for yourself all the passion and excitement millions of readers thrill to each and every month.

Save $5.⁰⁰ Each Time You Buy!

Each month, the Leisure Romance Book Club brings you four brand-new titles from Leisure Books, America's foremost publisher of Historical Romances. EACH PACKAGE WILL SAVE YOU $5.00 FROM THE BOOKSTORE PRICE! And you'll never miss a new title with our convenient home delivery service.

Here's how we do it. Each package will carry a FREE 10-DAY EXAMINATION privilege. At the end of that time, if you decide to keep your books, simply pay the low invoice price of $16.96, no shipping or handling charges added. HOME DELIVERY IS ALWAYS FREE. With today's top Historical Romance novels selling for $5.99 and higher, our price SAVES YOU $5.00 with each shipment.

AND YOUR FIRST FOUR-BOOK SHIPMENT IS TOTALLY FREE!

IT'S A BARGAIN YOU CAN'T BEAT! A Super $21.96 Value!

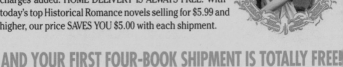

▐ *LEISURE BOOKS* A Division of Dorchester Publishing Co., Inc.

GET YOUR 4 FREE BOOKS NOW—A $21.96 Value!

Mail the Free Book Certificate Today!

4 FREE BOOKS

A $21.96 VALUE

Free Books Certificate

YES! I want to subscribe to the Leisure Romance Book Club. Please send me my 4 FREE BOOKS. Then, each month I'll receive the four newest Leisure Historical Romance selections to Preview FREE for 10 days. If I decide to keep them, I will pay the Special Member's Only discounted price of just $4.24 each, a total of $16.96. This is a SAVINGS OF $5.00 off the bookstore price. There are no shipping, handling, or other charges. There is no minimum number of books I must buy and I may cancel the program at any time. In any case, the 4 FREE BOOKS are mine to keep—A BIG $21.96 Value! Offer valid only in the U.S.A.

Name _____

Address _____

City _____

State _____ *Zip* _____

Telephone _____

Signature _____

If under 18, Parent or Guardian must sign. Terms, prices and conditions subject to change. Subscription subject to acceptance. Leisure Books reserves the right to reject any order or cancel any subscription.

A $21.96 VALUE

4 FREE BOOKS

Get Four Books Totally FREE — A $21.96 Value!

▼ Tear Here and Mail Your FREE Book Card Today! ▼

PLEASE RUSH
MY FOUR FREE
BOOKS TO ME
RIGHT AWAY!

Leisure Romance Book Club
P.O. Box 6613
Edison, NJ 08818-6613

AFFIX
STAMP
HERE

had gotten there, and why his arm was throbbing and hot.

He recalled being shut in the cellar by Maddy, and then something crawling up his shirt sleeve. Forgetting that he had killed it, he once again tried to get up, but again fell back to the floor in pain.

He was suddenly aware that the cellar door was no longer closed. Through a feverish haze he saw light from the kitchen spilling down the steps into the cellar, and then he felt panic seize him when he saw a dog coming down the steps, panting.

"No!" Farris said through clenched teeth when the dog stepped onto the earthen floor of the cellar and began sniffing around.

When the dog discovered Farris, it stopped and stared at him, growled threateningly, showing its sharp teeth. Then it began a loud, incessant barking.

A little girl, who looked to Farris no older than six, hurried down the steps and grabbed the black labrador around its neck. She screamed when she saw Farris lying there.

Farris felt utterly helpless as he lay there until the child's·father hurried down to the cellar, a pistol in his right hand, a lantern in his left.

Farris looked blearily at the tall, lanky man as he knelt over him, his pistol laid aside.

"Lord, man, what happened to you?" the stranger gulped out, seeing Farris so helpless and writhing in pain. He gasped when he held the lantern lower and saw the swollen arm. "How did you get down here? What happened to you?"

"Help . . . me . . ." Farris managed in a whisper, his eyes imploring the stranger. "Something bit me. I . . . think . . . it was a spider. I . . . think . . . I'm dying." Then he scowled up at the man. "What . . . are . . . you doing in my house?"

"Me and my family were uprooted by the flood," the stranger said. "We came to ask for a night's lodging. Watching my child and wife sleeping out in the dampness was almost more than I could bear. I saw your house. I came. I knocked. When I didn't get any answer—"

"You just let yourself in and made yourself at home," Farris said in a rush of words, then regretted what he had said the moment he heard the man's quick, shocked intake of breath.

"You can stay," Farris said hurriedly. "Lord, yes, you can stay in my house. Just please help me. I . . . don't . . . want to die."

His heart skipped a beat when the man did not respond right away, as though he was now thinking twice before helping a man who seemed at first to begrudge his presence inside his mansion.

"*Truly* . . . you . . . can stay as long as you wish in my home," Farris said quickly.

When the tall, lean man still said nothing, but remained silently kneeling beside him, his one hand stroking the fur of his dog, Farris added anxiously, "Will you? Will you stay?"

"Papa, answer the man," the child urged, her voice soft and sweet. "Surely you won't leave him down here to die, will you? The Bible teaches kindness, Papa. Papa, this man needs your kindness. He might be dying."

"Yes, Angel, I'm going to help the man," the stranger said, his voice drawn. "Now you and Blackie get back up those stairs. Tell your mama about the man and how she'll be needed to look after his wound. Tell her it's more than likely a spider bite. She'll know what to do."

"Thank you, oh, God, thank you," Farris said, sighing heavily.

He winced when the man slid his arms beneath him and lifted him as though Farris weighed no more than a sack of potatoes. He felt the man's muscles strain as he started carrying him up the steps.

Farris prayed that the stranger would not drop him. He was afraid that with one jolt of his body, his arm might drop off. It felt that heavy and yet so strangely lifeless.

Finally in the kitchen, where the sunshine streaming through the windows was a heavenly sight to Farris after having been in the dark, dank cellar for so long, he smiled.

"I never knew anything could look so wonderful," he said, then winced when the heat of the sun on his swollen arm made the heat of his flesh seem twice as bad as it was earlier. He closed his eyes, now drifting in and out of consciousness.

211

His eyes closed now, he became aware of a woman's soft, gentle voice.

"This downstairs bedroom next to the parlor will do better than those upstairs," Charlene Johnston said as she led her husband Ralph into the large, sun-drenched room. "That way, I won't have to go up and down the stairs so much when I look in on him to care for his bite."

"Mama, is he going to die?" Angel Johnston asked as she came into the bedroom just as her mother yanked the bedspread off, laying it across the back of a chair.

"Not if I can help it, he's not," Charlene murmured, grimacing when she finally got a good look at the arm as her husband stretched Farris out on the large oak bed.

The aroma of flowers drew Charlene's eyes to a huge vase of apple blossoms on the dresser against the far wall. Also on the dresser were an assortment of perfumes, their bottles fancy looking and expensive.

Her gaze shifted to a beautiful lacy chemise that hung from a wooden hanger on a peg on the wall. Then she looked down at the man again. "He must have a wife," she said softly. "Look over there, Ralph, at the perfumes and the lacy chemise. Also, see the apple blossoms? They've been picked recently."

Ralph knelt beside the bed and leaned close as he saw Farris's eyes flutter open. "Where's your wife?" he asked, as Charlene left the room for a basin of warm water and her black bag of medicine.

Farris fought to understand the man through his pain-induced haziness. "Wife?" he said, his tongue and lips now seeming strangely thick. He looked over at the man and found his vision was still blurred. "Maddy?"

He drifted off into another moment of unconsciousness.

Charlene hustled into the room, a towel draped over her arm, a basin of water balanced between her two hands. Angel came with her, carrying her mother's black bag.

"His wife's name is Maddy," Ralph said, rising to make room for Charlene beside the bed.

"So he awakened long enough to tell you that?" Charlene asked.

"Yes, but that's all he said," Ralph replied, kneading his chin.

Charlene bent low and studied the bite on Farris's arm. She tsk-tsked and slowly shook her head back and forth.

She went to her husband and took him by an arm. She led him back from the bed so that Farris could not hear her in case he woke up. "I don't think I can help him all that much," she whispered.

She brushed thick strands of coal black hair back from her face, so that they fell in long curls down her back. "That man is eventually going to lose that arm," she said, her voice drawn.

"For God's sake, at least look like you can help

213

him," Ralph said in a hurried whisper. "At least until we get a decent night's rest in out of the damp. I promise you, darling, we'll find a new place to build a home. I swear it won't be anywhere near that damn Ohio River."

"Yes, I know," Charlene said softly. "Ralph, I want to go back to Montana, but I know that's too much to wish for. Anywhere you take me and Angel will be all right with us, won't it, Angel?"

Angel, so tiny and frail, her dark brown eyes twinkling, smiled at her father. "Yes, Papa, anywhere," she murmured. "But I will so very much enjoy staying the night in this lovely place. Can I go and explore some more with Blackie?"

"Yes, but don't you or the dog break anything," Ralph said, giving Angel a soft pat on her behind.

"We won't, will we, Blackie?" Angel asked as she grabbed her dog around the neck and gave him a big hug, then took his leash and led him from the room.

Charlene went and stood beside the bed again. As she gazed at Farris's arm, trying to figure out what she could do, she rolled up the sleeves of her plain cotton dress.

Then she looked over at her husband. "Ralph, I'm going to need more than what I have in my doctor's bag to take care of something like this," she said, her voice drawn. "As you know, sometimes the medicines I was taught to use while attending school to become a doctor aren't enough. You know the herbs I've used while doctoring people well enough to go now into the forest and get those that I need for this arm. They are . . ."

Ralph listened, mentally making a note of what she required, then he left for the forest.

The woman's voice had drawn Farris awake again. He found midnight dark eyes gazing down at him from a face that seemed unnaturally dark for a white woman. It seemed more the color of an Indian's face than a white person's.

But not being able to see well enough to study her closer, he sighed and closed his eyes again, seeking merciful relief from his pain in the dark void of unconsciousness.

"I'm going to do what I can for you," Charlene murmured. She sank a cloth into the warm water in the basin. "I'm a physician."

Farris thought that she had said she was a physician, yet surely he had heard wrong. Women weren't physicians. Only men had the intelligence to become doctors!

"What I'm getting ready to do will hurt you terribly, but I must get your arm washed before I medicate it," Charlene said, slowly inching the wet cloth toward his arm.

When she placed the cloth on his wound, sending sharp pains through it which seemed to reach clean inside his heart, Farris screamed, then slipped again into unconsciousness.

Charlene cleansed the wound, then nodded a

silent hello to her husband when he came and spread out the various herbs that he had found in the forest on the bed beside Farris. He had known that she would want a small pot to boil them in. He placed this beside Farris on the bed also.

"I found everything you wanted," Ralph said, watching his wife sort through the green plants, choosing one and then another, placing those particular herbs in the pot.

Then when she was through deciding which ones to use at this moment, he took the pot away, filled it with water, and set it on the cooking stove where she had earlier gotten a fire going for the preparation of their evening meal.

"Yes, often the teachings of my elders prove that the Sioux medicines have more power than the white," she whispered.

Having been sent to college by the white people who adopted her when she was ten years old, she had learned the skills of white doctoring, yet she found herself falling back to the old teachings more often than not. She enjoyed utilizing that part of her heritage since all signs of her being Sioux had been taken from her the moment she stepped into the white world as the daughter of a white family.

"Nothing will ever totally kill the part of me that is Sioux," she whispered.

Chapter Twenty-one

Oh! There are spirits of the air,
And genii of the evening breeze,
And gentle ghosts, with eyes as fair
As star-beams among twilight trees.
                    —Percy Bysshe Shelley

Feeling fresh and clean from a bath in a nearby stream, Maddy was happy to be reunited with Black Wolf and Jaimie again. Jaimie was even now playing games with the children, while the adults sat around a huge outdoor fire, the Shawnee and Sioux acting as though they were one people, instead of tribes who had at one time been enemies.

Maddy sat beside Black Wolf, feeling strangely as though she belonged there.

And even though she caught some people of both tribes, men and women alike, giving her resentful glances, for the most part she had been accepted as Black Wolf's woman.

Just the thought of being his woman made a feeling of warm rapture overwhelm Maddy. She was so glad that he had understood why she had left him, that it was not because she didn't love him, but because she didn't want her presence to bring danger into the lives of his people.

She frowned slightly. If Farris Boyd managed to get out of the cellar alive, her presence among the Sioux might still bring them danger. For Farris would not stop searching for Maddy to make her pay for what she had done to him.

But with a few words of reassurance from Black Wolf that Farris was now the least of their worries, Maddy was trying to put the wretched man from her mind and enjoy the celebration that was in progress at the Shawnee village. It was a celebration to instill new hope in the hearts of the Sioux people, for tomorrow they would set out in search of a better land, one that would not be at the mercy of the Ohio River.

Maddy prayed that they would settle far, far away from this area, for no matter what Black Wolf said, until Maddy knew that Farris was dead, he would be her shadow everywhere she went. Even if he was not actually there, he would haunt her thoughts, filling her with a dread she could not let go of.

As the men of the two tribes talked, while a pipe was being readied to be smoked, several of the women saw to the food that was cooking, a freshly slain buck roasting over the huge fire. Maddy had not offered to help them, for she knew that they saw her as a guest.

She once again looked past the circle of people who sat on blankets on the ground around the fire, and watched Jaimie as she raced and wrestled with the young Indian boys her age. The girls reacted in various ways to the fact that Jaimie behaved more like a boy than one of them.

Some were impressed by Jaimie's abilities. Some were shocked.

Black Wolf's voice brought Maddy's eyes back to him. He held a clay pipe out before him that had been filled with a mixture of tobacco and red willow.

"On my pipe you see a bison calf carved on one side," he said, gazing slowly from man to man, then woman to woman. "It represents the earth that bears and feeds us. The twelve eagle feathers hanging from the stem symbolize the sky and the twelve moons, all of which are tied with a grass that never breaks."

He lifted the mouthpiece toward the sky. "I first offer the mouthpiece to the one above," he said, looking heavenward where the sky was just beginning to darken.

"Hear me, four quarters of the world, as I now offer the pipe to you!" he cried, holding it toward all the directions of the wind.

All eyes watched as a young brave took a burning twig to Black Wolf and held it to the bowl. Black Wolf sucked on the pipe until smoke spiraled from it, drifting in slow swirls heavenward.

Then he again looked at the warriors, whose eyes were intent on him. "My friends, let us now smoke together so that there may always be only good feeling between us," he said, handing the pipe to the man sitting to his left.

Slowly the pipe moved around the circle, each man taking his turn inhaling the smoke, then exhaling it.

When that was done, and food was served on wooden platters around the circle of people who were now freely talking and laughing among one another, Maddy was glad to accept a platter piled high with meat and vegetables. It had been many hours since she had eaten. She felt lucky to be alive. These past several days had been a challenge to her ability to survive.

She was proud that she had passed the test with flying colors!

Before she took her first bite she had to make sure Jaimie had also been given food to eat. She sorted through the children who were now sitting on the ground in clusters, smiling when she found Jaimie among the girls instead of the boys. She was eating and talking at the same time, her eyes filled with an excitement that proved she was happy with the new environment in which she found herself.

That made Maddy relax even more, for this was not a temporary way of life for them. Only moments ago Maddy had promised Black Wolf that she would marry him.

Content to the point that it almost frightened her, Maddy gave Black Wolf a half glance, then smiled broadly when she found him looking at her.

"*Mee-tah-ween*, my woman, is it not good to be together?" Black Wolf said, reaching a gentle hand over to her face. He placed his palm against her cheek, his thumb softly stroking the flesh beneath her chin. "For a while I thought—"

"Please don't say it," Maddy murmured, interrupting him. "It is behind us now. Let us look to the future."

"A future that your presence will brighten," Black Wolf said. "You are like the sunshine, bringing warmth and happiness into all the lives you touch. You will *zahn*, brighten my lodge."

"I can think of one man who would argue that," Maddy said, laughing softly as she thought of the moment she had sealed Farris Boyd in the cellar.

"If I ever see that *wasicho* again, it will be the last time," Black Wolf grumbled, knowing who Maddy had referred to without her having actually said the villain's name.

Farris's housekeeper, Maddy suddenly thought to herself, paling when she remembered that Farris had said a lady kept his house clean. On the days she came, she even served as his cook and maid. Surely she would hear him down in the cellar! Surely she would release him!

Unless she wasn't due to come for several days. Surely by then Farris would have succumbed to the spider bite that Black Wolf and Jaimie had told her about.

"You suddenly turned pale," Black Wolf said, frowning as he searched her face. "What causes you to look wary and apprehensive?"

"Nothing," Maddy said, forcing a laugh to give the impression that she was all right. "It's just whenever I think of that man, I . . . I . . . feel uncomfortable. But that will soon pass. I truly believe I have no reason ever to think of him again."

She wasn't about to tell Black Wolf her doubts about Farris. She would keep them to herself. Black Wolf had enough on his mind without having to worry about Farris Boyd being set free to hunt them down with hate in his heart.

"*Mee-tah-ween*, now that you are safe with me, you have no reason ever to fear anything or anyone again," Black Wolf said; then he picked up a piece of venison and gently placed it to her lips. "Now eat. When that hunger is fed, I wish to feed another."

"What do you mean?" she asked, eyes wide, then plucked the piece of meat between her teeth and smiled bashfully at him when she suddenly understood the meaning behind his words.

Now that promises of marriage had been made between them, she felt that there was nothing wrong in making love with him. Promises would have to do since there were no preachers nearby to seal their vows.

Yes, they would be married soon in the Sioux tradition, but even that was impossible just now. Black Wolf wanted to wait until they were settled on the new land they would soon seek in Kentucky. He wanted everything to be right, with no worries burdening them when they began the ceremony that would join their hearts forever.

"Our first time together will be a time of paradise," Black Wolf said as he leaned over and whispered into Maddy's ear. "I will make you *cheen*, desire more . . . and more . . . and more . . ."

Just hearing him talking in such a seductive way made Maddy's insides glow with anticipation.

She found herself hurriedly emptying her plate of food, which was unusual for her. She had always been teased by her family about being so slow as she ate her meals, so slow that everyone usually sat waiting for her to finish the main course before dessert could be brought to the table.

Tonight she wanted nothing more than to slide the empty wooden platter away so that she could show Black Wolf that she was ready for her "dessert" . . . which for Maddy, was *him*.

Allowing such thoughts to enter her mind made Maddy feel suddenly wicked, yet it was a delicious wickedness. She felt a strange, heady sweetness flood through her when Black Wolf also slid his empty platter away from him.

When he reached a hand out for Maddy, her hand trembled as she intertwined her fingers with his.

She knew that they would be sharing the lodge alone for only a while; Jaimie had been instructed earlier by Black Wolf that his lodge was now hers.

His tepee had been saved from the flood waters by his people and brought to the Sioux village along with the rest of his belongings.

After his people knew that he was alive, they had hurriedly erected his lodge and had placed his belongings inside it, arranging everything the way they knew he desired it.

Black Wolf had already reassured Maddy that Jaimie would not come to the lodge any time soon after the feast, for there was to be more dancing and games beneath the bright rays of the moon. Some of the dancing and games were planned to last until daybreak.

Jaimie had gotten Maddy's permission to participate in everything for as long as she wished. Knowing Jaimie, Maddy expected her to join the games and dancing until she dropped.

Maddy tried not to feel uncomfortable about the eyes that were following her and Black Wolf as they walked away from the crowd of Sioux and Shawnee gathered about the huge outdoor fire. She knew they were aware of where they were going, and why.

She knew that many of Black Wolf's people

resented her, just as most whites would resent Black Wolf.

But the word "forbidden" was a word Maddy no longer worried about. She had removed it from her vocabulary the minute she had accepted the fact that she loved Black Wolf without reservation.

It was a love that would endure all tongue-lashings from gossipmongers, white and red-skinned. Maddy was now a part of the Sioux world. She looked eagerly to the future now, whereas only a few short days ago she had wondered if she would even have one.

Black Wolf had given her reason to hope again, to love for the very first time in her life, to fight for their future together.

Her thoughts were interrupted when Black Wolf stepped up to a huge tepee and held aside the buffalo skin that covered the front.

Her heart pounding, her knees weak, Maddy smiled up at him, then stepped on past him into the soft firelight of the lodge. She only got two footsteps away from Black Wolf when he reached out and slid his arms around her waist, drawing her around to face him.

Their eyes holding, their pulses racing, Black Wolf and Maddy drew nearer to each other. Then suddenly he yanked her against his hard body.

His eyes flaring with hungry intent, Black Wolf held Maddy. Slowly gyrating his body against hers, he lowered his lips to her mouth and gave her a meltingly hot kiss.

A raging hunger that was new to Maddy caused her to take a ragged breath; the power of Black Wolf's body filled her with sweet abandon.

As he kissed her with a fierce, possessive heat, she clung to him.

Her head began a slow spinning as she felt the length of his manhood moving teasingly against her, slowly up and down, her body moving with his, writhing in response.

"*Tay-chee-khee-lah,*" Black Wolf whispered as he slid his mouth to her ear. "In Sioux I have just told you I love you. I want you as I have never wanted anyone. Do you feel the same heat? The same rush of fire within your veins?"

"Yes, and oh, so much, much more," Maddy whispered back, her breath catching as his hand crept up inside the skirt of her dress and soon found her moist, wet place.

When he began to stroke her throbbing center, she became aware of feelings there that she had never imagined possible.

Sighing, the pleasure building as waves of liquid heat pulsed through her, she held her head back, closed her eyes, and gave herself up to the rapture.

Suddenly she was aware that Black Wolf was no longer holding her just as she felt something else so delicious she thought she might faint from the pleasure. She gasped when she felt the bliss building, the flicks of his tongue on her womanhood, and then his lips there, threatening to rob her of all her senses except those that were guided by sheer pleasure.

As he stroked her in such a way, with Maddy trying not to think about the wickedness of this way of loving, she shivered with ecstasy as the pleasure peaked into something so wonderful she was totally bewildered by it.

Just as he slid his mouth and tongue away, and before she could climb down from that cloud of rapture, Black Wolf quickly undressed her.

His eyes filled with passion, he lifted her naked body and carried her back to his pallet of furs and blankets. As he stretched her out on the softness of his bed, he kissed her.

Her whole body pulsing with wondrous sensations, Maddy clung to him when he tried to pull away. "Please don't leave me," she whispered huskily. "Love me some more. I have never experienced anything so wonderful."

"You will soon realize there is something even more wonderful than what I have introduced you to," Black Wolf said huskily as he stood away from her and placed his thumbs at the waistband of his breechclout.

Slowly he lowered it. "Look at me," he said throatily, his eyes flaring with hungry intent. "See me. Know that the arousal you see is caused only by you. And only you can appease this need that is consuming me."

Maddy's eyes widened when she saw that part

of a man's anatomy that she had only seen before on the pages of books. She had read books that her mother had kept hidden in her trunks, books that she had discovered after her mother died.

Maddy was amazed to see now that the men in those pictures could not compare to Black Wolf. He was so large and so very well developed!

And . . . he . . . was hers!

She smiled and held her arms out for him when the breechclout dropped to the floor and he kicked it away. She knew that she was about to enter a world that no words in a book could describe.

She sucked in a wild breath when he slowly entered her, and in a moment she felt a quick, pinching pain.

"Do not be alarmed," Black Wolf whispered against her lips. "What you felt is natural. Be patient. That pain will soon turn to bliss."

As his lean, sinewy buttocks moved, slowly inching himself further into her, taking care not to hurt her anymore, sweet currents of warmth slowly began to spread through Maddy.

She twined her arms around Black Wolf's neck and kissed him, their tongues flicking between their lips.

And then he lowered his mouth and introduced her to another way of loving that made her go wild with pleasure. His tongue swirling around first one nipple and then the other, his tongue licking the flames within her, his hands sliding up to cup her aching breasts, caused an erotic heat to knife through her body.

Black Wolf fought to hold back the pleasure that was threatening to spill over within him.

He reveled in Maddy's nearness, in her touch, her kisses, her utter sweetness.

Everything Maddy offered was now his forever. The euphoria that filled his entire being was almost more than he could bear!

His steel arms enfolded her again as his lips bore down upon her mouth, his kiss now more demanding, more insistent. He could feel her hunger in her kisses. He savored the taste and feel of her lips and tongue. The pressure that he was feeling in his loins, the *heat*, was almost torture!

"I cannot wait any longer," he whispered against her lips. "Come with me, my woman. Together we will ride the waves of pleasure. Soar with me as though we are eagles mating in the sky! I love you, Maddy. I . . . love . . . you."

Maddy was beyond coherent thought. She heard his words as though they were being spoken from a deep tunnel.

All that she could concentrate on were these feelings that he was causing within her. They were now growing hotter, like a fire, consuming her.

Suddenly she felt something else. It was similar to the intense pleasure she had felt moments ago when his mouth had stroked her where she unmercifully ached.

But this time it was a thousandfold more pleasurable than the other time she had become immersed in wondrous bliss.

This time it was overwhelmingly beautiful, and, oh, so fulfilling!

Chapter Twenty-two

Up to the wonted work! come, trace
The epitaph of glory fled;
For now the Earth has changed its face,
A frown is on the Heaven's brow.
                    —Percy Bysshe Shelley

Even though she was carrying a lit lantern, Charlene Johnston moved guardedly as she stepped down from the stairs into the cellar. She knew the man upstairs had been bitten by a spider here in this very cellar, and where there was one spider, there were usually others.

Cautiously, and holding the lantern away from herself so that the light would reach farther ahead of her, Charlene slowly explored the cellar. Her eyes went over the canned foods, to choose what she could prepare for the evening meal.

Brushing cobwebs aside, shivering when some of them clung to her hands, she worked her way around the small room and chose glass jars of green beans, stewed tomatoes, and peaches. They would go well with the rabbit that

231

her husband had shot earlier, and which was already slowly frying in a pan on the beautiful wood-burning cooking stove in the kitchen.

She set the lantern on the bottom step and took the food up to the kitchen, then returned for the lantern. She stopped abruptly when she saw the light from the lantern reflecting on something on the floor.

She bent to look, her eyes widening when she saw two halves of a broken bayonet.

"How did this get here?" she whispered to herself.

She picked up one of the halves and took a better look, recognizing it as the sort of bayonet that soldiers attached to guns.

Her jaw tight, she gingerly put one half of the broken bayonet into her apron pocket, then grabbed the lantern and left the cellar.

"What took you so long?" Ralph asked, standing over the stove, turning the rabbit in the hot, splattering grease.

He swung around when his wife did not respond, raising an eyebrow when he saw a strange, twisted look on her face.

He laid the fork down on the counter and went to Charlene. Gently he placed his hands on her shoulders. "Tell me what's wrong," he said. "You look upset. Was there something in the cellar that disturbed you? If so, Charlene, tell me what."

Her eyes locked with her husband's, Charlene slowly slid her hand into her pocket and, careful not to cut herself, placed her fingers on the duller edge of the bayonet and pulled it out for him to see.

"Damn, how'd that get in the cellar?" Ralph gasped, taking the piece of blade from his wife. He turned it slowly over in his hand and studied it more closely. "It's the sort—"

"Yes, the sort used to kill many of my people," Charlene said before Ralph could finish his sentence.

"What'd you find, Mommy?" Angel asked as she ran into the room, eyes wide as she stared at what her father was holding. "A knife?"

"No, it's not a knife," Charlene said thickly.

"Then what is it?" Angel persisted, reaching a hand up to touch it, giving her mother a quizzical stare when she stopped her.

Farris heard the commotion in the kitchen. From what he could tell, the strangers were talking about something that had been found in the cellar. Yet from where he lay in his bed, all he could hear was a mumble of words.

Too curious to just lie there, not knowing what was happening in his own kitchen, Farris decided to see what the problem was.

Groaning and dizzy, his arm as heavy as lead, he rolled over to the edge of the bed. He stopped to take a breath, then struggled to his feet.

With every step he took, the pain in his arm threatened to make him faint. But finally he made his way out into the corridor, then pressed his back against the wall for support and inched his way toward the kitchen.

When the large dog he had encountered in the basement rushed toward him, its teeth bared, Farris cried out for help.

All three came at once from the kitchen.

Angel giggled as she grabbed her dog by the collar. "A big man like you afraid of my puppy?" she said, her eyes mocking Farris. "Shame on you, mister man."

"You take that damn mutt out of my house," Farris said, his eyes narrowed angrily. "Now. Do you hear me? Now!"

"I don't think you are in any condition to order anyone around, much less my daughter," Ralph said tightly, glaring icily into Farris's eyes. "Now get on back to your bed and mind your business. You're lucky we happened along. If not, you'd have died in that cellar."

Farris was only half hearing what Ralph said. His eyes were fixed on his bayonet. "My prized bayonet! Who did that to my bayonet?" he said, his voice rising in pitch as he looked from Ralph to Charlene. "Which one of you broke my bayonet? Don't you know its value?"

"I found it in the cellar already broken, but even before it was, it had no value," Charlene said stiffly. She placed her hands on her hips. "Now or *ever*."

She gave Ralph a half glance. "Go and throw it in the garbage, Ralph," she said without taking her eyes off Farris.

Ralph started to walk away, but with his good arm Farris managed to reach out and grab him by the arm. "Don't you dare," he hissed out. "That's *my* property. Even though it's broken, it's still a part of history that must be protected."

"History?" Ralph said, turning the half of the bayonet from side to side, looking questioningly at it. Then he gazed into Farris's eyes. "Whose?"

"The United States Cavalry, that's who," Farris rushed out. "You damn idiots. Don't you know nothin'? This is the bayonet that killed Chief Crazy Horse." He laughed wickedly. "I'm the man who slammed it into the chief's savage body."

Farris noticed that suddenly everyone became quiet. He saw the surprised looks in their eyes quickly change to hatred.

"You are the man who brags all over the country that you killed my chief?" Charlene hissed. She took a slow step toward Farris. "You tell everyone that you are a big man because you killed Crazy Horse with this ugly bayonet?"

"Your . . . chief?" Farris stammered, his gaze taking in her appearance, the dark hair and eyes. . . .

"Yes, *my* chief," Charlene said, proudly lifting her chin. "I am not altogether Sioux, but a portion of me is. I am a *breed*, a breed who would do anything for the Sioux side of my heritage."

Farris's body jerked when she suddenly slapped him in the face, then pointed toward the door at the end of the corridor. "Leave!" she cried. "Leave now!"

Stupefied to realize she was an Indian, and astonished at her ordering him to leave his own house, Farris was momentarily rendered speechless.

Then he stiffened his jaw. "This house is *mine*," he growled out. "Nobody, especially no *breed*, tells me to leave. *You* leave. At once. All of you. Get out of my house."

Charlene grabbed her husband's pistol from his gunbelt, which hung low and heavy around his hips. She aimed it at Farris. "I can make you do anything I want," she hissed out. "For you see, white man, I'm the one holding the firearm, not you. Leave now, or be shot."

She laughed and nodded toward the bayonet blade. "Or better yet," she said, her eyes gleaming. "You can die as Chief Crazy Horse died." She smiled at her husband. "Ralph, kill him with the bayonet. But kill him slowly. I'd like to see him grovel and beg for mercy as he dies."

"No!" Farris cried, already staggering to the door. "Don't kill me. I'm leaving."

His body red hot with fever, his arm paining him, Farris continued to stumble toward the door. Just as he reached it and pulled it open, he heard a rush of feet behind him.

His breath was knocked out of him when he felt someone give him a big shove, causing him to fall to his knees and roll through the doorway onto the porch.

Turning on his side, he glared up at Charlene. "You'll pay for this," he ground out. "Some day . . . somehow . . . I'll make . . . you pay . . ."

Charlene threw her head back in a fit of laughter, then sobered and glared down at Farris, her hands on her hips. "I doubt you'll live long enough to carry out your threat," she said tightly. "Don't you know how bad your arm is? It's in the process of turning gangrenous."

She tossed the bayonet blade down beside him. "Now get on out of here and take this . . . this . . . thing with you," she said, turning with a swish of skirts and going back inside the house.

Farris flinched when she slammed the door between them, wincing when he heard the sound of the lock being turned. "The witch," he whispered, then crawled slowly down the stairs, a step at a time, stopping to rest on his back when he finally reached the ground.

When his arm became even more painful, he reached over to grab it, then stopped when he felt the stickiness of the ooze that was seeping from it.

He lay there for a while to rest, then once again got to his knees and crawled slowly toward the tethered horses.

When he finally reached them, he grumbled when he found that his was gone. "Damn her," he whispered harshly to himself. "Maddy took my stallion! Just you wait . . . Maddy, just you wait until I get my hands on you!"

He chose another horse and reached for the

stirrup. Grabbing it, he pulled himself slowly up to his feet.

Groaning, with waves of dizziness threatening to send him into the dark void of unconsciousness again, he gazed down at the piece of his bayonet, cursing whoever had broken it.

Then he slid the bayonet into his saddlebag.

"I'll find the guilty party," he whispered, knowing that Maddy couldn't have broken it. She didn't have the strength.

It had to be someone else who had gone into the cellar between the time when Maddy had been at the house and before the family had gotten there.

"But, damn it, who?"

After tying the saddlebag closed, he moaned as he pulled himself up into the saddle, sighing with relief when he was finally in it.

As he rode slowly away from his home, his thoughts were still on the bayonet. Finding it broken was even more traumatic to him than momentarily being forced from his home, for, in time, after he settled things with Maddy, he would regain his strength and evict the interlopers.

But his bayonet could never be repaired, nor could his pride, for never again would he be able to show people the bayonet and boast about it being the one that killed Chief Crazy Horse. The moment the bayonet blade had been broken in half it had lost its importance . . . its glitter.

"That Maddy is somehow responsible," he

whispered to himself. "I hope I live long enough to find her."

Oh, how she would regret having double-crossed him!

Chapter Twenty-three

How calm it was! the silence there
By such a claim was bound
That even the busy woodpecker
Made stiller with her sound
The inviolable quietness.
                    —Percy Bysshe Shelley

Everything seemed unreal to Maddy since her life had changed so drastically. The way of life she had always known was gone, and now she was a part of Black Wolf's life, and his people's.

Yet today she was momentarily returning to her past life by going to the cave and retrieving all of the possessions that she had left there. She was also going to her parents' graves to pray over them, and take one last walk through her family's water-ravaged cabin.

The Ohio had receded until it was safe to travel once more. Not wanting to ride a horse ever again if she had anything to say about it, Maddy was with Black Wolf in his canoe when her cabin came into view.

The sight of the mud and debris clinging to

the sides of her family's home caused a deep sorrow within Maddy. It was hard to believe that almost everything that home had stood for was gone. Except for Jaimie and a few possessions, it was all gone, a thing of the past now.

But oh, what a wonderful future she would have with her beloved Black Wolf, she reminded herself. He was making her world right again, as well as his people's.

She gazed at his powerful, bare copper back as he continued to draw the paddle through the water, now heading the canoe toward shore.

Yes, he was a powerful, strong man, but he did have so many burdens to carry on those muscled shoulders. She wondered how he felt about it all, whether or not he felt too challenged by everything to be comfortable about it.

She knew him well enough to know that he would never wear his worry openly for anyone to see. He always talked of hope, trying to instill it in his people's lives, for without hope, what was left?

Maddy felt hopeful now for the first time since her beloved father's death.

She clung to the sides of the canoe as Black Wolf beached it on the rocky shore.

When he stepped out and dragged the canoe to higher ground, Maddy waited. She knew that he would lift her from the canoe and carry her to the thick grass before putting her on her feet.

He always treated her like some delicate, frail flower, and she enjoyed being pampered. It made her feel more feminine. She loved being feminine, especially now that she had a man who seemed to want that in a woman.

Had she been like Jaimie, and boasted of riding horses, shooting guns, and winning foot races over boys, she did not think that Black Wolf would love her as much. And she wanted nothing now but his love.

"Come, *mee-tah-ween*, we will go now to the cabin," Black Wolf said, lifting Maddy into his arms.

"You are so sweet to bring me," Maddy murmured, clinging around his neck as he carried her up the steep embankment.

Surprisingly, he did not set her on the ground when he reached the tall, drier grasses. Instead he held her against him as he slowly carried her toward the cabin.

"You have lost much, also, because of the river," Black Wolf said, gazing down at her. He felt so much for her, he found it hard not to stretch her out on the ground and make love to her all over again.

Through the night they had made love more than once.

He had delighted in showing her the many ways to make love, glad that she allowed them.

His lips tasted her even now, her sweetness, her softness.

His heart thundered inside his chest as he remembered how quickly she had learned the art of using her mouth on his body.

It made a volcanic heat rise within his loins even now to think of those moments when they had flown together on wings of rapture to that bliss that only men and women in love could reach.

"What I am seeing in your eyes doesn't have anything at all to do with the river or my cabin, does it?" Maddy murmured, her pulse racing as his eyes seemed to be devouring her.

She knew what he must be thinking about. Their long, sensual night together. They had shared so much through the night, and although he had thought it was all new to her, she had read about those ways of making love in her mother's hidden, wicked books and knew that men and women shared such sensual exploits.

It had been wonderful to bring the pages of those books alive while on Black Wolf's bed of blankets and pelts. But she was so glad that she had known about what he thought he was introducing her to, for, Lordie, she might have been too shocked to allow it!

"No, I am not thinking about cabins or caves," Black Wolf said, chuckling throatily. "I was thinking about last night and the woman who shared my bed."

"That woman was *me*," Maddy said, giggling, her eyes dancing.

"Yes, and you are all woman," Black Wolf said huskily. "Were I to lay you down amidst the grasses at this very moment, would you open your legs again to me? Would you touch me with

243

your hands like you did last night? Would you lead me inside you with those delicate, sweet hands?"

"Yes, I would do all of those things," Maddy murmured, the wonderful, delicious pressure that she now knew was normal causing a wetness at the juncture of her thighs.

"If there were not so many people on the river today traveling to their devastated homes, I would make love to you, my woman, for all the birds, forest animals, and sky to witness," Black Wolf said huskily. He leaned over and gave her a soft, quivering kiss. "But tonight? When we are *ee-shah*, alone, in the privacy of our lodge? We will then do what is in both our hearts and minds."

"Our lodge?" Maddy said, her eyes widening. "You are referring to your tepee being also mine?"

"What is mine is now yours," Black Wolf said, slowly sliding her to her feet.

He wrapped her in his muscled arms. He drew her up against his hard body and gazed adoringly into her eyes.

"We are as one, are we not?" he asked softly. "We will soon speak vows of forever to one another?"

"Yes, we are as one," Maddy said, feeling so loved at this moment. "But the vows aren't necessary. I now know that when one loves, it isn't always necessary to seal that love by saying words. It is how one treats one's beloved that matters. And, oh, my darling, you have treated me like a precious jewel. I could never want for anything more."

"But I plan to give you everything that is in my power to give you," Black Wolf said, reaching a gentle hand to her cheek. "Just you wait and see, *mee-tah-ween*. Once we are settled in our new home on our new land and my responsibilities to my people have been fulfilled, then I will place you before everything else. We will wake up in the mornings and fall asleep at night in one another's arms. We will make love both morning and night."

"But what about Jaimie?" Maddy murmured. "We can't do any of that in Jaimie's presence, and Jaimie will be sharing our lodge, won't she? She's my responsibility now. I don't want to let her down."

"Yes, she will share our lodge, but there will be a curtain drawn between Jaimie's sleeping quarters and ours," Black Wolf said. He brushed a soft kiss across Maddy's brow. "And we will make sure she is asleep before we begin our lovemaking. Lovemaking is something we want Jaimie to learn naturally by doing."

"I'm so afraid she won't ever fall in love with anyone," Maddy said, frowning. "She is so boyish. What if that never changes?"

"She will change when she gets those feelings that make a woman realize she is a woman," Black Wolf said, placing his hands on Maddy's cheeks and sliding her hair back from her face.

He chuckled. "You are too much woman for your sister not to be also."

"You awakened those feelings in me," Maddy said, blushing.

"As some brave will awaken them in your sister's heart one day," Black Wolf said.

"If my sister does fall in love, I hope it is with someone just like you," Maddy said, flinging herself into his arms and hugging him. "I love you so much, Black Wolf. Without you, life would be meaningless."

He held her for a long moment, then took her by the hand and led her toward the cabin. "Are you certain you wish to go inside?" he asked, giving her a quick glance.

"Yes, I must," Maddy said, swallowing hard. "I must take one last look at where my family laughed and shared so much love. Although it is all gone, it still remains alive inside my heart and will until the day I take my last breath."

"Memories can be good or bad," Black Wolf warned. "You will make bad memories by going inside and seeing the devastation of what once was."

"I never thought of it in that way," Maddy said, stopping now to gaze at the cabin. "Perhaps you're right. Maybe it's best not to go inside and see how the river has ruined everything. It *will* form a bad memory. Why should I put that on myself?"

"Then let us go on to your family cemetery so that you can say your last words over your family's graves," Black Wolf said, his fingers twining more tightly with hers as they walked away from the cabin, toward the hill that would take them to the graves.

"With all of your responsibilities lying heavy on your shoulders, I am touched that you would take this time with me today so that I can take care of mine," Maddy said, giving him a soft smile.

When he gazed down at her and their eyes met, everything within her went warm with rapturous bliss. "How can I be so lucky to have you?" she murmured. "Black Wolf, I do love you so much; sometimes I wonder if all this is truly happening."

"It is all real enough," Black Wolf said, chuckling. "Last night could not be a dream imagined by someone while sleeping. And tonight you will again know how real it is when I take you to my blankets."

"I wish it could be now," Maddy murmured, then went somber when she saw the graves up ahead in the shade of a lovely birch tree.

She slipped her hand from Black Wolf's and ran softly to the three mounds of dirt.

Tears filling her eyes, she fell to her knees between her mother's and father's graves. She placed a hand on each grave, splaying her fingers out over them.

"Oh, Mother, oh, Father, how can it be that this is our final goodbye?" Maddy whispered, tears spilling from her eyes. "I doubt I shall ever return here. Tomorrow Jaimie and I will cross the Ohio and travel far away with Black Wolf and his people."

She looked up at Black Wolf, whose shadow fell over the graves. "Mother and Father, here stands the man who has brought much happiness into your daughter's life," she said, smiling up at Black Wolf. "I wish you could see his handsomeness. Do you sense his kindness? He is as no other man can ever be. He is everything to me."

Black Wolf fell to his knees beside Maddy and placed a loving arm around her waist. He drew her next to him and began a slow, soft prayer, one that his mother had taught him long ago to be spoken over the graves of the dead.

He chanted and sang as his eyes lifted to the sky, and the prayer sent goosebumps rushing over Maddy's flesh. Never had she been as moved by anything as she was moved by what Black Wolf was doing.

She leaned against him as she listened, then joined him and sang softly with him when he had repeated the song enough times for her to know it.

When it was all over and Maddy had placed some wild flowers on each of the graves, she rose, hand-in-hand with Black Wolf, and walked away.

"What you did touched my heart so deeply," she said, giving him a grateful smile. "I've never met a man as compassionate as you."

"My feelings grow from what my parents taught me, for they were everything good on this earth, as I am certain your parents were in *your* eyes," Black Wolf said, nodding. "The prayers and songs you heard me say over your parents' graves are the same I have said and sung over mine."

"And now we both have to leave our parents' graves and will never visit them again," Maddy said, swallowing hard.

"My father's grave is now the river," Black Wolf said somberly, glancing over his shoulder toward the Ohio. "When the water swallowed our island it also swallowed my father's grave."

"How sad," Maddy murmured.

"Yes, there are many things in this world that can be described as sad," Black Wolf said thickly.

He stopped and slid his arms around Maddy's waist and swung her around to face him. "But I am no longer sad," he said. "I have *you*. You are my happiness, my hope for the future. With you at my side, everything is possible."

"I'm not sure how I feel, knowing that you depend on me so much," Maddy said, searching his eyes. "It's such a responsibility."

"Our love and what comes from it should never be a responsibility, but something wonderful to be rejoiced over," Black Wolf said, twining his fingers through her hair, bringing her lips to his. "*Mee-tah-ween . . .*"

Maddy sighed with heady pleasure when his

lips came down on hers and kissed her.

Her heart soaring and singing, she clung to him and returned the kiss with abandon.

And then they went onward and entered the cave. After several trips to and from the cave to the canoe with what was left of her family's possessions, they were once again traveling in the river, but this time downstream.

Maddy took one last look over her shoulder at her family's cabin, then lifted her chin and looked straight ahead.

"Tomorrow, Black Wolf," she said, reaching a hand to his sleek, copper shoulder. "I can hardly wait until tomorrow."

"Yes, tomorrow we leave the Shawnee village," Black Wolf said as he glanced over his shoulder at Maddy. "It is good to see you looking forward to a new life with my people. I will make you happy, *mee-tah-ween*. It is a promise I do not make to you lightly."

"I know," Maddy said softly. "And my promise to you, that I will make you happy, is something spoken from deep inside me."

"Then all is well, Maddy, in both our lives," Black Wolf said, laughing gaily into the wind.

"Yes, very well," Maddy said, laughing softly with him.

She could not help taking another look over her shoulder at what she was leaving behind. She wondered how it could be, but she seemed to be seeing her mother and father standing on the embankment, side by side, waving a last goodbye to her.

Chapter Twenty-four

I like a look of agony,
Because I know it's true;
Men do not sham convulsion,
Nor simulate a throe.

—Emily Dickinson

His arm dangling lifelessly at his side, Farris slid awkwardly from his horse, groaning when he fell to the ground with a thud between two other horses.

Worn out from the miles he had been forced to travel to get to the doctor's house, he waited a moment before attempting to get to his feet. He was hidden between the horses so that, thus far, no one had noticed him.

Breathing hard, he was glad that he had made it to Doc Charlie's house. Surely Doc Charlie could give him something for the pain and infection. New medications were being invented every day. During the Civil War the many deaths due to infected wounded limbs had prompted the United States Government to put more money into researching ways to cure infection.

Cassie Edwards

"Can I help you, young man?"

The kind voice of a woman drew Farris's eyes quickly around. He had been so engrossed in his pain that he had not noticed her approaching him. He *had* noticed the many horses, wagons, and buggies outside of Doc Charlie's house and judged that the doctor was busy today tending to the many casualties resulting from the ravages of a river gone wildly out of control.

He winced when he saw a frail woman standing over him instead of someone who would have the strength to assist him. The elderly woman wore thick-lensed, gold-framed glasses. Her skin was drawn taught across her face. Her hair was swirled into a tight gray bun atop her head. The long cotton print dress she wore hung loosely from her small, short body. Tucked beneath her left arm was a beaded purse and in her right hand was a wooden cane.

"Here, young man, let me give you a helping hand," the woman said, gasping when she got a better look at his arm as she stooped down closer to him.

"Oh my," she said, visibly shivering as she stared at the inflamed, swollen, pus-covered arm. "How did that happen, young man?"

"A . . . spider . . . bite," Farris stammered, ignoring her proffered hand, for he knew that if she tried to help him, he might pull her down on top of him. She didn't look strong enough to swat a fly, much less help lift a man from the ground.

He groaned and bit his lower lip as he slowly pushed himself to his feet.

"I know you," the woman said, taking a step away from him. "Why, you're Sheriff Boyd, aren't you? I've seen you strutting around River Town with your badge all shined up and gleaming in the sun."

"Yes, I'm Sheriff Boyd," Farris said, finally on his feet, yet so unsteady he knew that climbing the steps to the wrap-around porch would be a challenge.

He stared up at the two-storied white clapboard house. Like his own, it had been saved from the river because Doc Charlie had been wise enough to have it built high above the flood line.

"River Town is all but gone," the woman said glumly. "My daughter's millinery shop was one of the first to go. The river just seemed to swallow it whole. And. . . ."

The lady rambled on and on as she walked stiffly beside Farris with her cane, yet he paid no heed to what she was saying. He was concentrating too hard on getting up those damn porch steps. His knees were so wobbly and weak he wasn't even sure he could make it to the porch, much less up the steps.

But he must! He had to have Doc Charlie's help.

And he had to keep his strength, if by willpower alone, to be able to continue his search for Maddy. If he had his way about it, today would be the last day of her life!

"Jaimie, too," he whispered to himself.

Yes, Jaimie had proven to be a thorn in his side from the moment he had first tried to court Maddy.

The brat! She was always there gawking or plying him with questions about this and that. She was a useless twit. The world would be a better place without them *both*.

"Young man, did you say something?" the elderly woman asked, grabbing his good arm.

When he turned with a start and glared at her, he could tell that the look he was giving her startled her.

She stared with wide gray eyes through her thick lenses up at him, then mumbling beneath her breath, moved on past him, her cane tapping as she placed it on each step. Although she appeared to be at least seventy years old, she was feisty and spry enough to manage the steps and was soon inside the house.

"Good riddance," Farris grumbled.

Grabbing the rail, he pulled himself up the steps one at a time. Sweat pearled his brow at the pain in his arm.

Finally he made it to the porch. Leaning against the wall, he gaped at people who came and went from the house. They stared at his arm, then nodded a hello to him and went on their way.

"Idiots," Farris mumbled. "They don't care

about nothin' but their own hides. I'll show 'em when I'm well again and can use the powers of sheriff to get back at those who shun me."

Feeling rested enough to go on inside the house, Farris went to the door and opened it, stopping and staring disbelievingly at what he found inside the grand old mansion. The rooms on each side of him had been turned into a hospital. Cots were on the floor of both the library and parlor.

The injured lay beneath blankets on makeshift beds, and those who had been left homeless from the flood sat around in groups. Some were talking. Others were smoking and gambling. Children huddled around their mothers, sobbing.

"Sheriff Boyd?" Doc Charlie said as he stepped up to Farris. He immediately saw Farris's arm. He bent low and studied it, then gave Farris a wary stare. "Doesn't look good, Farris. A spider bite caused this?"

"Yes, but I can't tell you what kind of spider," Farris said, gazing at the short, squat doctor. He was dressed in a black suit, his long gray hair framing his round, paunchy face. "Can you help me, Doc? Can you give me something for the infection? Can you give me something for the pain?"

Doc Charlie placed a gentle hand on Farris's right arm. He led him down a long, dark corridor. "We'll see," he said. "Let me take a better look at it in my office. The lighting is better there. I'll give you a thorough examination and then give you my opinion on what should be done about that arm."

"Opinion? What *should* be done about the arm?" Farris said incredulously. "Damn it, Doc, do as I said. Give me something for the infection. Doctor the wound itself. Give me pain medication. Then I'll be on my way."

"It's not always as simple as that," Doc Charlie said, leading Farris into his spacious office at the far end of the house.

Bright light from the outdoors was pouring in through the many broad windows of the room. Over a long examining table covered with white padding hung a huge kerosene lamp giving off even more light.

"It's got to be that simple," Farris grumbled, going to the table in the middle of the room and inching himself onto it. "I've things to do, Doc. Things that can't be put off to another day."

"As you saw in the outer room, Farris, the best of plans can be altered in one eye blink," Doc Charlie said, his eyes still on the arm. "Lie down on the table, Farris. Let me take a good look at that arm. Then I'll tell you what the day truly holds for you."

"What the hell does that mean?" Farris said. He tried to sit up, but the strong arm of the doctor held him down.

"By gum, Farris, you chose to come to me for doctoring," Doc Charlie grumbled. "I sure as hell didn't go out soliciting for the likes of you on the busiest day of my doctoring career. And although I don't believe in your way of running a sheriff's office, since you did come for my help, I'm going to do the best I can for you."

"You'd better do better than that, or by God, I'll make sure you'll never doctor anyone again," Farris spat out, resenting the doctor holding him down by force.

"I don't take much to threats," Doc Charlie said, glaring at Farris, their eyes locking and holding in silent battle. "But being as I'm a Christian and don't turn my back on anyone in trouble, I'll forget you threatened me. What's important, Farris, is taking care of that arm. If we don't, you'll not live long enough to hand out threats to too many more people."

"That's big talk for such a little man," Farris hissed.

When the doctor began cleansing his arm with something that smelled like alcohol, Farris let out a loud yelp.

"You're a big man, you can stand the pain," Doc Charlie said, smiling smugly down at Farris.

"Stop *now*, you sonofabitch!" Farris cried.

Doc Charlie jerked the medicine-soaked cotton swab away from Farris's arm. He glowered at Farris. "Name calling is the last thing a man who is at the mercy of a doctor should do," he said, slamming the cotton swab into a basin. He placed his fists on his hips and leaned down closer into Farris's face. "But the decision I have made about your arm is one made from skills, not from resentment or vengeance."

"What . . . decision?" Farris asked, his eyes searching the doctor's. "What are you saying?"

"I'm saying that your arm is too bad to save," Doc Charlie said, wise enough to take a step away from Farris. "If you wait another day you will surely die soon from gangrene. I've got to remove that arm, Farris. *Now*."

"Remove my arm?" Farris shouted, his pulse racing. Shakily he sat up on the table. "No. You can't. You've got to do something else that will help me."

"Farris, you were in the cavalry," Doc Charlie said, his voice drawn. "You saw enough gangrene to know what it can do, and how quickly." He nodded toward the arm. "Can't you see, Farris? It's already in its first stages. I recognized it the moment I saw it but I hoped that under a better light I might see some possibility of saving it. Farris, it's impossible to save that arm. Let me take it off now so that I can go on about my business. You aren't my only patient, you know."

"Just like that? You can so coldly tell me that you want to remove my arm so . . . so . . . you can move on to your next patient?" Farris cried, his voice rising in pitch. "Damn you, Doc. Damn you all to hell. I won't let you cut off my arm. I won't . . . let . . . you."

Doc Charlie shrugged idly. "If that's your decision, so be it," he said, turning to leave the room.

"Wait!" Farris screamed. "Don't leave me like this! Fix my arm! I've already got a lame leg from the damn war. I can't lose my arm!"

Doc Charlie spun around and faced Farris. "Farris, didn't you hear anything I said?" he said. "I'm telling you that if you don't let me remove that arm, it's your life that's at stake here. Your life, Farris. You . . . will . . . die."

Farris left the table and went to Doc Charlie and grabbed his collar. "I'm not going to lose my arm or my life," he said between clenched teeth. "Doc, give me something for the pain. I've got business to tend to!"

"I don't know what business could be so important that you are risking your life over it," Doc Charlie said, placing his hand on Farris's and removing it from his collar. "But since I'm a decent person with feelings for humanity, I will give you something for the pain. But I pray that you think this decision over more carefully. Come back anytime. I'll be here to remove the arm and then care for you at my house for as long as it takes for you to heal from the surgery."

"Thanks but no thanks," Farris mumbled. "Just give me the damn medicine. I'll be on my way so that you can go and cut off somebody else's arms or legs."

Doc Charlie went to a cabinet and opened it. He reached inside and took out a narrow, long, dark bottle. He turned and slammed it into Farris's outstretched hand. "This is against my better judgment, Farris, but I know you'd not leave without it, so here it is," he said sourly. "It's laudanum, Farris. Take it sparingly. It has some crazy side effects if taken in too large a dose."

Chuckling beneath his breath, Farris unscrewed the cap from the bottle and, defying the doctor by staring at him with amusement in his eyes, took several deep swallows of the foultasting medicine, which sent shivers up and down his spine.

Laughing throatily, he put the cap back on the bottle and tucked the bottle in his rear pants pocket. "Thanks for nothin', Doc," he said with a toss of his head. "Put the cost of the medicine on my tab. I'll be back later to pay for it."

"Farris, if you leave now, and don't come back real soon with a request for surgery, you'll not be alive to pay for the medicine I gave you today, *or* the examination," Doc Charlie said solemnly. "But I won't demand payment. You just go on and do whatever it is that's more important than your life. I pity you, Farris. I . . . pity . . . you."

"No need for that," Farris said, walking past the doctor and out into the corridor.

Knowing that what the doctor had said was more than likely true, yet still ignoring the warning, Farris went on outside, managed to get on his horse, and rode away toward River Town.

His only chance to find Maddy was to question the townspeople to see if anyone had seen her or her sister.

Being so extraordinarily beautiful, Maddy always attracted attention. Surely there would be several people who would have noticed her.

With each mile he rode, it was harder to stay in the saddle. His arm seemed to hang like a ton of lead from his shoulder. But the laudanum had at least dulled the pain, and he managed to keep going until he finally reached River Town.

The water had receded, and mud stretched like a dull brown blanket up and down the streets of the small town. The buildings were deserted, and only a few people were trudging through the ankle-deep mud to inspect their establishments.

Farris managed to get his horse down to the riverfront, where people were still coming and going in boats. One by one, he questioned people about whether they had seen Maddy and Jaimie.

One man who stood away from the others, loading his boat with his belongings, finally gave Farris the answer that he hoped would lead him to Maddy and Jaimie.

"Yep, I saw 'em," the man said, taking a corn-cob pipe from his mouth. He stared at Farris's arm, shivering with distaste at the sight, then looked away from him and motioned with his pipe toward the river. "I saw a young woman and a child that fit your description in a boat on the river with an Injun. Word is, Sheriff, that the Sioux island was completely flooded. Surely they all drowned. So why not go and look at the Shawnee village for the two lasses you're seekin'? The Shawnees' village is high above the flood line. Could be the lasses are there."

His arm too painful to travel in a boat alone, Farris whipped the man's pistol from his gun-belt and aimed it at him. "You take me to the Shawnee village," he growled. "And don't even think about shouting for help. My trigger finger is gettin' itchy."

"Don't shoot me," the man said, dropping his pipe as he raised his hands in the air. "I'll do whatever you say, go wherever you tell me to go."

"Idiot, drop your hands to your sides. Get in that boat," Farris said quickly, giving a wary look over his shoulder toward the other people on the riverbank, to see if anyone had noticed.

"All right, whatever you say," the man said, his voice anxious.

"First help me in," Farris said, taking a step toward the boat. He could see the man grimace as he quickly took hold of his good arm, avoiding getting too close to the one that oozed with pus.

Finally in the boat, Farris sighed deeply, hung his head and closed his eyes, for the moment resting, because he had much ahead of him that would require strength. He feared his vitality was slowly draining from him. He could feel the heat of his brow and knew that the fever was raging hot again. He knew the chances were small that he would survive much longer.

But he would rather die than be forced to live without one of his arms. And before he died he would make sure someone else's days were as numbered as his. Maddy's! Jaimie's!

Perhaps even the Indian that had been with Maddy, if Farris had his way about it!

Chapter Twenty-five

My brain is wild, my breath comes quick,
The blood is listening in my frame,
And thronging shadows fast and thick
Fall on my overflowing eyes.
                    —Percy Bysshe Shelley

The huge outdoor fire sent its flames heavenward, spreading orange streamers of light across the dark sky. Although Maddy was bone-tired from a long, strenuous day of labor, doing things she would have never thought she was capable of doing, she was thrilled to be a part of the festivities at the new Sioux village as she sat beside Black Wolf on a pallet strewn with wildflowers.

The sacred tepee of bison hides for the village shaman had just been erected. Its hides were darkened by age, having traveled from as far as Nebraska to the island in the midst of the Ohio, and now to the Sioux's new village in Kentucky.

Somewhere, some time ago, someone who was a skilled painter had drawn vision pictures on the old sacred tepee.

Maddy turned and looked over her shoulder

at the tepee, which sat only a few feet behind her. Earlier she had walked slowly around the tepee, gazing in wonder at the "vision pictures." A flowering tree had been painted on the south side, while on the north side there were white geese. The daybreak star had been painted on the east side. Horses, elk, and bison had been painted over the entranceway at the front of the tepee, as well as a flaming rainbow.

"It is a magnificent lodge, is it not?" Black Wolf said as he caught Maddy looking at it.

He, too, gazed at the sacred tepee, recalling the day his cousin Red Feather had painted the vision pictures on it.

A wave of melancholy swept through Black Wolf as his thoughts dwelled on Red Feather. He had been twelve when he displayed his talents to his people as he painted the vision pictures on the shaman's lodge.

It saddened Black Wolf to the very core to remember that the day after the paintings were completed, Red Feather had been killed by renegades from another village.

The killers had been hunted down and caught. Black Wolf's cousin's death had been avenged by the quick deaths of those who had killed him. But Black Wolf had learned that day that no matter how revenge is carried out, it never lessens the burden of sadness in one's heart over the death of a loved one.

From that day forth, he never saw the value of

revenge. It was a feeling that ate away at one's insides.

Yes, he took revenge when it was necessary. But he did not live for the opportunity to do so as did some warriors he knew.

Being his people's leader, he put more emphasis on filling their lives with things worthwhile instead of dwelling on reasons to hate and ways to avenge themselves on those who had caused the hate.

"Yes, the tepee is magnificent," Maddy said, bringing Black Wolf out of his reverie.

She looked around her at the merrimentn of Black Wolf's people. She reached over and took Black Wolf's hand. "It's such a wonderful night, Black Wolf," she murmured. "Everyone is so happy."

She watched the brightly painted dancers who performed before the great fire to the music of many drums and eagle-bone whistles. Earlier, when the dancers had just begun to dance in their beautiful attire, Black Wolf had explained some of the clothes and dance steps to her.

She had openly admired one particular style of dress, which had small bells sewn all around the skirts. Black Wolf had told her that dress was called the "jingle dress." It was very colorful and accented by a belt, fan, leggings and moccasins. The jingle dress created a musical accompaniment to the dance as the bells tinkled softly with each movement of the woman.

Another dance that was fascinating to Maddy

was the Gourd Dance. The men, wearing red and blue blankets, were the only ones who participated in this dance. They wore the blankets so that the red color always lay over their right shoulders. The gourds were attached to beautifully beaded handles.

She smiled when she found Jaimie dancing among the people with the other children her age. They stamped their feet and bobbed their heads in time with the music as they whirled amidst the adults.

Maddy's smile waned when she focused on what Jaimie was wearing. Several of her Sioux friends had given her clothes to wear. Among them were beautiful fringed dresses, but Jaimie had chosen to wear what her friend Eagle Wing had given her . . . fringed breeches, shirt, and moccasins.

When Maddy had tried to encourage Jaimie to wear one of the dresses, Jaimie had said that she would be more comfortable in breeches. It made it easier for her to run and play, and to ride horses. Dresses had a way of twisting around one's legs while doing those things, an encumbrance she did not wish to deal with, especially not now when she was trying to show the Sioux children that she could handle any challenge that was placed before her.

Although Maddy did not approve of this competitive side of her sister, thinking that it might get her in trouble one day, Maddy had given in to Jaimie's wishes.

How could she not when Jaimie had returned home from the hunt, victorious?

And not only that, she had brought home the news that Black Wolf had given her an Indian name because of the successful hunt. Running Deer!

Proud that Jaimie was being accepted so quickly by the Sioux community, Maddy stood back and watched her sister's beaming face, feeling that things were working out, after all. Jaimie had grieved so much over the loss of her father. She had been the son her father had never been blessed with.

Now, for the first time, Jaimie seemed truly able to put this grief behind her and be happy.

Maddy looked over at the huge fire and smiled. The deer that her sister had killed had been chosen to be the one that would be cooked and eaten at the festival of hope tonight. It hung now over the outdoor fire, on a spit that a woman was slowly turning.

The fragrance from the juices dripping into the fire, wafting tantalizingly through the crowd of people, made Maddy's stomach growl from hunger. It was a celebration tonight of many things . . . of their new home, of the hunt, but especially of hope.

Maddy had her own private reason for celebrating . . . her intense love for Black Wolf and knowing that soon they would publicly declare their love in marriage vows spoken between them.

She had never thought that she could be so content. After her father had died and she had laid him next to her mother and infant brother, she had thought that her world had come to an end.

The days after that had been spent moving mechanically from chore to chore.

She had almost forgotten how to hope until the day she had met Black Wolf and discovered that she loved him.

"You look beautiful tonight," Black Wolf whispered close to Maddy's ear.

He leaned away from her and gazed at her. The doeskin dress that Raven Hair had given her, with its lovely beads sewn in the design of forest flowers, fit her body well. The softness of the fabric accentuated her beautifully rounded breasts and her tiny waist. The fringe at the hem lay around her tapered ankles. Moccasins adorned with the same beads as the dress covered her tiny, delicate feet.

Maddy saw Black Wolf's eyes roaming slowly over her. She blushed when she saw his gaze linger on her breasts before moving on down.

"Thank you," she murmured, smiling at him when his gaze came back to her face.

She quivered with ecstasy when he plucked a flower from those that were spread on the platform and gently placed it in a lock of hair above her ear.

Black Wolf leaned closer and again whispered into her ear. "You would be more beautiful alone with me beneath the stars than here before the blazing fire," he said huskily. "Before the feast, let us leave and spend time alone."

Knowing what "time alone" might mean, almost certain of it by the huskiness of Black Wolf's voice, Maddy blushed as she glanced up at him.

"Yes, let's be alone," she murmured, then looked quickly at the crowd.

She watched the dancers and singled out Jaimie. Jaimie was still engrossed in having fun with her friends. She wouldn't notice Maddy's absence.

Maddy turned smiling eyes back to Black Wolf. "Will you be missed?" she asked softly.

"Perhaps yes, perhaps no," Black Wolf said, his eyes gleaming into hers. "But if I am, no one will question where I have gone. Remember, *mee-tah-ween*, I am chief and my movements are my own."

"Then let's go," Maddy said, her pulse racing.

Taking her hand, he led her from the platform and soon they were running, laughing, through a large grove of birch trees.

They took a turn to the right and ran through a grove of cottonwoods. She was still amazed at why the women had chopped and stripped some of the cottonwood trees today. She had watched them feed the bark to the horses. She had been told that the horses liked the bark and it made them sleek and fat.

She had watched poles from the same trees

being made for a corral for the Sioux's many horses. Even now, back at the corral, there was a tepee for the horse guard, who sat by a hole in the hide to watch for horse thieves.

She was proud to have learned so much already about the Sioux customs and was hungry to learn more. It was like going to school without having to open books!

"Come with me up this slight hill," Black Wolf said, gripping her hand more firmly as they ran away from the trees into open land, then up a hill adorned with thick, bluish-green grass.

When they reached the top of the hill, where the stars twinkling like diamonds in the dark heavens seemed so low one might be able to pluck them, Black Wolf turned to Maddy and swung her into his arms.

"*Mee-tah-ween*," he said huskily, then twined his fingers through her hair and drew her lips to his. Tilting her head up, he brought his mouth down hard on hers and kissed her with a savage wonder. Her lips trembled against his as she returned the kiss.

Then his hands swept down and yanked her against him.

Caught in his embrace, a surge of ecstasy welled up inside Maddy, filling her, drenching her with a rush of hot desire.

Desire raged through Black Wolf, too, all of his senses yearning for the sweetness Maddy was offering him. Her body moved sinuously against his in promise.

271

He kissed her with urgent eagerness, his hands trembling as he reached down and lifted the hem of her dress, then slowly slid his hand up the inside of one of her legs until his fingers came to her wet, ready place.

Slowly he stroked her heat, smiling to himself when she opened her legs to him so that she could be more easily pleasured.

When Black Wolf thrust a finger into her hot moistness Maddy felt her breath catch and hold. The nub of her womanhood throbbed unmercifully as she was again awakened to a world of sensuality.

Overwhelmed with longing, a sweet, painful longing, Maddy arched toward Black Wolf. His finger began moving rhythmically in and out of her, the tip of his tongue now tracing the curve of her cheek.

"Black Wolf . . . Black Wolf . . ." she whispered, holding her head back as his tongue explored further along her face, and then moved down the slender column of her throat.

Wanting his tongue on her breasts, wanting his all, his everything, Maddy suddenly stepped away from him. While his eyes held hers, she slowly slid her dress up past her thighs, then sucked in a wild breath when he reached out to her and yanked the dress over her head.

Transfixed now by the smoldering desire in his eyes, Maddy reached over and slid his breechclout down across his muscled thighs.

His readiness sprang out into the open, making her breath catch.

Breathing raggedly, Maddy reached a hand out for his thick shaft. As they still gazed at one another, saying so much to each other without speaking a word, her hand moved on Black Wolf's pulsing satin hardness. His heat melted into the flesh of her palm.

When she heard Black Wolf groan with sensual pleasure, she moved her hand away from him and went into his embrace again and kissed him.

As they kissed, Black Wolf's hands drew Maddy against the warmth of his nakedness; then as he held her against him, he led her down to the ground and blanketed her with his body.

Silence vibrated around them as he shoved himself inside her and began his rhythmic thrusts. His teeth and lips feasted on her breasts, and then his tongue swirled around the nipples, then sucked one and then the other.

Their bodies strained together hungrily. Their lips came together again in a fierce, fevered kiss.

Sweeping his arms around her, he brought her closer against him, reveling in the yielding silk of her body.

He felt the searing, scorching flames of heat building in his loins.

His arms tightened around Maddy.

His lips quivered against hers.

"Come with me to paradise," he whispered, taking one last leap inside her, his senses reeling in drunken pleasure as ecstasy exploded inside him.

Maddy felt him reach his peak of passion, then closed her eyes dreamily and clung to him as her own body answered his and exquisite sensations spiraled through her body.

Afterwards, they were still clinging together when the hoot of an owl in a tree made them realize where they were . . . outdoors, with all nature a witness to their rapture.

Also, now that they had descended from their flight of joyous bliss, they were aware that the drums and rattles in the village had been silenced.

"Lord, Black Wolf, surely we've been missed," Maddy said, scrambling out of his arms.

She crawled over to where her dress had fallen and grabbed it. "We must hurry back there," she said anxiously. "I certainly don't want anyone coming to look for us."

"No one interferes with the private moments of a chief," Black Wolf said, yet he also dressed hurriedly.

He ran his fingers through his hair to straighten it, then gazed at Maddy who was now fully dressed. Her mussed hair was the only telltale clue that they had gone to heaven and back in one another's arms.

He went to Maddy and wove his fingers through her hair as their eyes locked in silent wonder. Slowly he combed the tangles out of her hair, then bent to the ground and picked up the flower that had fallen from above her ear during their lovemaking.

Smiling, he replaced the flower in her hair, then drew her against him and kissed her again, one long, last kiss, before returning to his people and performing as a chief again instead of lover.

Laughing softly, they drew apart and, hand in hand, returned to the village.

Large platters of food awaited them on a platform of flowers. They took the wooden platters and sat down with them and ate, but their eyes kept meeting as they remembered that just moments ago they had been alone, their lovemaking filled with savage wonder.

Maddy wished to herself that it would always be this wonderful for them, that no one would ever interfere in the joy they brought one another. For a moment she allowed troubling thoughts to enter her mind as she wondered how Farris Boyd was, and whether or not he was still in the cellar.

She prayed silently to herself that he was!

He, alone, could ruin everything, for she knew that if he had survived and was free of the cellar, he would not stop until he found Maddy and . . . and . . .

She did not venture further with that morbid thought, for she knew where it would take her.

She was visibly shaken by her fear of Farris, and Black Wolf was instantly aware of it. He reached a hand to her cheek. "What is on your mind that takes away from the pleasure of the moment?" he asked thickly.

Maddy gave him a weak smile. "Nothing," she said, the lie necessary, for she did not want to bring any worries into Black Wolf's life, not now when everything seemed suddenly so right.

"Then smile, don't frown," Black Wolf said, but he knew that she *had* been thinking about something that troubled her.

He would not confess to her that he, also, had been troubled by something . . . by whether Farris Boyd was truly out of their lives forever.

That man was all that was evil on this earth!

Chapter Twenty-six

The Devil, had he fidelity,
Would be the finest friend—
Because he has ability.
But Devils cannot mend.
                    —Emily Dickinson

The man Farris had forced to take him upriver was tied to a tree nearby while Farris sat on a butte overlooking the Shawnee village. For hours now he had watched for Maddy and Jaimie in the village, disgruntled because he hadn't seen them.

The moon was high and bright tonight and its light made it possible for Farris to continue to watch all of the activity in the village. It seemed to be a normal night for the Indians.

He squinted his eyes as several children danced and sang around a huge outdoor fire. He was watching for Jaimie to come from one of the lodges to join the fun. But still no Jaimie.

His gaze followed several women as they came from their lodges to sit on blankets close to the fire to watch the children play. Some women had brought their sewing materials to work by the light of the moon and the fire. Other women just sat there leisurely chatting among themselves, waving occasionally to one of the children.

But still Farris saw no sign of Maddy.

"They're probably hiding in one of those damn tepees," Farris grumbled to himself. "They are probably hiding because they know no bolted door can keep me from them."

He cackled insanely, then continued muttering to himself. "And it didn't, did it?" he whispered harshly. "Come hell *or* high water, I'm going to find you, and when I do—"

"Talkin' to yourself like that proves you're nuttier than a fruit cake," the captive man said, laughing throatily. "I don't know how on earth folks saw you fit to be River Town's sheriff. You sure must've put on some performance to get elected."

"What's that you're sayin'?" Farris said, turning around with a start. "Did I hear you call me a fruit cake?"

The man's face stiffened. He glared at Farris. "Your arm stinks," he spat out. "You're going to be dead soon from gangrene, and good riddance, I'd say. River Town has gone through enough damnation without you returning as our sheriff."

"No one asked your opinion about anything," Farris said, moving to his feet. His left arm dangling, pain shooting through it like lightning strikes, he shuffled his feet over to the man and raised the pistol. With the butt of the gun, he knocked the man unconscious.

"That should silence you for some time, if not forever," Farris said, laughing throatily.

He reached down and, groaning with pain as he used the swollen fingers of his left arm, he finally managed to take the man's gunbelt from him, and then the knife sheathed on his leg.

After the knife was sheathed on his own leg and the gunbelt was around his waist, Farris holstered the pistol, then went back to the edge of the butte and stared once again at the village.

"I'm damn tired of waiting," he growled. "I'm going to go and take a closer look. I'll find her if she's there. I'm the sheriff of River Town. The Shawnee know that I have jurisdiction over this land, which they took over without a treaty. Just because they built a fence around their village doesn't mean that I can't perform my duties as sheriff inside it."

His head spun with the pain in his arm; he was hardly able to bear it, but his determination to find Maddy combined with the laudanum to mask the pain. Farris slipped and slid down the side of the steep hill, falling face first on the ground when he finally reached the bottom.

Cursing, Farris slowly got back to his feet. His lame leg had twisted beneath him when he had fallen, and it was hurting him now, too.

Speaking in a low whisper, repeating curse words over and over again, he moved on toward the palisaded village. The fence was now only a few feet away.

"I've got to stay conscious," Farris mumbled as weakness overcame him. His shoulders swayed as he stopped and tried to steady himself. He breathed hard and hung his head.

"Lord, I ain't never been much of a prayin' man, but I'm askin' you to help me stay strong enough to find Maddy . . ." he mumbled, then jerked his head up with a start in the middle of his prayer when he heard footsteps approaching.

He paled when several armed Shawnee warriors stepped out from behind the tall fence and faced him with raised rifles.

"What do you want here?" Red Sky asked, his glossy black hair fluttering around his shoulders in the night breeze.

Red Sky's eyes shifted to Farris's arm. He quickly lowered the rifle to his side and went to Farris. "You have come for help," he guessed. "Come with me to my village. Our village shaman will take a look at your arm."

"Shaman? You mean a medicine man, don't you?" Farris gulped out. "No. I don't need your medicine man."

The tall, muscled warrior glared at Farris. "If you have not come to the Shawnee for help from our shaman, then why are you here?" he said, leaning his face closer to Farris, then stepping away when the stench of the injured arm was too overwhelming.

Seeing that he was treading on dangerous ground by showing his utter distaste of the Shawnee's medicine man, Farris realized that he had to at least pretend to want his help.

"I didn't mean what I said," he stammered out, his eyes narrowing as he glanced from Indian to Indian. "I *have* come for your help. Yes, your medicine man can look at my arm."

Farris's face turned dark with hatred as he watched the muscular warrior discuss the matter with three others.

Let them think I'm agreeable to their plan, then once I'm inside the fence I'll pretend to listen to what the medicine man says as he performs his crazy hocus pocus over me, he thought to himself. What can it hurt? All he'll do is shake a rattle or two over my arm and think that's enough to cure it.

Then when the tribe was asleep, Farris would search through the tepees for Maddy and Jaimie.

It made him smile to think they might not be there because they wished to seek shelter there, but as *captives*. It would give him much pleasure to see their frightened faces. And if they *were* captives, wouldn't they go willingly with Farris from the village beneath the protective cover of night?

"Come," Red Sky said, beckoning to Farris. "Follow us. We will take you to our Shaman. He will do what is right for your arm."

What . . . is . . . right? Farris thought, lifting

an eyebrow. Then he smiled when he reassured himself that the savage medicine man would only do his chanting and rattling over his arm, thinking that would be enough to make it well.

"Crazy hocus pocus," he whispered beneath his breath.

He smiled to think that the Indians blamed white people for the decimation of their tribes.

If they were smart enough, they'd see that having such things as medicine men to care for their ailments was the true cause of so many of them dying. The savages had no real medicine.

As Farris stumbled along behind the warriors through the wide gate into the vast Indian village, he was quickly aware of how quiet everyone became when they saw him.

Those he walked past gasped and covered their noses with their hands. His stench was now overpowering and vile.

Others gathered their children into their arms and ran into their lodges. Even the village dogs shied away from him, their tails tucked beneath their hind legs.

Farris walked onward with the warriors, finding that each step was now a great effort. Not only was his arm killing him, he had not eaten for many hours.

He would ask for food before the medicine man performed over him. Surely the savages would see that he needed to be fed as well as doctored.

The smell of roasting meat came to him

through the night air, directing his eyes to the outdoor fire that had burned down to low, orange flames. Over it many slabs of meat hung from large racks, their juices dripping tantalizingly into the fire.

"Food," Farris said, reaching a hand toward the meat. "I . . . need . . . food."

Red Sky turned to Farris. He stepped back and placed a gentle hand on his good arm and led him to the fire, then down onto a pallet of blankets beside it.

"When our shaman is summoned from his sleep, food will be brought for you," Red Sky said, nodding to a woman who was peeking from one of the tepees.

The middle-aged woman, whose gray hair hung long to the ground, came quickly to the tall warrior.

Farris leaned closer to them as he tried to hear what was being said, feeling fortunate that, thus far, everything seemed to be going as planned.

He watched the older woman nodding and smiling up at the tall warrior. Perhaps he could question the woman about Maddy and Jaimie.

She seemed the sort who was willing to please. Would she even feel that way toward a white man who was in trouble?

He could tell her that Maddy was his wife and Jaimie was his daughter. He would beg her to sneak him into the tepee in which they were confined, if they were indeed being held hostage.

If Maddy and Jaimie were there as the guests

of the Shawnee, as Farris was, then surely he could convince the woman that he must see them.

He watched eagerly as the woman returned to her tepee, then came from it again carrying a large wooden platter piled high with food.

As she set the platter down beside him, he hungrily eyed the meat, roasted corn, and slices of apples. He was so hungry, he forgot his plan to question the woman.

With his free hand he grabbed up the meat and crammed it into his mouth and ate until he felt uncomfortably full. When he shoved the platter aside, he found that he was alone beside the fire except for the woman, who had knelt close to him on her haunches as she watched him eat.

All of the warriors had gone to their individual tepees. No one was in sight except for the gray-haired woman.

Farris smiled at his luck.

As the woman leaned over to take the platter, Farris gently held her wrist. "I need your help," he said, speaking low and making sure his voice carried no further than the woman. "Will you help me?"

He saw confusion enter the woman's eyes.

He watched her as she started talking in sign language with him. He had learned enough sign language during the war to know that she was telling him that she hadn't learned the art of speaking the white man's language.

Disgruntled, his scheme ruined, Farris sighed deeply and released his hold on her wrist. He picked up the platter and shoved it into the woman's hands, nodding for her to leave.

The fire's warmth felt good on his face, so Farris turned toward it, then turned with a start when the tall Shawnee came and knelt beside him.

"The shaman awaits you in his medicine lodge," Red Sky said, his voice gentle.

He placed an arm carefully around Farris's waist and helped him up from the ground.

Farris didn't like this savage's arm at his waist. But he could not deny that it felt good to be helped to walk. Although he had eaten, he still felt weak and lightheaded.

He was afraid the gangrene had set in and was spreading, contaminating his body, organ by organ.

Yet he could never think that removing his arm was the best thing for him. He still felt that he would rather die than be disfigured like those he had seen during the war. It had been utterly disgusting to see a man hobble around on one leg or have a stump at the shoulder where an arm had been.

No, looking like that was worse than death itself!

"How did you injure your arm?" Red Sky asked as he led Farris toward a large tepee painted with bolts of lightning all across the front.

"A spider bite," Farris ground out. "It was a poisonous spider, one that leaves decay behind where it has bitten."

"I am unfamiliar with such a spider as that," the tall Shawnee said, frowning as he looked down at the foul-smelling arm. "Are there many such spiders in this area? If so, describe it to me."

"This was the first I encountered and hopefully my last," Farris said angrily. "I never saw the damn thing."

"I shall warn my people to be wary of spiders," Red Sky said, his voice drawn. "Especially the children. They run often in the forest, laughing and playing."

He stepped away from Farris and held the entrance flap of the huge tepee aside. "Enter," he said, gesturing with his free hand toward the opening. "I will leave you with Cloud Whisper. His medicine works well. Trust it."

Farris gave the tall Shawnee a guarded glance, then moved past him and went on inside the tepee.

Soft firelight greeted him from the flames in the firepit in the center of the lodge. He stopped when he found himself face to face with an elderly man dressed in a fur robe, his long and flowing gray hair reaching to the floor of the lodge.

"Come and lie down beside the fire as I examine your arm," Cloud Whisper said, his voice deep and full of authority. He stared at the arm as Farris walked past him toward the blankets. "Your arm has lost its natural appearance. It has become a lifeless thing, has it not?"

"Yes, your description fits it to a T," Farris said, chuckling sarcastically.

His laughter waned when the elderly man came and knelt closer to him, his twitching nose proving that he disliked the odor of the arm.

Farris gazed at the medicine man as he looked more closely at his arm. He was elderly, with skin drawn taut over his bones. Yet Farris noticed that the medicine man's eyes seemed to be those of a young man. His dark eyes had not lost their intelligence.

Suddenly, Farris felt a small ray of hope that perhaps the medicine man might be able to help his arm. Thus far he was not using rattles or medicine bags, nor was he chanting.

Yes, perhaps Farris had been wrong to poke fun at the abilities of medicine men. At least he could hope, couldn't he?

As Cloud Whisper continued to silently study Farris's arm, his eyes moving slowly over it, Farris looked around the inside of the tepee and saw many beaded bags hanging from the lodge poles, as well as many animal hides.

As he had seen on the outside walls, streaks of lightning had been drawn on the buffalo skin covering.

Before he could study the other things in the tepee, the spinning in his head finally took its toll on him. Although he was trying to fight it, he drifted off into the black void of unconsciousness.

In his dream he watched from somewhere above his body as a huddled figure slowly sawed on his painful arm with a strange metal object with zigzag teeth. In his dream, Farris fought to reach out and stop the huddled figure, but it was as though some unseen force was holding him back.

Through a misty swirl that suddenly appeared in his dream, he saw much blood. He even heard the pitiful cries of a man in terrible pain. . . .

Suddenly Farris awakened from the dream and discovered that the screams were his screams. The huddled figure was the medicine man. The arm being amputated had been his arm!

"No!" he screamed as he gazed down and saw the pool of blood on the blankets where his arm had been.

Through a veil of pain that seemed to cover his eyes, he saw a woman taking the arm away in a basin.

"Bring it back!" he cried. "Don't take my arm! It's mine! It's . . . mine . . . !"

When he tried to get up and go after the woman, the pain and weakness pulled him back to the bed of blankets.

He looked with desperate eyes up at Cloud Whisper. He reached a hand up toward the medicine man.

"Why?" he cried. "Why did you do that?"

"It was the only way to save your life," Cloud Whisper said, moving to his feet.

"You've disfigured me!" Farris screamed, tears pouring from his eyes. "I'll kill you for this! Do you hear me? I'll . . . kill . . . you for this!"

Sobbing, he fell into a merciful, exhausted sleep.

Chapter Twenty-seven

Fair coquette of Heaven,
To whom alone it has been given,
To change and be adored forever.
                    —Percy Bysshe Shelley

Wanting to feel the same excitement that she knew Jaimie had always experienced while fishing with their father, Maddy was with Black Wolf and Jaimie on a fishing expedition.

They had traveled on foot to a stream that Black Wolf had recently discovered while hunting deer. The bed of the stream lay in a steep and rocky chasm, but there was a way down to the water over a rough trail like a stairway.

With a quiver full of short, sharp spears attached to his back, Black Wolf helped Maddy down the steep stairway of rock while Jaimie leapt down the steps ahead of them, springing from rock to rock like a swift-footed deer.

"We will soon be there," Black Wolf said, steadying Maddy as her foot slipped on a rock.

Maddy had learned this morning why Jaimie always insisted on wearing breeches while enjoying her outdoor activities. The buckskin dress that Maddy wore today constantly tangled around her legs, sometimes threatening to trip her.

She stopped and took a deep breath before venturing onward.

She searched through the thick leaves of the tall cottonwoods that hung over the stream down below, now no longer able to see Jaimie.

"Jaimie!" she shouted. "Running Deer! Jaimie! Please don't get so far ahead of me and Black Wolf!"

Sometimes Maddy called Jaimie by her given name, and sometimes by the name given to her by Black Wolf. Every day it was becoming more natural to call her sister by the Sioux name, for day by day Jaimie was becoming more Sioux than white.

Her sister fitted into the Sioux way of life much better than Maddy, since the lives of the Sioux were guided by nature and the outdoors.

Maddy was learning, day by day, to appreciate things of the outdoors. But it was not easy for a woman who had never spent any time outdoors except to plant the family garden or hang the wash on the line.

But she was trying. Oh, Lord, she was trying, for she never wanted to disappoint Black Wolf.

"Sis, I'm fine," Jaimie shouted back, her voice sounding like a long echo as it wafted up from the deep chasm of water. "Hurry! It's breathtaking! I've never seen so many fish! Some are even jumping out of the water as though they are trying to speak to me!"

"Yes, they are saying catch me and eat me," Black Wolf said, chuckling as he took Maddy's hand when she resumed her slow journey down the rocky slope.

"After today I will appreciate what you have to go through to catch fish," Maddy said, the sound of a meadowlark's song coming to her from the vast meadow up above her that stretched out far and wide and green from the chasm of rock.

"I hoped that you would enjoy the adventure of it," Black Wolf said, and then wished he had not spoken when Maddy gave him a discouraged look.

"I'm sorry if I'm disappointing you," Maddy murmured, sweat pearling her brow from the effort of keeping up with Jaimie and Black Wolf. "I have never taken much to outdoor activities. Believe me, after today, you will see that my time is best spent in the kitchen, cooking the day's catch, not helping to catch it."

"And you look beautiful as you go about your womanly chores," Black Wolf said, stopping to draw her into his arms. He steadied her against him as one of her feet slipped again on the damp rock. "But you also look beautiful beneath the blue sky and sunshine. You look beautiful no matter where you are or what you are doing."

"I don't feel beautiful," Maddy sighed. "I feel like a wilted piece of lettuce."

"Lettuce?" Black Wolf said, arching an eyebrow. "I am not familiar with that word."

"You've never eaten lettuce?" Maddy asked, her eyes widening in wonder.

"I am not at all familiar with lettuce," Black Wolf said. "It is something you eat?"

"When it isn't wilted like I am today," Maddy said, laughing softly. "Black Wolf, lettuce is a pale green plant grown in a garden. Its leaves grow together in a sort of ball. There are many ways to eat it. I will buy lettuce seeds at the trading post and plant lettuce for you to see and for us all to enjoy. During the summer months my mother always had lettuce for our evening meals. It's quite a refreshing vegetable. Sometimes sweet . . . sometimes bitter—"

"Maddy! Black Wolf! Hurry! I'm so anxious to fish!" Jaimie cried, drawing Maddy and Black Wolf apart.

Again they worked their way down the rocky stairway. Black Wolf had awakened Jaimie and Maddy before dawn. They had eaten a quick breakfast of toast that Maddy had browned over her morning cook fire.

Her thoughts went to the cow she had left at Farris's house. She hungered every day for the milk and butter from her cow. She grew angry all over again every time she thought of how Farris had stolen the cow and their horses, and how she had been forced to leave them behind in order to flee his premises.

And then she had left Illinois with Black Wolf, leaving the cow behind, forever.

She wondered who was now milking her each morning. Could it be Farris? Had he survived?

She forgot her troubled thoughts when she was finally able to see Jaimie standing down below by a stream that was so crystal clear she could see many fish swimming slowly through it over the rocky bottom.

"I've never seen so many fish in one place," Maddy exclaimed as Black Wolf helped her down to the stream.

Jaimie ran up to Maddy and took her hand. "Get on your knees," she said excitedly. "Put your hand in the water. The fish are curious. They will come up to you. It's like they are kissing your hand!"

Maddy smiled up at Black Wolf, then fell to her knees beside Jaimie.

The water was silky and cold as she reached a hand into it. As the fish swam toward her hand, she at first felt nervous, but, curious to see how it would feel to have a fish nibble on her fingers, she left them there.

Several fish came up to her hand and circled around it, their mouths nibbling softly on her flesh. "They must be hungry," Maddy said, glancing up at Black Wolf. "If father were here, oh, Lord, what a time he would have with the bait he made to place on the hooks of his fishing lines. He'd be able to empty out this stream in the blink of an eye. We'd have delicious fish for several days."

"My way is as efficient," Black Wolf said. "Come and stand beside me, *mee-tah-ween*, while I teach Jaimie how the Sioux catch fish."

"Maddy, do you wish to be taught first?" Jaimie asked, obviously hoping that her sister would become involved in the fishing expedition. "Fishing is such fun, Maddy. Truly it is."

Maddy stood next to Black Wolf, her eyes watching the fish as they swept down from the surface and swam leisurely along the bottom.

"I'm not sure it'd be fun at all catching those fish," she murmured. "They are so innocent as they await their fate."

"It is as natural a thing for man to feed on fish as it is for you to eat that lettuce you told me about," Black Wolf gently explained. "Your God and my Great Spirit placed the fish in these streams for us to catch to sustain our bodies."

"Yes, I know," Maddy said. "But now I also know just why I never went fishing or hunting with father. I doubt I could kill anything, even a fish."

"Would you rather go elsewhere while we catch the fish?" Black Wolf said softly, understanding this gentle side of the woman he adored, and loving her more for it.

Yet on the other hand he admired Jaimie's courageous attitude toward the hunt. Having both Maddy and Jaimie in his life was having the best of two worlds in women.

"No, I don't want to look like a weak ninny," Maddy said, stiffening her back. "I shall stay, but I still don't wish to join you in the actual catch."

"Come on, Black Wolf, *please* show me how to use a spear," Jaimie said, her cheeks flushed with excitement. "I hardly slept all night thinking about it. I've always used a fishing pole. Using a spear will be exciting."

Maddy stepped back while Jaimie went closer to Black Wolf as he pulled one of the short, sharp spears from the quiver on his back.

Clutching her hands together behind her, Maddy scarcely breathed as she watched and listened while Black Wolf prepared Jaimie for her first catch of the morning.

"Take the spear, Running Deer," Black Wolf said, sliding the spear into Jaimie's eager hands.

"It's so smooth," Jaimie said, running her hand slowly up and down the spear.

"I fashioned this spear from a limb of the cottonwood tree," Black Wolf said proudly. "I meticulously sanded it for many hours until it was as smooth as silk against my fingers. I knew then that it would enter the flesh of a fish without tearing at it. It will make a clean, smooth entrance. It will kill mercifully quickly."

"It's as smooth as the petals of a rose," Jaimie marveled, then clutched it in her right hand. "Tell me, Black Wolf, how to do it. I'm ready."

"You will thrust with the spear as hard as you can," Black Wolf instructed. "And strike deep,

Running Deer, for the fish are always farther
down than they look."

"And do I hold onto the spear after it enters
the fish's body?" Jaimie asked softly, eyeing the
fish she planned to spear.

"Yes, you will thrust it into the fish, then pull
the fish out just as quickly," Black Wolf said,
bending to a knee beside the stream. "Thrust
now, Running Deer. I will help bring it in after
you spear it."

Jaimie drew back the spear, then lunged it
into the water as the fish swam past. Jaimie's
eyes widened when the fish continued to swim
away from her. Her aim had been wrong. She
had missed!

It had seemed so easy and yet she had missed.

"What happened is a natural occurrence,"
Black Wolf said, giving Jaimie a reassuring look.
"You missed because the clear water is deeper
than it seems."

"I'll do better next time," Jaimie said, drawing
the spear back again and waiting.

Maddy covered her mouth with a hand as she
waited for Jaimie to thrust again, hoping that
this time she would catch a fish, for she knew
how Jaimie longed to do so. She also knew how
Jaimie could pout for hours if she did not suc-
ceed at something she tried.

She laughed softly when Jaimie thrust
quickly, and just as quickly brought the spear
back heavy with a fat trout. It was so heavy that
Black Wolf had to reach out and cradle the fish

in his hands in order not to lose it from the end of the spear.

"I did it!" Jaimie screamed, her exuberance startling birds from the trees overhead. She turned to Maddy. "Oh, Maddy, you *must* try it. It's such a wonderful feeling to know you have speared the fish. Think about how much you love to eat fish. It won't be so hard then to catch one."

Black Wolf slid the fish from the spear and placed it in a lined basket that was half filled with water to keep the fish fresh for their evening meal.

He turned to Maddy. His dark, mesmerizing eyes beckoned her to him. "You wish to try it just once?" he asked softly.

Knowing that she was outnumbered, and having witnessed the excitement of the catch for the first time in her life, Maddy was tempted to share the fun with Jaimie and Black Wolf. She could tell by the look in his eyes that he wanted her to become more involved with the fishing expedition.

"All right," she murmured, going and standing beside Jaimie. "I shall give it one try. But that's all. I don't want to make a fool of myself more than this one time, for I truly doubt I will be able to spear a fish."

She looked down at Black Wolf, who seemed pleased as punch over her decision. He waited, ready to help pull in her fish.

Fearing looking the fool, Maddy clutched the

spear as Jaimie slid it into her hand. Her heart pounded as she stared at the fish in the stream. She tried to remember what Black Wolf had said about striking deep, for fish were always farther down than they looked.

She focused on one fish in particular. She knew by its peculiar streaks of orange and green that it had been the first fish to come and nibble softly on her hand. It had felt so funny and tingly, yet she had felt a strange sort of bonding with the fish.

As it swam in a slow circle, then came toward her shadow in the water, as though it recognized her and wanted to play with her again, Maddy felt nervous perspiration bead her brow.

How could she kill that fish? It was coming to her so innocently, so trustingly.

She dropped the spear in the water, gasping when she saw it sink to the bottom, then turned apologetic, embarrassed eyes up to Black Wolf. "I'm sorry," she said, her voice catching. "I . . ."

Black Wolf came to her and gently took her by the hand and drew her up into his arms. "Do not fret so over that which your heart does not allow you to do," he said softly, the compassionate understanding in his eyes causing Maddy's insides to melt.

"Then you aren't angry?" she asked, swallowing hard. "Black Wolf, I . . . I . . . dropped the spear."

A loud splash behind her drew her quickly

from Black Wolf's arms. She paled when she saw Jaimie in the water, taking a dive headfirst down to the bottom to retrieve the spear before the current floated it away.

"She will be all right," Black Wolf said, drawing Maddy softly to his side. His arm around her waist comforted her. "She is as good a swimmer as you."

Maddy looked quickly up at him. "At least in that way I have proven that I am not completely ignorant about outdoor activities," she murmured, recalling how she had saved him from drowning in the river. "I do so much enjoy swimming." She looked back at the stream just as Jaimie bobbed back to the surface, the spear in her hand.

"I got it!" Jaimie said, her eyes beaming as water dripped from her hair. "Maddy, you must try again! Please?"

Black Wolf felt Maddy stiffen at Jaimie's suggestion.

When Maddy gave him a questioning gaze, he slowly shook his head. "Do not do anything you do not wish to do," he said softly.

"No, I truly don't want to spear a fish," she murmured. "Are you certain my cowardice does not make me look weak in your eyes?"

"I do not call caring for wild life as you do cowardly," Black Wolf said, turning her to face him. He framed her face between his hands. "I call it admirable and sweet. I would expect nothing less from you."

Maddy flung herself into his arms. "Thank you," she whispered. Then she gazed up at him and smiled. "I *will* cook what you and Jaimie catch, though."

"Maddy, here's the spear," Jaimie said, stepping up to Maddy, her clothes soaked and smelling of fresh, clean stream water.

Maddy turned to Jaimie and placed a gentle hand on her damp cheek. "Honey, I'm not going to use it," she said softly. "You can, though. Go ahead. Enjoy fishing. I shall watch."

"Are you certain?" Jaimie asked, searching her sister's face.

"Yes, very," Maddy said, smiling. She looked over Jaimie's shoulder at the stream and saw the fish that she had not been able to kill swim past.

She then gave Jaimie a pleading look. "But, Jaimie, don't catch the one with the strange markings," she was quick to say. "It's special, Jaimie."

"All right, Sis," Jaimie said, shrugging.

"Ready to proceed?" Black Wolf asked, placing a hand on Jaimie's shoulder.

"Yes, are you?" Jaimie asked.

"Yes, and after we catch six we will stop and return home," Black Wolf said, falling to his knees. He looked up at Maddy with a soft beckoning in his eyes.

She understood that he wanted her to at least join the fun by kneeling beside him.

Smiling, she dropped to her knees and found herself actually enjoying the sport of fishing. Yet all the while she kept an eye on her special fish so that it would not accidentally become a victim of Jaimie's spear.

Yes, today was fun, but tomorrow would be the best day of all, perhaps even the best day of her life.

She was going to marry Black Wolf!

Chapter Twenty-eight

My perfect wife,
Oh, heart, my own, oh eyes, mine too!
                    —Robert Browning

The fire had burned down low, casting dancing
shadows along the inside walls of Black Wolf's
lodge. Wildflowers were strewn across the mats
on the floor around the thick, soft pallet of furs
on which Black Wolf and Maddy lay, clinging to
each other.

"The wedding ceremony was beautiful,"
Maddy murmured, tracing the outline of Black
Wolf's lips with a finger. She had memorized
how he had said to her, "I take this woman for
my wife," in the Sioux tongue: *Mee-tah-wee-choo* . . .

In fact, she knew many Sioux words now and
sometimes spoke Sioux as well as English. She
was proving to Black Wolf that she could be an
astute student of anything that he wished to
teach her!

"Your people have so quickly accepted me and
Jaimie," she murmured. "Are their feelings sin-

cere, or is it because you are their chief and they feel they have no other choice than to behave toward me and my sister as they are behaving?"

"A little of both," Black Wolf said, hating to admit that truth to Maddy. He knew that there were many among his people who would never warm up to any white-skinned woman, not even if she was as sweet and kind as Maddy. White people had taken too much from the Sioux, bringing heartache into their lives.

Black Wolf had learned long ago that there were good and bad people of all skin colors. Farris Boyd was one of the worst of his race. Black Wolf hoped he had been silenced forever.

"*Mee-heea-nah*, my husband, suddenly you have grown so quiet," Maddy murmured, moving to her knees beside him.

She gazed into his eyes as he looked up at her. "I see a haunted expression in your eyes," she murmured. "I'm sorry if I am the cause, for having asked questions that are troubling to you. This is a precious moment between you and me . . . our *wedding* night. I should have only spoken of the magic of romance."

"Magic of romance?" Black Wolf said, his eyes lighting up as he smiled. "You see romance as something magical?"

"Isn't it, Black Wolf?" Maddy said, sighing as she stretched herself atop him, reveling in the touch of his body against hers, so hard . . . and again, so ready.

Her hands went to his face. Gently she splayed

her fingers on his cheeks. "Isn't our love for one another magical, as though it came from a wonderful book where romance plays the key role?" she murmured.

"Magical in that sense, yes," Black Wolf said, reaching up and cupping her breasts within his hands. "But never in a supernatural way. Our love is real. It is for always."

His thumbs circling her nipples, causing them to harden against his flesh, brought a sigh of pleasure from deep within Maddy.

She could see the silent, urgent message in Black Wolf's dark, stormy eyes. His needs matched hers.

She gave herself up to rapture and covered his lips with hers, giving him a soft, quivering kiss, opening her legs to him as she felt his manhood searching for her soft, moist place.

She lifted her hips and moved them in a slow, undulating movement as she helped him place his ready hardness inside her. When he was deep within her and his thrusts began, he kissed her with a fierce, possessive heat. Maddy drew a ragged breath and moved her hips rhythmically with Black Wolf's.

She was glad that they had the tepee all to themselves for the rest of the night. The only thing troubling her was where Jaimie was spending the night: in Eagle Wing's lodge.

Although Jaimie had said that it had been Eagle Wing's sister, Yellow Flower, who had invited her to stay the night in her parents' lodge, the fact remained that Jaimie was spending the night in Eagle Wing's lodge.

Maddy knew of Jaimie's fascination for this young brave.

Maddy could only take into account how young Jaimie was and hope their youth would be enough to keep the two children's infatuation only that, at least until they were much older and understood the seriousness of their feelings.

Maddy had to smile, knowing that if anything could turn her sister into a true lady, it would be romantic feelings for a young man.

There was no denying how such feelings could change Jaimie forever.

Surely Jaimie would throw away the breeches and wear dresses so that she could look beautiful for the man she loved. Also, Maddy hoped that one day Jaimie would let her hair grow long and beautiful again, as it had been before she had taken a pair of scissors to it.

Still kissing her, Black Wolf encircled Maddy with his arms and held her close to him as he turned her so that he was now above her.

He plunged into her, withdrew, and plunged again, as feelings of intense ecstasy feathered up his spine.

With a thick, husky groan he slid his mouth from her lips. Waves of liquid heat pulsed through him when he filled his hands with her breasts.

He swept his tongue around her smoky pink nipples, causing them to tighten. Slowly he licked her, the rose-taste of her flesh sweet and tantalizing against his tongue.

As Black Wolf's tongue tasted and his hands kneaded her breasts, a sensual heat knifed through Maddy's body, dizzying her with the hot, demanding pleasure.

That first time they had made love, she had not been prepared for such intense passion. The smoldering memories flooded her now, making her smile and tremble in anticipation of what was to come.

Each time with Black Wolf was better than the last. Now silvery flames licked through her body.

Suddenly, he was moving faster within her, using quick, sure movements, and she knew that he was almost ready to join her on that wondrously joyous flight to paradise. She could already feel the euphoria filling her entire being . . . growing, building, spreading.

And then she could not hold back any longer. She clung to Black Wolf and cried out as the ecstasy overwhelmed her, so glad that he was joining her as his body stiffened, then began jolting and quivering as he sent his seed deep inside her.

Even when it was over, his steel arms still enfolded her, cradling her close. "I want you again," he whispered huskily against her lips. "Tonight, *tah-wee-choo*, wife, I cannot get enough of you. Do you feel the same? Do you want me as much?"

"I do, *oh-wahn-yah-kay-wah-shtay*, handsome

husband," Maddy whispered, almost beyond coherent thought in the rapture of the moment. "Yes, oh, yes, I do. Please, let's make love again."

"I do not want to tire you," Black Wolf said, leaning over her so that their eyes could meet and hold.

"Never," Maddy said, reaching a hand to his cheek and stroking it. "And if you do, I can take a nap tomorrow."

"You should anyway, so that tomorrow night we can repeat what we do tonight," Black Wolf said, his eyes dancing into hers.

"Tomorrow night we will not have as much privacy as tonight," Maddy said softly.

"After *Tahn-kah* is asleep behind her privacy curtain and we are in bed behind ours, we will be free to do as we wish," Black Wolf said, his hand moving down the soft curve of her waist, then lower where his fingers found her throbbing womanhood.

He saw her quick intake of breath and the pleasure that filled her eyes when he began stroking her heat, smiling to know that she was such a sensual woman.

It was every man's dream to have a woman who shared lovemaking with the same feverish intensity as he.

Maddy was everything to him . . . everything!

"Jaimie . . . Running Deer . . . isn't here now," Maddy said, breathing hard as ecstasy built within her. "It is only you . . . only you and I, *mee-heeg-nah. Tay-chee-khee-lah*, I love you."

She questioned him with her eyes as he rose, got a wooden basin, and set it beside her on the floor. He poured water that had been warming in the coals of the fire into the basin.

"What are you doing?" Maddy asked, arching an eyebrow.

"*Tah-wee-choo*, just lie back and close your eyes," Black Wolf said huskily. "*Tah-tah-ee-chee-yah*, relax. Just enjoy."

She questioned him with her eyes a moment longer, then sighed deeply and closed her eyes, her heart leaping inside her chest when she felt him drizzle the warm water over her body, first across her breasts and then in slow circles over her flat tummy.

When she opened her eyes and started to question him again, he reached a hand to her eyes and gently closed them.

"Enjoy," he repeated huskily. "Just . . . *tah-tah-ee-chee-yah* . . . and enjoy."

Maddy slowly nodded, then gasped with pleasure when she felt the water being drizzled over her womanhood.

She spread her legs and felt the euphoria building once again as he bathed her with the palm of his hand, one of his fingers occasionally sliding inside her, stirring the flames within her.

And then she felt something else on that sensitive, pulsing place.

His tongue.

Slowly he licked her, his tongue sometimes flicking inside her, almost driving her wild. Then he would blow on her, his hands now at her buttocks, lifting her closer to his mouth.

The rapture was so intense, Maddy bit her lower lip and tossed her head feverishly from side to side.

And then she felt something even more wonderful. He had blanketed her with his body.

In one deep thrust he was inside her. She lifted her legs around him and locked her ankles together behind him. She twined her arms around his neck and brought his lips down onto hers, his tongue now surging through her lips, seeking . . . probing . . . sucking.

Oh, Lord, she could hardly think anymore. Her body was growing hotter and hotter, like a consuming fire.

She could even hear the flames roaring in her ears!

Black Wolf held her tightly against him, his kisses bruising her lips, his fingers biting into her flesh as wild ripples of pleasure swam through him.

Again their passion crested.

Maddy arched her back.

She clenched her fists.

She gasped with pleasure against his mouth.

Afterwards, trembling, they fell apart. Maddy lay on her back, her body throbbing like one vast heartbeat.

Black Wolf lay on his back, his eyes closed, all liquid inside, his longing and needs fed. Never had he felt so alive! So fulfilled. His senses were dazzled by the intenseness of their shared feelings!

Opening his eyes, he turned on his side and faced Maddy. Slowly he stroked the soft white flesh of her breast, then moved his hand lower and splayed his fingers over her womanhood, which was still wet with his sperm.

"Never could I have ever imagined such a love as this," he said thickly, drawing Maddy's eyes open.

She smiled up at him and reached down and pressed her hand against his hand, causing his palm to cup her even more tightly.

"Stroke me again," she begged. "But only stroke me."

She giggled. "I am too tender for anything else but that tonight," she softly confessed.

"I am not asking for more tonight, myself," Black Wolf said huskily, his free hand taking hers and placing it on his manhood. "Move your hand very slowly on me, for I am also tender to the touch."

Together, their eyes closed, they stroked one another, their hands only stopping and falling aside when they fell into a soft, relaxed, wonderful sleep.

"*Tah-wee-choo*, my *tah-wee-choo*," Black Wolf whispered in his sleep.

Chapter Twenty-nine

As a man calls for wine before he fights,
I asked one draught of earlier, happier
  sights.

—Robert Browning

Two weeks had passed since the Shawnee shaman had removed Farris's arm. He had spent
many fitful, feverish nights in the medicine
man's lodge, sometimes not caring if he lived or
died.

But the stronger he got from the shaman's
treatments, and the dedication of the Shawnee
women who had spoon-fed him nutritious broth
until he had gotten strong enough to sit up and
eat on his own, the more he was determined to
live.

He had vengeance on his mind.

Nothing and no one would stop him from
finding Maddy as soon as he was strong enough
to travel.

Hating the Shawnee for having removed his
arm, Farris found it difficult to pretend they

were friends and that he was grateful to them for having saved his life.

But all of this was necessary. It was a part of his plan . . . a plan to get them to trust him so that they could help him find the Sioux camp where he now knew Maddy was living.

"I have brought you cooked venison and some cooked vegetables that I found growing wild in the forest," Wild Daisy said as she walked into the lodge that had been built just for Farris.

He was well enough now to live by himself; the shaman came only occasionally to check on him.

"As well as your company?" Farris said, smiling slyly up at Wild Daisy, whom he had pretended to have deep feelings for. In truth he felt nothing but loathing for her as he did for all redskins.

But getting her on his side was part of his scheme. She was one of the women who had fed him, and her father was the cousin of the Shawnee chief. She was so pretty, young, and sweet, she could persuade anyone to do anything.

"If you wish, I can sit with you again while you eat," Wild Daisy said, placing the platter of meat and vegetables beside Farris, as well as a wooden jug of water.

"Yes, do sit with me," Farris said, patting his hand on the blanket spread out on the floor close to the lodge fire.

Lifting the skirt of her floor-length buckskin

dress, Wild Daisy settled on the blanket close to Farris.

"Your shoulder where the arm was removed," Wild Daisy said softly, looking at the bandaged stump; "does it hurt less today than yesterday?"

Farris frowned at the petite, lovely girl of sixteen winters, whose copper face was soft with sincere compassion.

"The pain is gone," he said thickly.

He grabbed a piece of meat from the platter and stuffed it into his mouth.

As he chewed he watched the young girl, wondering how any chief could trust him with her. He was a man who had been without a woman for too long. It would be so easy to take advantage of the girl's innocence and the chief's trust in him!

"I am so glad the pain is all but gone," Wild Daisy said, clasping her hands eagerly on her lap. She cast her eyes downward, then looked quickly up at Farris again. "But if the pain is gone, you will be leaving soon."

"Yes, I hope to leave soon, today if possible, and return to my parents' home in Kentucky," Farris said, wiping grease from his mouth with the back of his hand. "As I told your chief yesterday, I would like to go home and finish my healing there. I asked him for an escort. He agreed to it."

"You are close to your parents?" Wild Daisy asked, scooting closer. "Perhaps especially your mother? You are so gentle around women."

Farris almost laughed in her face, for everything he had told her was a lie. His parents didn't live in Kentucky. They were both dead.

Telling everyone that he wished to return to his parents' home in Kentucky was just another part of his plan to travel to Kentucky so that he could find the Sioux village and, therefore, *Maddy*.

He had listened well to what everyone had said while in one council or another beside the large communal fire.

Their voices had traveled first into the medicine man's lodge while Farris had been confined there, and then into Farris's when he had been moved to a lodge built for him, so that he could recuperate alone.

When he had heard Maddy's name mentioned, he had listened every time the people gathered around to talk. He had discovered that she was now Chief Black Wolf's woman.

A messenger from Black Wolf's village had brought word to the Shawnee that Black Wolf and Maddy had married.

Farris had learned that their village had been established in Kentucky, and that their lodges had been erected far enough away from the Ohio never to be uprooted by its ravaging waters again.

His plan was to ask for a Shawnee escort into Kentucky since he couldn't man a boat alone, or even mount a horse without assistance.

While the Shawnee traveled with him, he

hoped to find the Sioux village. It was known now to him that warriors from the Sioux village and the Shawnee made trips back and forth to one another's villages. They had become fast friends, allies.

If Farris had to, he would force the Shawnee warrior at gunpoint to take him to the Sioux village. Then he would kill the warrior and go the rest of the way alone.

By then he should be strong enough to handle a horse. He would never let the fact that he was now a man with only one arm stop him from finding and killing Maddy!

"You are so lost in thought," Wild Daisy said, placing a gentle hand on Farris's one arm. "Is it something I said that made your mind wander?"

"No, it's just that I am so eager to see my mother again," he said, the lies easy to tell now that they had begun. He slipped his arm away from her hand and pretended to wipe tears from his eyes with the back of his hand. "I have sorely missed her. I never should have come to Illinois. I should have stayed in Kentucky with Mother and Father. Now when I return, I won't even be able to help them with the chores. I . . . am . . . a helpless cripple."

Tears flowed freely from Wild Daisy's eyes. She went to Farris and hugged him. "Do not cry," she murmured, a sob lodging in her throat. "You may have lost an arm, but you are not a cripple. You will learn to do everything with one arm that you always did with two. I know. I have seen it among my people. I was a small girl when the white pony soldiers came to our village where we used to live. The pony soldiers maimed and killed many of my people. But they did not kill the spirit of those who survived the massacres. You will have the same sort of spirit and courage."

She went to her knees before him. "There was some gossip about you having killed and maimed many Sioux," she said, her eyes wavering as she gazed into his. "Some say you killed Chief Crazy Horse. Others say that is not so, that you only tell tall tales like that to draw attention to yourself. Is that so, Farris? Do you tell tales like that to draw attention?"

"Your people know about Chief Crazy Horse?" Farris blurted out, turning pale.

"Yes, but they say it is not true that you killed him," Wild Daisy said.

She reached a gentle hand to his face, wincing and pulling her hand away when her fingers were scraped by the thick beard that had grown during his two-week stay at her village.

"You are such a gentle man," she said softly. "*I* know that you did not kill Chief Crazy Horse. You just needed attention, did you not? I have seen men and women who lied because they felt lonely and wanted attention."

"Yes, you are right, I said what I said, did what I did, because I was lonely," Farris said, believing the lie necessary to his survival.

She would return to her parents' lodge and tell

them what he'd said. They, in turn, would go to the Shawnee chief and relay that message to him. He knew now that their chief was all things to them; whatever order he handed out was done, and swiftly.

Yes, Farris would say whatever he needed to in order to survive.

"Because you miss your mother?" Wild Daisy asked softly. "You can admit to me that you miss your mother. Loving a mother so much does not show weakness in a man. It shows character. It proves he is a man of compassion."

"You see me as a man of character, do you?" Farris asked, dismayed to find that he was drawn to this young girl, whose innocence made him forget the color of her skin.

Today he did not see her as an Indian. She was genuinely sweet and pretty. And young, he reminded himself.

He forced himself to ignore his feelings for Wild Daisy. Having any feeling other than loathing was foolish. It was dangerous.

He focused on something else, on what Wild Daisy had said about his mother. Yes, he did miss his mother.

He had loved her with the deep love a son feels for his mother. But he could never go back home and embrace his mother again. She was gone forever!

And so was Maddy! She was now married. And . . . to . . . a redskin.

He thought of his plan again, of how he would

kill the Shawnee warrior after the Sioux camp had been pointed out to him. Yes, he would have the strength he would need to carry out his plans. He needed only one hand to draw the blade of a knife across someone's throat. That was exactly how he planned to kill the Shawnee warrior.

He would then use the same knife on Maddy, Jaimie, and Black Wolf!

Someone lifted the entrance flap, casting a large shadow on the floor of the lodge. Farris's eyes flew up to find the Shawnee chief standing there. He stiffened as the chief came into the lodge and stood behind Wild Daisy.

"Return to your morning chores," the chief said, placing a gentle hand on Wild Daisy's head. His eyes locked with Farris's. "I have much to discuss with him."

"Very well," Wild Daisy said as the chief slid his hand from her head. She got to her feet beside him, then turned and smiled down at Farris.

Farris returned the smile, watching her until she left the lodge.

Then he looked warily at the chief as he settled down on his haunches before Farris.

"Today is the day you will leave my village," the chief said, his voice tight. "I do not feel completely comfortable with my decision, for I am aware of your tales of having killed Chief Crazy Horse. I discussed it among my warriors and we have decided this is best."

319

"What have you decided?" Farris asked, his voice drawn.

"That you are to leave for Kentucky soon," the chief said. "You asked for an escort. One will be given to you. He will travel with you until your home is reached. After he witnesses your reunion with your parents he will then return home to us."

"You are very kind," Farris said, almost choking on the words, for he had hated relying upon the goodwill of these savage redskins!

"It is not from kindness that I do this for you," the chief said, his eyes narrowing. "It is best that you are far from my people. If I ever discover proof that you killed Chief Crazy Horse, or *any* people with red skin, I, personally, will send an arrow through your heart."

"I . . . never . . . even rode with the cavalry," Farris said, hoping *this* lie would be convincing. "Everything I said before was a lie. I . . . I . . . was a coward. That was why I chose the career of being a sheriff. In a sense that has helped me regain my faith in myself as a man."

"If all that you say is not true, you are the most skilled liar I have ever known," the chief said, rising to his feet. "But I will not waste any more time pondering over this. My people need my leadership. They come first. Now you come with me. I will show you the horse you will ride. You already know the warrior who will ride with you. It will be Red Sky."

The chief started to walk away, then turned

on a heel and looked down at Farris before he got to his feet. "I must tell you that I am uncomfortable over one thing about sending you into Kentucky," he said, his jaw tightening. "My friend Black Wolf and his people are there. If all that you have told me is false and harm comes to Black Wolf because of it, I will hunt you down and personally kill you. And know this, Farris Boyd, when I choose to kill out of vengeance, it is deliberately slow . . . and . . . painful."

A cold fear grabbed Farris in the pit of his stomach as he stared wide-eyed up at the chief.

Chapter Thirty

Let knowledge grow from more to more,
But more of reverence in us dwell.
                    —Alfred, Lord Tennyson

Maddy was sitting beneath the shade of a towering oak tree with many other women, happily learning the art of how to sew and bead buckskin clothes.

Although she had been skilled at sewing since she was a small girl who imitated everything her mother did around the house, Maddy was amazed at the artistry displayed by the Sioux women as they carefully sewed intricate beadwork on the buckskin dresses, blouses, and skirts.

As she watched Raven Hair finish a dress that she had started sewing long before Maddy had joined the Sioux, she became puzzled by something about the bead design, yet was hesitant to ask her friend about it. She was afraid that her question might seem a criticism.

And Maddy wanted nothing more than to be as one with these women; she never wanted to appear to be criticizing anything they did. In truth, their skills sometimes made her feel useless and ignorant. They seemed to know so much more about being a woman than she.

"Sis, Sis!" Jaimie cried as she ran toward Maddy, her eyes wide with excitement.

Maddy, who had been carefully stringing beads, laid her work aside and waited for Jaimie. She wondered what might have happened to bring such brightness into her sister's eyes.

Like Maddy, Jaimie discovered something exciting and new about the Sioux each day. Maddy was exuberant about what she was learning, but did not show it as openly as her little sister, who always showed her feelings about everything.

It was so good to see the excitement return in her sister's eyes after it had been taken away so suddenly by their father's untimely death.

When Jaimie finally came and threw herself down beside her on the blanket, Maddy saw that she was too breathless to speak right away.

"Jaimie, what is it?" Maddy asked, gently pushing a fallen lock of red hair back from her brow. "What has got you so worked up?"

"I've been with the young braves and the warriors in the council house," Jaimie said, her eyes beaming. "Maddy, I've learned today how to make bows and arrows!"

Maddy tried not to show her disapproval, having discovered long ago that no matter what she did, Jaimie was Jaimie and if her sister still wanted to learn things that were meant only for boys, there was no use in trying to talk her out of it.

"That's interesting," Maddy said, sighing. She smiled awkwardly at Raven Hair, who was listening to the conversation, her eyes showing that she was impressed by this child who turned her back on the activities of the young Sioux girls.

"Black Wolf taught me," Jaimie went on. "But, Maddy, I'm not talking about the huge bows you see the warriors carrying. I'm starting out with a smaller one. Black Wolf told me that when he was but ten winters of age he carried a boy's bow. He said that it's not the size of a bow that indicates a man's strength. It's the power he holds in his head."

Maddy gave Raven Hair another nervous glance, starting when she found that not only Raven Hair was listening, but all of the other women as well. They stopped sewing, their eyes and ears eagerly taking in this conversation between their chief's wife and her sister.

Taking Jaimie by a hand, Maddy urged her to get up from the blanket and walk out of speaking range of the women. Maddy felt she must scold Jaimie this time. Things were quickly getting out of hand. Now was the time to put an end to Jaimie's foolishness.

"Did you hear yourself?" Maddy scolded as she leaned down into her sister's face. "When you speak of bows and their size you mention *men* using them, not girls. Jaimie, you are not a boy or a man. You are a girl. I forbid you to do anything else with the boys of the village. Come right now and sit down with me and learn to sew!"

"Sis, *please* don't insist that I do something I absolutely abhor," Jaimie said, shuddering with disgust. "Why should it matter so much that I love things boys and men love?"

"Because it is unfeminine and disgusting in the eyes of the Sioux women," Maddy harshly whispered back to her, still afraid the women could hear her. "It's embarrassing me, Jaimie. Don't you care?"

"Yes, Sis, I care," Jaimie said, her lower lip curving into a pout. "But don't you care about me? If you force things on me that I hate, you know I won't be happy. I'd ... I'd ... much rather leave here and live somewhere else if I can't be happy."

Maddy paled. She took a step away from Jaimie. "You ... what ...?" she gasped.

Jaimie saw how what she had said had hurt Maddy. She flung herself into her sister's arms and hugged her. "I'm sorry," she murmured. "I don't mean to upset you. But please, *please*, Maddy, let me grow up in the way that makes me the happiest. I never want to resent you."

"It means this much to you to make bows and arrows?" Maddy asked, swallowing hard as she stroked her sister's back through the buckskin shirt that she wore with buckskin fringed breeches instead of a dress.

"Yes, and there's more, Maddy," Jaimie said guardedly.

Maddy sighed and stepped away from Jaimie. She searched her sister's face, then took her hands. "What is it?" she murmured. "Tell me. I promise not to jump down your throat this time."

"I must go and cut my own wood for the bow I will be making," Jaimie blurted out. "That's the way it's done, Sis. Everyone cuts their own wood for their own bows."

"I don't know, Jaimie," Maddy said, her eyes wavering. "That seems to be asking a lot of a little girl."

"I helped cut down trees when we built our cabin in Illinois," Jaimie said. "I can handle an axe or a hatchet as well as anyone, and you know it."

"Yes, you were quite a help for Father back in those days that seem so long ago," Maddy said softly. "But still, Jaimie, this is *now*. Father isn't here to keep you safe."

"I've learned how to fend for myself, Maddy," Jaimie said, stiffening her upper lip. "You know that."

"Yes, and I'm proud of you," Maddy said; then she drew Jaimie into her arms. "I love you, little sister. I just don't want anything to happen to you."

"It won't," Jaimie said, then eased from

Maddy's arms. She looked up at her. "Are you saying that I can go? Can I go now? I'm so eager to start making the bow."

Maddy looked beyond Jaimie. "Where are the others who will be going with you?" she asked, then looked quickly down at Jaimie when she didn't respond.

"Jaimie, there will be others going with you, won't there?" she asked quickly.

"No, there won't," Jaimie said, lowering her eyes.

"Jaimie . . ." Maddy said, her voice breaking.

Jaimie looked directly at Maddy. "I must go alone," she blurted. "That is the only way I can prove that I can find the right tree for the bow without it being pointed out to me. That's a part of the test, Maddy. I must do it the way it is done by the Sioux."

"Test?" Maddy said, raising an eyebrow. "Has it now become a test?"

"In a sense," Jaimie said, shrugging.

Then Jaimie looked pleadingly up at Maddy with her deep green eyes. "Oh, Sis, please say I can go," she begged. "I'm so anxious to prove myself."

"Jaimie, you already *have*," Maddy argued.

"Not in this respect," Jaimie replied. "I must prove that I am as capable as the next person to find my own tree for my own bow."

"You mean as capable as the next 'boy,' don't you?" Maddy said, sighing heavily.

"Well, yes, I guess so," Jaimie said, gazing into

her sister's eyes. "But does that truly matter?"

"I'm tired of trying to make you understand," Maddy said.

She placed a gentle hand on her sister's shoulder. "Go on, Jaimie," she said, although reluctantly. "I won't delay you any longer."

Her voice broke. She looked away from Jaimie, then gazed down at her again. "But, Jaimie, please be careful," she murmured. "We aren't yet very familiar with this area. We're not sure about who lives even a mile away. Don't take chances. If someone of a suspicious nature comes near, run, Jaimie. Run back home. Do you hear?"

"Yes, I hear," Jaimie said, her excitement having returned since she knew that she was going to be able to do as she pleased. "Thank you, Sis. Oh, thank you. You will be the first to try out my new bow!"

"You know I'm anxious for *that*," Maddy said, laughing softly.

She watched Jaimie rush into the large council house, then leave again carrying a hatchet. She saw her sister run with her long, thin legs into the forest, gazing after her until she no longer could see her.

"She will be all right," Raven Hair said as she came and stood beside Maddy. "Your *tahn-kah* is a young woman with a strong will. She carries much courage inside her heart. Do not fret so over her. Soon she will begin developing into a woman. With that will come the feelings of a woman. You do remember, do you not, when your breasts began to fill out and the soft tendrils of hair began to grow at the juncture of your legs?"

"Yes, very well," Maddy said, recalling how proud she was to have discovered the first signs of becoming an adult.

"When the flow of the moon enters your young sister's life, then, most of all, she will begin looking differently at the boys than she does now," Raven Hair said. "She will see Eagle Wing as someone to love instead of someone to challenge."

"I know he already looks at Jaimie through the eyes of a man rather than just a friend," Maddy said, going back to the blankets with Raven Hair and sitting down beside her.

"Then he will be the teacher of things besides bows and arrows for your sister," Raven Hair said, ignoring the frown this brought to Maddy's face. Instead, she spread out the dress she had just completed beading for Maddy to see.

"It's finished and, oh, so lovely," Maddy murmured, running her hand over the soft fabric of the dress, and then the lovely beadwork in a design of forest flowers.

She gave Raven Hair a sideways glance, then studied the design of the beads again.

"There is a question in your eyes as you study my dress," Raven Hair said. "Why is that, Maddy? Do you not approve of what I do? When you say it is lovely, is it not said in sincerity?"

Embarrassed that Raven Hair should think she was lying to her, Maddy felt her face flood with color.

She reached for Raven Hair's hand. "Never think that I am not sincere with you in all things," she said earnestly. "I am your friend. I would never be dishonest about my feelings toward you or anything you do."

"Then why is there question in your eyes when you look at my dress?" Raven Hair asked, her eyes searching Maddy's. "You see something wrong in the way I sewed it, do you not? You just do not want to tell me because you are afraid it will hurt my feelings."

"No, I never want to hurt your feelings," Maddy said softly. "That's why . . . that's why . . . I didn't want to question you about something I noticed about your beadwork."

"What is it you see that I do not see?" Raven Hair asked, staring down at the artwork of her beading on the bodice of the dress. Slowly she ran her hand over it, then looked at Maddy with questioning eyes.

"I noticed that here and there you have used a single bead of a different color that interrupts the pattern of your design," Maddy explained. She pointed out the single bead that was of a different color. "*Here*, Raven Hair. Why did you do it that way? I wish to know so that I can do my beading exactly like you. I so love the design on this dress . . . on *all* of your dresses."

Raven Hair's eyes lit up. She laughed softly,

then threw her arms around Maddy's neck and hugged her. "I am so glad you do not find my dress ugly," she said, then eased away from Maddy and reached for her work.

Carefully Raven Hair stretched her dress out over her legs, looking from the beadwork to Maddy.

"This one bead of a different color is my identifying signature, a way to tell my work from another woman's," Raven Hair explained. "It is also an admission to the Sioux Creator of our human frailty and imperfection."

"Truly?" Maddy said, eyes wide. "What you said about your Creator is so lovely, Raven Hair. Oh, so lovely."

"It is good that you have taken to the Sioux customs so quickly," Raven Hair said, laying her dress aside.

Raven Hair gestured toward the other women, who had returned to concentrating on their work. "There is so much for you to learn," she said. "See how one woman works hides into a cradle board?"

Raven Hair moved her hand and gestured toward another woman. "That woman is working a hide into new moccasins that will match the shirt and breechclout she has already made for her husband," she explained.

She gestured with her hand again, elsewhere. "See how one woman is carefully preparing a robe out of a bear pelt?" she said. "This will take her many long hours of labor, but she doesn't see it as tedious. She, too, sews for her beloved husband. A good robe requires a skilled craftswoman."

Raven Hair softly shrugged. "Men carve bows, make arrows, or repair horse gear, while women cook, sew, or carry water," she said.

The mention of bows and arrows caused Maddy's attention to waver. She looked over her shoulder and into the shadows of the forest, hoping that Jaimie would return soon. While her sister was out there alone, Maddy could not rest easy.

Chapter Thirty-one

When to the sessions of sweet silent thought
I summon up remembrance of things past,
I sigh the lack of many a thing I sought.
                                    —William Shakespeare

As she cut carrots in small slices and placed them in a pot of water over her lodge fire, Maddy was still worrying about Jaimie. Although Jaimie had been gone for only a short while, it seemed an eternity since she had given her sister permission to go and get the wood she needed to make herself a bow.

"This isn't Illinois," she whispered to herself, where, except for Farris Boyd, she had learned to trust her neighbors. As she had warned Jaimie, this was a new area, where few acquaintances had yet been made.

"It was foolish of me to allow her to go unescorted," Maddy whispered aloud. "Black Wolf shouldn't have allowed it either. He has been confronted with more untrustworthy people than I have, and yet . . ."

She laid her knife aside and rose to her feet.

She went to the entrance flap and shoved it aside.

Should she go for Jaimie? Or should she give her a bit more time?

"She's just a little girl," she whispered, leaving the tepee. She walked around to the back, searching with her eyes through the forest. "She shouldn't be out there alone."

Low growls of thunder rumbled in the distance.

Maddy looked heavenward with a start.

Searching the sky for storm clouds, she stiffened when she saw them building in great mountains of black in the east.

"A storm," she whispered, shivering at the memory of what the recent storms had done not only to her and Jaimie, but also to Black Wolf and his people.

But the Ohio River was nowhere near. And if the small creek winding through the forest beside their village flooded, it could not reach so far over its banks that it would threaten the Sioux in any way.

In fact, a flood might be welcomed. They had built their lodges several feet up a small embankment from the water. Having the stream closer would give the women better access to water for drinking, cooking, and bathing. The fish that leaped in that water would be closer at hand for catching.

But a storm might be dangerous to Jaimie! Should she be caught in a torrential downpour she might get disoriented and not be able to find her way back home.

"*Tah-wee-choo*, wife, what brings you to the back of our lodge?" Black Wolf said as he stepped around and saw her there. "I went inside. I saw the dinner only half prepared. I became worried about why. Your tracks led back here. Why?"

"It's Jaimie," Maddy said, turning to gaze up at him. "I don't think we should have allowed her to go alone into the forest."

Another rumble of thunder made her spine stiffen.

She glanced quickly up at the sky. "And a storm is approaching," she said, her voice drawn. "I am plagued by nightmare visions of the last terrible storm. What if this one is as bad and lasts as long?"

"I have made certain that our village is where no water from streams, creeks, or rivers can ever be a threat to it," Black Wolf said, taking her hands and squeezing them reassuringly as she turned her eyes up to him. "Until the river stole our island from us, my people always welcomed the rain. It gives more than it takes, my woman. It nourishes. It cleanses. It refreshens. So look forward to rain, do not dread it."

"Even while Jaimie is out in the rain?" Maddy asked, looking up at him with concern.

"She is not something that will melt in the rain like a piece of maple candy the Sioux children enjoy during maple sugar making season," Black Wolf chuckled.

"Black Wolf, I'm serious," Maddy said, firming her jaw. "I'm honestly worried about Jaimie. I think we should go and find her and bring her home."

"She is on a mission," Black Wolf said, his voice changing to one of authority, which he usually used only in council. "We must not interfere on her quest to find the perfect wood for the bow she plans to make for her hunts."

"Oh, Black Wolf," Maddy said, sighing heavily. "Why can't you see her as a little girl instead of one of your young braves? She should be with me inside the tepee learning how to make stew, not out there perhaps lost in the forest on her quest for wood. She should only go into the forest with us women as we search for the perfect plants with which to make perfect food."

Black Wolf was taken aback by Maddy's anger and sarcasm. He had never seen this side of his wife and was not sure how to react to it. He did not want to say anything else that would upset her, for he had noticed that, of late, she had begun to look pale.

Even her eyes were sunken and had black circles beneath them.

When he had questioned her about it, she had waved him off and told him that he was imagining things. He had begun to wonder if living the harder life of an Indian was causing her paleness . . . her weariness.

Maddy's eyes widened and she placed a hand over her mouth when she realized how snappishly she had spoken to her beloved husband. She was stunned that such words, such sarcasm, had crossed her lips.

She adored Black Wolf. Normally she trusted his judgment in all things.

"I'm so sorry," Maddy rushed out, flinging herself into his arms. "I don't know what made me say those things . . . in . . . the way I said them. Lately I've not been myself. I've not been feeling. . . ."

Her stomach began to churn as it had earlier in the morning prior to joining the women in their sewing circle. Just after Black Wolf and Jaimie had left to go into the council house to make bows and arrows with a large group of men and boys, Maddy had hardly made it to the back of her lodge before she had thrown up all of her breakfast.

Now the same awful feeling was suddenly sweeping over her. She took a quick step away from Black Wolf and, while holding her hand over her mouth, ran to the edge of the forest.

Then she bent low and felt the sting of the vomit as it raced up into her throat. She hung her head and tears filled her eyes as she threw up so intensely she felt she might faint.

Black Wolf had seen the fear in his wife's eyes and was momentarily stunned when she began to run away from him.

But when she stopped and started retching,

his heart skipped a beat. Then he ran to her and cradled her brow in his hands until she was finished.

Breathing hard, and wiping her mouth clean with the tail end of her buckskin dress, Maddy stayed in the bent position for a moment longer in case more came up from the depths of her stomach.

"Maddy, what has caused this?" Black Wolf asked as she straightened her back and looked apologetically into his eyes. "How long have you been feeling ill? I began noticing yesterday a difference in your appearance. Tell me where you hurt. Tell me what you think the illness is? I will take you to our village shaman. He will make you well."

"There is nothing your shaman can do about my particular illness," Maddy murmured.

Now she was almost certain about the secret she had kept from Black Wolf for the past several days since her moon flow had not started on time. She felt it was safe to tell him that she was almost certainly with child.

His and *her* child.

Yes, surely she was pregnant.

She had all of the signs that she remembered her mother having when she had first become pregnant with Maddy's younger sister and her stillborn brother.

"Are you saying that you do not believe in the healing arts of our shaman?" Black Wolf asked, gazing incredulously into Maddy's eyes.

338

Maddy reached gentle hands to his cheeks and framed his face between them. "Darling husband, I believe it is safe to say your shaman cannot heal my special kind of sickness," she said, laughing softly. "I am experiencing the sort of sickness that women have when they are in the early stages of pregnancy. Black Wolf, I do believe I am with child!"

The thunder rumbled again in the distance, but neither of them heard it. Her worries about Jaimie had just as quickly been forgotten as Black Wolf grabbed Maddy into his arms and swung her around, laughing.

"I take it that you are happy with the news?" Maddy said, giggling as he placed her on her feet.

She paled when she discovered that he had not let go of her any too soon. Again she bent low and threw up.

When she was through again, Black Wolf lifted her fully into his arms and carried her back inside their lodge. As though she were a delicate doll, he placed her on their bed of blankets.

"I shall care for you, oh, so tenderly, my love," he said huskily, stroking her brow with his trembling fingers. "A child." He slid his hand down and gently placed it on her abdomen. "Our child grows inside your womb even now. Is that not a miracle?"

"A miracle of miracles," Maddy said, smiling adoringly up at him.

A voice outside their lodge brought Black Wolf to his feet. He swept the entrance flap aside and found Lone Beaver standing there.

"My chief, everyone has arrived in the council house for council," Lone Beaver said, looking quickly over his shoulder and up at the sky as the thunder rumbled again. He winced when he saw that the black clouds had roamed closer overhead.

Lone Beaver then looked with concern at Black Wolf. "A storm approaches," he said thickly. "Should we prepare our people for the worst?"

"Nothing bad is going to come with that storm except for perhaps some strong winds," Black Wolf said, watching some whiter clouds blowing ahead of the darker ones. "Send word around camp to our women to secure their lodges against the threat of wind. Then go to the council house. I shall be there soon."

Maddy had heard him mention the wind. She was already on her feet. "I shall ready our lodge," she said, starting to walk past Black Wolf.

He grabbed her wrist and stopped her. "*I* shall secure our lodge," he said sternly. "Go back to your bed. Rest. At least until you are past this moment of sickness."

"I believe I am going to be pampered," Maddy said, smiling sweetly up at Black Wolf. "And I think I just might learn to enjoy it."

Blinding streaks of lightning against the black sky caused her to cringe. And suddenly Jaimie was back on her mind. "Black Wolf, you *must* send someone out for Jaimie," she said, begging him with her eyes.

"She is a smart child and will know that it is best to return home," Black Wolf said. "Do you want to humiliate her by sending someone for her? Give her time, *Tah-wee-choo*. She knows what is best. How could she not? She had the best of teachers." He cupped her chin and lowered his mouth to her lips. "You, my wife. You were her teacher."

He kissed her, then swung away from her and went all around the outside of the tepee, securing the stakes.

Maddy rolled the inside of the buckskin down and secured it with folded blankets on all sides.

Then she went to the entranceway and found that Black Wolf had gone on to the council house.

Hugging herself, she watched the sky. She silently prayed that Jaimie would have the sense to come on home. She could go back later for that darn piece of wood that she needed for that darn bow!

She felt guilty the very moment she let those thoughts enter her mind. Her sister was happy for the first time for so long. How could she resent that?

And her sister had blended in so well with the Sioux people. There should be no room for resentment in her life when, in truth, neither

Maddy nor Jaimie had ever felt as blessed as now.

Sighing, Maddy went back inside and resumed preparing supper. She stiffened and tried to ignore the thunder that still persisted in the distant sky.

"Everything is going to be all right," she whispered, trying to reassure herself.

And how could it not be? The good Lord had reached down and blessed not only her, but also Jaimie.

And now there was another blessing to give thanks for.

"Our child," she whispered, the very thought of the child growing in her womb making her feel blissfully, exquisitely happy.

No, nothing bad is ever going to happen to me and Jaimie again, she thought to herself. Nor to Black Wolf and his people.

But all the same, if Jaimie didn't return soon, she would go out looking for her. . . .

Chapter Thirty-two

Sin? O, yes, we are sinners,
I know—let all that be.
                            —Alfred, Lord Tennyson

Red Sky, the Shawnee warrior who had led Farris Boyd to Black Wolf's village, lay dead in the bushes, his throat slit.

Moments after the warrior had pointed the village out to Farris, Farris had cleverly called Red Sky's attention to something else, giving Farris time enough to grab his knife from its sheath and cut his throat.

With only one hand to drag the body, Farris had struggled to hide it in the depths of the forest, where he hoped no one would find the dead Sioux. At least not until after Farris had done what he had come to do.

Farris had been watching the activity at the Sioux village for some time now, smiling cunningly when he saw Maddy sitting among a circle of women beneath a tree, looking so content, so unwary of someone spying on her with vengeance in his heart.

Later he had watched Jaimie run into the forest only a few feet from where he was hiding. He had wondered about the hatchet she was carrying, wondering what the little tomboy was up to this time.

He had almost gone for Jaimie then, but had thought better of it. Maddy was his first priority. With jealousy eating away at his insides, he had watched Maddy and Black Wolf talking outside the lodge, then disappear inside it.

Disgruntled, Farris knew now that he could not go to the tepee and make himself known to Maddy, not while Black Wolf was there. His plans were to kill Black Wolf later. He would enjoy looking into Black Wolf's eyes when he told the redskin that Maddy was dead!

Farris started to settle down beneath a tree, then stopped when a sudden alarm swept through him.

He turned and gazed in the direction that Jaimie had gone.

The dead Shawnee warrior. If Jaimie continued walking in that direction she might discover Red Sky!

And when she did, surely she would let out a scream that would alert the whole Sioux camp that something was wrong. They could come like swarms of bees into the forest and discover not only the dead Shawnee warrior, but also Farris, the one who killed him.

"The stupid, nosy little bitch," Farris grumbled as he rose shakily to his feet and limped away from his hiding place, hoping to catch Jaimie before she ruined everything.

And wouldn't this be the perfect opportunity to do away with her, while her sister was with her Injun lover? Once he found Jaimie, he would silence her forever!

The stitches that had been sewn in his shoulder after the arm had been removed had come undone. Blood was dripping through the bandages.

The pain was almost too unbearable to take another step.

Yet he had come this far. He couldn't let the damn stump at his shoulder stop what must be done.

He just couldn't let Maddy get away with destroying his life. Yes, she alone was responsible for the loss of his arm. If she hadn't locked him in that damnable cellar, the spider wouldn't have bitten him. He wouldn't have lain there for hours before someone came and found him!

"I owe you, Maddy," he muttered to himself, forcing back the lightheadedness that threatened to send him to the ground in a black void of unconsciousness. "I . . . will . . . have my revenge before . . . I . . . die!"

He paid no heed to the thunder in the distance.

Cackling beneath his breath, he stumbled onward. Finding it too hard to grab things to steady himself, he reached back and slid the knife into his sheath. He then moved onward, from tree to tree, having to rest frequently as the blood dripped from his shoulder, weakening him.

"Where are you?" he whispered, tears flaming his eyes as the pain worsened in his shoulder. "Jaimie . . . where are you?"

Chapter Thirty-three

Up the small stream he went; he did imprint
on the green moss his tremulous step, that
caught strong shuddering from his burning
limbs.

—Percy Bysshe Shelley

The rumbling of thunder caused Jaimie to stop
suddenly. She looked through the leaves of the
trees and saw that the sky was still blue, the sun
bright.

That had to mean she had some time left before the storm hit. Perhaps it wouldn't even
storm. Often in the summer, storms only teased
a person. They would linger in the distance and
send off roars like a lion, but nothing more.

That's the way this storm will be, she hoped
to herself as she moved onward.

She knew she shouldn't go much farther,
though. She didn't want to lose her way back to
the village. She was not familiar with the lay of
this land as she had been back home where she
had wandered alone everywhere.

But today she was learning and she would remember the next time she wandered here. She would remember a certain tree, a certain bush, a certain clump of rocks. She would remember the way the stream snaked along the ground and the flowers that grew on the embankment. She would remember the wild grapevines and the wild strawberries that wove together beautifully along the ground.

Having become so immersed in watching for things to remember in the future, Jaimie was not aware of what lay in her path as she pushed through thick forsythia bushes heavily laden with yellow flowers.

"Lordie!" she cried as she almost fell to the ground when she tripped over something.

Thinking it was a limb, she looked down to kick it out of the way, but a scream froze in her throat when she discovered what it was.

A . . . dead . . . Indian!

And she recognized him. It was Red Sky! He was from the Shawnee village where she and Maddy had stayed.

A noise behind her made Jaimie whirl around.

She dropped the hatchet and took a quick step over the dead Indian when she found Farris Boyd standing there, a bandage on his shoulder all soaked in blood, and blood dripping onto the ground in great pools of red beside him.

Seeing Farris there, with one arm missing and utter hatred in his eyes, Jaimie knew that he was the one who had killed the Shawnee warrior.

Knowing this, and realizing his intense hatred for her, Jaimie was so terrified her feet wouldn't move.

It was as though they were frozen to the ground!

"I gotcha," Farris spat out, finding the strength to move quickly behind her, his one arm gripping her around the throat, squeezing. "I've waited a long time for this, Jaimie."

Wild-eyed, gagging, Jaimie grabbed at his arm, trying desperately to move it.

But she was weakened quickly by lack of oxygen as her wind was cut off.

Black dizziness engulfed her and she floated away into unconsciousness.

Laughing, Farris moved his arm from Jaimie's throat and watched her crumple to the ground. Smiling crookedly, he gazed down at Jaimie. He started to reach for his knife, to stab it into her, but a loud clap of thunder made him turn with a start.

He knew that if the rain came in torrents it would be bad for him. If he got chilled by the rain, and his arm got soaked and the bandage fell off, exposing his stump to the elements, he might pass out and never come to again.

"She's dead anyhow," he mumbled, gazing down at Jaimie, seeing how she lay lifeless among the dried, dead leaves.

Finding it harder and harder to move, he stumbled away from Jaimie's body.

Looking through a pain-induced haze, he

wandered onward and found a hiding place behind a thick cluster of cottonwood trees close to the Sioux village.

He eased down beneath the trees. Holding his face in his one hand, he breathed hard into it, his heart pounding as each shock of pain coursed through him.

"I'm not going to last much longer," he whispered harshly.

When he heard Maddy shouting Jaimie's name at the edge of the forest, his head jerked up.

His eyes danced as he moved slowly to his feet.

"Come to Daddy," he whispered, laughing throatily. He grabbed his knife. "Come on, Maddy. Surely you want to search for Jaimie. Don't take the time to get your husband. Come into the forest alone. Come on, Maddy. I'm waiting for you. . . ."

And when Maddy did as he silently bid her to do, he waited and slid his knife back into its sheath.

When Maddy came up close to the trees, Farris jumped out, grabbed her around the throat enough to cut off her ability to scream, then began dragging her away with him.

No matter how hard Maddy tried to scream, she couldn't make a sound. She reached up and tried to yank his arm away. But the grip was too tight.

She was at Farris Boyd's mercy. She wondered if he had found Jaimie. She went cold inside as she thought of what he could have done to her dear, beloved sister!

She noticed immediately that one of his arms had been removed. Blood dripped from the bandage. She prayed that he would be rendered too weak soon to complete his act of vengeance against her.

If not, she knew that these would be the last moments of her life, also . . . her unborn baby's!

Chapter Thirty-four

He is made one with Nature; there is heard
His voice in all her music, from the moan
Of thunder, to the songs of night's sweet
bird.

— Percy Bysshe Shelley

Her throat aching terribly, finding it hard to swallow, Jaimie coughed and choked as she awakened.

Small droplets of rain fell upon her face as the storm began, the lightning fierce as it flashed and ominously lit up the black sky through the foliage of the trees.

Groaning, dizzy, Jaimie slowly propped herself up on an elbow.

For a moment she was disoriented. She found it hard to think straight, to put things together in her mind.

She put a hand to her throat and slowly rubbed it, then flinched when finally she recalled what had happened to her.

"Farris!" she whispered hoarsely.

Her heart racing, she guardedly looked on all

sides of her as she rose slowly to her feet, her knees wobbling. She couldn't believe that Farris Boyd had actually been there.

How had he known where she and Maddy were? It was obvious that he had followed them to harm her and Maddy.

"Surely he thought I was dead or he wouldn't have left me," she whispered to herself.

"Maddy!" she said aloud, so hoarse she hardly recognized her own voice. "Oh, Lord! Surely he's gone for Maddy!"

She tried to run toward the Sioux village, then stopped and gagged when she again found the dead Shawnee warrior, flies buzzing around the bloody wound in his neck.

Now she understood too well how Farris had found the location of the Sioux village. He had forced Red Sky to lead him there, and then slit his throat to silence him.

Feeling lucky that Farris had not used the same knife on her, Jaimie put a trembling hand to her throat. Just touching it caused the pain to increase, and she realized that it must be terribly bruised.

Lightning flashed overhead. Thunder rolled. Rain began to fall in thick sheets, mingling with the blood beside the dead warrior.

Jaimie hated to leave Red Sky there, his body so unprotected against the elements, insects, and animals.

But as weak as she was, she would do well getting herself back home. It would be next to impossible for her to dig a grave with her hands.

"I must do something," she whispered.

She fell to her knees on the ground and scooped wet leaves over the warrior, blanketing him enough with the leaves to at least keep him unseen until the Sioux could come and retrieve his body so that he could be returned to his people for a proper Shawnee burial.

Wiping mud from her hands on her breeches, then brushing back her dripping wet hair from her eyes, she began running toward home.

She prayed that she would find Maddy safe and sound there. Surely Farris knew not to enter the village in broad daylight to abduct her.

Tonight. Oh, surely he would come tonight for Maddy! Jaimie must warn Maddy, as well as Black Wolf.

Black Wolf would send many warriors out into the forest to search for the crazed, one-armed man.

"One . . . armed . . ." she whispered, stopping when she recalled that one of his arms was gone.

The arm that had been swollen when she and Black Wolf had found him in the cellar, unconscious. Surely it had gotten infected. No doubt Farris had had no choice but to give permission for it to be removed or he would have lost his life instead of just an arm.

"He has to hate me and Maddy even more now," Jaimie whispered, again running toward home. "Surely he blames us for everything bad that has recently happened to him."

She lifted her eyes heavenward and cursed the rain and lightning. She knew that as long as she was outside during such a storm, she was in danger of being injured by lightning. Her father had taught her that when she was a small child. He had always warned her to get inside the house when it stormed, away from things that attracted lightning.

"I wish a lightning strike would hit Farris," she whispered, her eyes narrowing angrily.

Finally through a break in the trees a short distance away she could see the village. She could see that all entrance flaps were closed and that the sides of the lodges had been rolled down and secured against the rain.

She imagined Maddy inside their lodge beside the warm fire, but she expected that Black Wolf would not be with her. She had heard Black Wolf discussing with his warriors a long council they planned after everyone left the council house that afternoon.

If Black Wolf isn't with Maddy, surely she *is* vulnerable, Jaimie worried, again noting the inactivity in the village, and how the lodges were closed up tight to protect their occupants from the rain.

It could be a perfect time for Farris to enter the village and abduct Maddy. No one was around to see him. Or . . . to stop him!

But being one-armed, he was at a disadvantage. If Maddy saw him enter her lodge, he could not move quickly enough to disable her before

Cassie Edwards

she grabbed a firearm. Yet would Maddy think to arm herself? She hated guns!

And Maddy didn't know how to fire a gun. Worst of all, Farris knew that Maddy hated guns and was ignorant about loading and firing them. He had heard Jaimie scold her about her non-skill with weapons.

Yes, Maddy could be in danger this very moment, and if Jaimie caught Farris red-handed inside their lodge, she would not hesitate to kill him. She wasn't afraid of guns or of a little bloodshed, especially blood spilled from the likes of Farris Boyd.

He was a fiend. A cold-hearted killer.

She would never forget that first time he had bragged to her about having killed the great Sioux, Chief Crazy Horse. There had been such an evil gleam in his eyes. She had even seen an anxious twitch in his right cheek.

Yes, he had received a distorted, sick pleasure from repeating his story to anyone who would listen. Jaimie had hated it the first time she heard it.

Indians had always intrigued her. And she, like her sister Maddy, had felt a deep sorrow over the injustices done them by whites and the federal government. Everything but their dignity had been taken from them.

Now having lived among the Sioux, Jaimie knew that no one could ever take away or kill their dignity.

Oh, how she admired them and the way they

had been able to continue living a dignified life after having so much taken from them by whites! She was so proud to be a part of them.

Now running free of the forest, slipping and sliding on the mud of the cleared ground, Jaimie fought the onslaught of rain as it pummeled her face.

Another fear grabbed her. Only recently she had experienced such hideous storms. The rain had come in such torrents when the Ohio flooded.

She glanced over at the small stream that flowed near the village. To her relief it was only partially over its banks. And by the way the water was rushing freely onward, she doubted there would be any danger of it flooding the Sioux village.

Yes, Black Wolf had chosen the site of his new home well. Floods had been uppermost in his mind when he had decided on this strip of land, knowing that his people should never have to worry about high water again.

Her chest heaving, her heart pounding, Jaimie ran into the village. Her gaze fell on her lodge, where she could see the glow of fire through the buckskin hides.

She squinted as she looked more closely through the rain to see if anything seemed amiss about the tepee, whether the entrance flap was loose and blowing in the wind, which might mean that Maddy was not there to tie it closed.

When she saw the ties hanging free and fluttering in the wind, Jaimie's heart seemed to drop to her feet, for now she knew almost for certain that Maddy wasn't there.

Tears spilling from her eyes, Jaimie looked heavenward. "Please keep her safe, Lord," she whispered. "My sister deserves your protection. She is a student of the Bible. She prays often. Please let nothing happen to her. Oh, Lord, please don't let her be with that madman!"

Almost stumbling into the lodge after shoving aside the entrance flap, Jaimie grew cold when she discovered the silence of the tepee, the absolute emptiness of it.

She looked around for signs of a scuffle, puzzled that she saw none.

Yet that gave her hope. Perhaps Black Wolf had come for Maddy and had encouraged her to go to the council house to join him during the fierceness of the storm.

Her heart racing, and whispering another prayer, Jaimie rushed out into the rain again. She was panting when she ran inside the council house without stopping to ask permission to enter, even though she knew it was the custom when warriors met in council. What they discussed in council was of the utmost importance. It was always private until they chose to spread the word to others.

When she didn't see Maddy in the council house, but saw only the many warriors who sat in a circle around the huge fire in the center of the floor, Jaimie swallowed back a sob of fear.

Her eyes locked with Black Wolf's. She could tell by his expression that he knew something was wrong.

Black Wolf's heart skipped a beat when he saw Jaimie standing there so frightened and wet. When the fire's glow showed him the bruise on her throat, he leapt to his feet and went to her. He was almost too afraid to ask how it had happened.

He was almost afraid to ask where Maddy was. The anxious fear in Jaimie's wide eyes told him that her sister was in some sort of trouble.

"Farris is somewhere near!" Jaimie said hoarsely, then she quickly explained the events that had brought her there in such a frightened frenzy.

She grabbed Black Wolf desperately by an arm and dug her fingers into his flesh. "Black Wolf, Farris choked me," she cried. "He left me for dead. And he killed Red Sky. I stumbled over the Shawnee warrior in the forest. And, Black Wolf, Maddy isn't in our lodge. I fear that Farris came and stole her away! And, Black Wolf, Farris only has one arm now! Blood was dripping through the bandage! What do you think happened?"

Black Wolf's head was spinning as he listened to Jaimie's rushed words, growing cold and heatedly angry at the same time.

When he realized the worst . . . that his woman was surely at the mercy of a madman, he gently unlocked Jaimie's hand from his arm.

He gave her a fierce hug and assured her that things were going to be all right.

Black Wolf then spun around on a heel and began shouting out instructions to his warriors.

"We must find my wife!" he shouted. "Hurry to your lodges! Arm yourselves heavily! Meet me outside soon on your horses!"

He swept Jaimie up into his arms and left the council house in a hard run.

When he entered his lodge, he slid Jaimie to the floor, then knelt down before her.

"Running Deer, get out of those wet clothes," he said. "Wrap yourself in a warm pelt and sit beside the fire. Listen well, *Tahn-kah*, when I tell you to stay here while I search for Maddy. Do not leave this lodge. Farris left you for dead once. When he realizes you are still living and breathing, he will not stop at anything to find and kill you. I will post guards outside our lodge. You will be safe here."

"But I want to go with you," Jaimie said, hating it when her voice came out in a nagging whine.

"Not this time, *Tahn-kah*," Black Wolf said, slowly running his fingers over her bruised throat. "I know how you enjoy being a part of the hunt, Running Deer. But this time we hunt for human flesh. It will not be a pretty sight when we find and kill Farris Boyd. It is not something a girl your age should see."

"I am as brave and courageous as any warrior," Jaimie cried, taking a quick step away from him. "I must go, Black Wolf. Please let me go with you. It's my sister out there at the mercy of that evil man. Please let me help find her."

"*Tahn-kah*, arguing with me is only slowing me down," Black Wolf said, searching her eyes. "Do you understand that? Do you not see that the time I take to convince you to stay here is time that I could spend searching for your sister?"

Feeling ashamed for being so stubborn, Jaimie lowered her eyes. "I'm sorry," she murmured. "Go on. I'll do as you say. I'll sit by the fire. I'll wait."

She quickly raised her eyes and gazed at Black Wolf, then flung herself into his arms and hugged him. "Please bring my sister home safe, Black Wolf," she sobbed out. "I love her so. Until you came along, Maddy was all I had. She is everything to me, Black Wolf. Please find her."

"She will be safe in our lodge tonight," Black Wolf promised, holding Jaimie for a moment longer. Then he eased her away. "Now do as you said you would do. Remove the clothes. Wrap yourself in a pelt. Sit by the fire. I will return home soon with Maddy. I promise you that, *Tahn-kah*. And I never make promises lightly, nor do I ever make promises I cannot keep."

Jaimie watched him hurry around the tepee, taking up his bow and quiver of arrows, positioning them across his shoulder, then slinging a gunbelt around his waist that was heavy with pistols.

She saw his fierceness in how he yanked up his rifle. Then he left the lodge after giving her a nod of reassurance.

Black Wolf quickly mounted his horse, then motioned to his warriors and told them to fan out in all directions, some on foot and some on horses.

He told them to find their Shawnee friend Red Sky. His body must be returned to his loved ones for proper burial!

As he rode from the village, he recalled something that was etched in his mind with indelible clarity. He was recalling what his father had told him about how Crazy Horse had died.

Many pony soldiers had gone to Chief Crazy Horse's village with false tongues. They had told Crazy Horse that if he went with them to Fort Robinson, he would not be harmed. He had been told that the man in charge at the fort only wanted to talk with Crazy Horse.

When they had arrived at the fort, they took Chief Crazy Horse to the fort's prison, which had iron bars in the windows.

When Crazy Horse saw what the pony soldiers' intentions were, that he would be locked away forever from his people, the sunshine, the blue sky, and the land he loved with all of his being, he took a knife from his robe and went after the lying soldiers.

He had been quickly stopped . . . by a bayonet.

Black Wolf tried to block the image of the bayonet in his cousin's chest from his mind, but every time he thought of Farris Boyd, he thought of Chief Crazy Horse's death.

"Farris Boyd, today *you* die!" Black Wolf cried to the heavens as he waved his rifle in the air.

The rain had stopped. The sky was turning a mellow blue overhead.

"*Mee-tah-ween*," he whispered, a sob lodging in his throat. "*Tah-wee-choo*, my wife, let me be in time. . . ."

A keen sorrow swept through him as he thought of someone else . . . Red Sky. This gentle-hearted man did not deserve to die, alone without friends and family, his life snuffed out by a white man.

One thing brought a slow smile to his lips. Jaimie had said that Farris had only one arm now. Black Wolf knew that this put the evil man at great disadvantage. Perhaps Maddy might even be able to save herself from him.

Yet just as quickly he recalled how she hated weapons and knew nothing about them, and his smile changed into a deep, dark frown.

It made him feel sick inside to know that he had not kept his word to her. He had vowed to protect her.

If anything happened to her, he would hold himself at fault, as though he, himself, had slain her!

His eyes grew fierce. He would still keep that promise to her. He would find her, and pity Farris Boyd if he had harmed her in any way!

Chapter Thirty-five

A heavy weight of hours has chained and
  bowed
One too like thee: tameless, and swift, and
  proud.

—Percy Bysshe Shelley

Deep in the dark bowels of the forest, drops of
rain dripped slowly from the leaves of the trees.
Maddy realized that the shadows were length-
ening around her and knew that soon it would
be totally dark.

Shivering not only because she was chilled
and wet from the rain, but also because she was
standing face to face with a madman, she stared
at Farris as he held her at knifepoint. When he
had released his hold from around her throat,
she had briefly hoped it was because he had decided to spare her life.

But she had quickly discovered how wrong
she was. When she had turned to face him, he
already had his knife out of its sheath and he
quickly placed it at her throat.

She knew not to move when the sharp tip of the knife sank into her flesh deep enough to draw blood.

"You can't get away with this," Maddy said, speaking carefully, so she didn't jar the knife. Her skin already burned where the knife had penetrated.

She hated to think what it might feel like to die from a knife wound as her father had died, and Black Wolf's father . . . and Santa.

It would be an unmerciful death.

"I haven't come this far to find you to let anything interfere with my killing you," Farris growled out. "But before I do, I just want to watch you squirm a little bit more. Killing you too quickly would take the joy out of it for me. You bitch, because of you I lost my arm. Because of you, I've lost everything."

His eyes narrowed as he cackled. "Of course, you'd rather I had lost my life down in that damn cellar, wouldn't you?" he said. "You didn't know that someone would come along and take a look in the cellar, now did you?"

"Who found you?" Maddy asked warily, hoping to keep him talking long enough for Black Wolf to discover her missing from their lodge, or Jaimie.

Surely Jaimie had returned to their home by now, or the council house, after having found whatever sort of wood she had been seeking in the forest. Yet it was Jaimie's failure to return that had caused Maddy to enter the forest in the first place.

Another thought came to her that made her knees grow weak.

What if Farris had found Jaimie before he found Maddy? Could he have . . . ?

She swallowed hard, not allowing herself to think the worst about her beloved sister. Surely Jaimie had gone in another direction away from where Maddy had gone to search for her.

Yes. She was home safe now sitting by the fire.

"Who came into my beautiful home without permission?" Farris hissed, leaning his face closer to Maddy's. "They just barged in, you know, like they owned the place."

He laughed sarcastically. "The nerve," he said thickly. "Can you imagine? Just making yourself at home in another man's house?"

"Who . . . are you . . . talking about?" Maddy prompted, paling at the thought of what Farris might have done to whomever had freed him after they had been kind enough to release him from the cellar.

Even if they had trespassed, surely Farris wouldn't have killed them. Yet he was planning to kill her, wasn't he? And he *had* slain Chief Crazy Horse and bragged about it as though there were no sin at all in killing!

Yes, this man was capable of doing anything, even killing a whole family of settlers if that suited his purpose.

"Can you believe that one of those who came

into my home was a half-breed?" Farris snarled. "She even went so far as to pretend to be a doctor, thinking that would erase the Indian side of her nature."

He spat on the ground beside him. "The whore," he hissed. "She even was dressed like a white woman, and had a kid that looked white like her white husband."

Then he leaned his head back from Maddy, his one hand still holding the knife at her throat as he raked his eyes slowly over her. "You've turned into a savage squaw, ain't you, Maddy?" he said, laughing throatily. "You not only married one, you're dressed like one."

His eyes danced as he gave her a long stare. "How's an Indian in bed, Maddy?" he asked. "Better than a white man?"

"How dare you ask such a question?" Maddy hissed out. "Do you think I'd ever tell you anything about my personal life?"

She laughed softly. "But at least you know that I married Black Wolf," she said smugly.

She knew that she was pushing her luck by saying what she was going to say, but she couldn't resist taunting him.

"How does it feel to have a woman you wanted choose a red man over you?" she asked, her voice thick with contempt. "You one-armed, crazy man, even when you had both arms and were healthy, I abhorred the very sight of you. You made my stomach turn then. You disgust me even more now that you are made even uglier by having only one arm."

It took all of the willpower that Farris could muster not to sink the knife into Maddy's throat. Her insults sank so deep into his heart he felt a dark fury he could barely control.

"You speak awful bold for a woman with a knife at her throat," he said, cackling. "Why, Maddy? Why are you tempting me to go ahead and kill you? Have you found no wedded bliss with that savage redskin? Have you discovered just how filthy they are once you've lain beneath one of them? Or is it because you've caught fleas from your savage husband?"

He gazed up at her hair, then looked into her eyes. "Yep, I bet you've got damn fleas crawling all around on your scalp," he said. "What a shame, Maddy, for you to have chosen this life over what I offered you. You'd have never wanted for a thing."

He laughed again. "For certain I could afford to buy you enough soap to keep your head clean of fleas," he said.

"You are the most despicable, loathsome man I've ever known," Maddy said, her eyes filled with fire. She glanced at the bloody stump where his arm used to be. "And now you are only half a man. No woman will ever go to bed with you again, even if you live long enough to try."

"Do you know, Maddy, I had no plans to rape you before I killed you, but now, because of what you said, I'll rape you just for the pleasure of feeling you squirming beneath me," Farris said, his eyes gleaming. "Then, young lady, I'll slowly sink my knife into your heart and watch your life slip away."

"At least you won't be using a bayonet on me like you did my husband's cousin," Maddy said bitterly.

She looked nervously past Farris, praying that she could delay Farris long enough for Black Wolf to find her!

Oh, Lord, she prayed, let him know that I'm missing. Please let him be out there even now searching frantically for me.

If only he knew. . . . !

"Your husband's . . . cousin?" Farris said guardedly, lifting an eyebrow. "I only recall killing Black Wolf's father, not a cousin."

"You . . . killed . . . his father?" Maddy said, the color rushing from her face. "It was you? You killed him?"

Farris shrugged nonchalantly. "I certainly did and I must say it was like I was back in the cavalry getting my jollies killing redskins," he said throatily.

Then his eyes narrowed as he glared at Maddy. "Now, who were you talking about when you said I'd killed Black Wolf's cousin?" he asked, his eyes searching hers.

"You stupid idiot, don't you know that Black Wolf is Chief Crazy Horse's cousin, and that his father was Crazy Horse's—" Maddy stopped what she was saying when she saw alarm enter

Farris's eyes, and his hand lowered momentarily from her throat.

She gulped hard, for surely now she had said more than she should have. Now that Farris knew Black Wolf was related to Chief Crazy Horse, he would probably kill Maddy quickly and flee the area before Black Wolf came and found him.

Her heart thumped wildly as she realized that only she could save herself from being stabbed to death by this one-armed lunatic. Maddy reached down deep inside herself and found the courage, and the will to act upon it.

Breathing hard, she lifted the skirt of her dress out of the way and kicked the knife from Farris's hand.

Wild-eyed and growling like an animal, Farris bent to retrieve the knife, but, not yet used to the lopsided feeling of being one-armed, he fell awkwardly to the ground.

Seizing the opportunity, Maddy bent down and picked up the knife. But before she could step far enough away, Farris grabbed her ankle and yanked her down to the ground beside him. The knife flew out of her hand as she fell.

Growling, Farris released his hold on her ankle and grabbed the knife. Chuckling, he hovered over Maddy with the knife.

But before he could plunge it into her, a lone gunshot filled the air.

Her eyes wide, her throat dry, Maddy saw that

the bullet had entered Farris's chest, the impact knocking him backwards.

Another shot split the air.

It entered Farris's side, throwing him sideways.

Stunned to see Farris lying there, sprawled awkwardly on the ground, his one hand clawing the air as he moaned in pain while his lifeblood poured from the two bullet wounds, Maddy slowly sat up and stared at him.

When she heard a rush of feet toward her, she turned her head to see Black Wolf running from the trees, smoke wafting from the rifle he carried at his side.

Sobbing, Maddy rushed to her feet and ran to Black Wolf and clung to him. "Thank God you came," she cried. "I would surely have been dead by now. He . . . hated . . . me so much."

She could hear horses approaching and saw many of Black Wolf's warriors ride into the open. Lone Beaver was holding the reins of Black Wolf's steed as it trailed along behind him.

"He is not dead yet," Black Wolf growled out, looking past Maddy's shoulder at Farris.

Maddy turned from Black Wolf's arms and stared down at Farris, who had managed to roll over on his back, his eyes gleaming as he looked up at her. Then he looked over at Black Wolf, his one hand clutching his shirt where the bullet had pierced the cotton fabric, the blood still oozing from it.

"And so you finally have your revenge on the man who killed Chief Crazy Horse," Farris stammered out. "Had I known earlier who you were, Black Wolf, I'd have killed you the same way I killed your—" Farris stopped, choking on blood as it started to stream from the corners of his mouth.

He then spoke in a low, strained whisper. "Had I known your father was related to Crazy Horse, I'd have done more than stick a knife in his belly. I'd have spit on the breechclout when I took it from him," he said scornfully. "I'd have made sure I killed him with the same bayonet that killed Crazy Horse!"

"You are the one responsible for my father's death?" Black Wolf said in horror.

"The . . . very . . . one," Farris said, managing a low, maniacal laugh.

The pain knifed through him, and he gazed up at Black Wolf pleadingly. "Finish me off, Black Wolf," he begged. "Come on. Do it. The pain. I . . . ain't . . . ever . . . been able to stand pain."

It took all of the willpower that Black Wolf had practiced since he was a mere youth not to pick up the knife that lay at the man's side and plunge it into his heart.

He felt Maddy clinging to his arm, purposely holding him back.

He gave her a quick glance and saw her silent plea that he not react irrationally to what Farris had disclosed to him.

He then stared down at the dying man.

No. He would do nothing to bring death more quickly to Farris Boyd. He would let it come slowly, painfully, unmercifully.

He even wished that there was some way to keep him alive longer. But no man who had lost as much blood as Farris had lost could live for much longer.

As he gazed down at Farris, waiting for his death, he remembered something his father had told him about Chief Crazy Horse's death.

Yes, his cousin's life had been snuffed out by a bayonet. But Farris was not the man who had killed Chief Crazy Horse.

Black Wolf suddenly remembered the details of his cousin's murder. Crazy Horse had been killed by a *half-breed* . . . a man who was part white and part Sioux, who had aligned himself with the white pony soldiers, doing their dirty work.

Farris Boyd had *not* killed Crazy Horse, only enjoyed bragging about it as though it were an honorable achievement, instead of an act of cowardice.

Black Wolf's thoughts were interrupted when Farris spoke again.

"And, Maddy, I think it's time for you to know just how much I did love you," Farris said, his breathing now more shallow, each word an effort. "Maddy, I killed your father. I did it because I'd do anything to have you. Your father was an obstacle. I killed him to get him out of the way.

Maddy, darlin', I'd . . . have . . . given . . . you the world."

Stunned and sickened to know that this man had killed her father in such a vicious, senseless way, Maddy turned her eyes away from him and held her face in her hands, crying.

She remembered with much guilt in her heart how she had at first thought that Black Wolf might have killed her father.

Oh, how could she not have guessed it was Farris Boyd? As she thought back now, she saw how it had been no coincidence that just after her father died, Farris had come and pushed the subject of marriage on her . . . saying that now she was alone without a man for protection, *he* offered it to her.

She should have known! she thought. How could she have been so blind? How could she have been so downright stupid!

Then she thought of something else . . . how her father's clothes had been removed by his assailant.

She paled when she thought of a third murder. Santa's! He had been knifed to death. His clothes had been removed!

Three men killed in the same fashion. Surely Farris had also killed Santa!

"Why did you remove the clothes from those you killed?" Maddy blurted out, now staring down at him. "And . . . did you kill Santa?"

"Who?" Farris gasped.

"Santa, but you would have known him as

Jonathan Harper," Maddy said somberly.

"Oh, yes, *Colonel* Harper," Farris said, his breathing now coming in short rasps. "Yes, I killed the sonofabitch."

"But why?" Maddy cried, a sob lodging in her throat as she recalled how pitiful Santa had looked, lying there naked, the insects swarming over his body. "Santa was so kind. He never harmed anyone."

"When he was a colonel in the cavalry, he was a tyrant of a leader," Farris gasped out. "One day he horsewhipped me for disobeying an order. I knew then that I'd never rest until I saw him dead."

"The clothes . . ." Maddy gulped out. "Why did you remove the clothes from those you killed?"

"To make them die with less dignity," Farris stammered out, breathing hard.

"You are even sicker than I ever imagined," Maddy said, tears streaming from her eyes. "You are a fiend . . . someone who has . . . no . . . heart."

Farris managed a low, deep laugh, then he turned his gaze to Black Wolf. "Ah, Black Wolf, what . . . a . . . pleasure it . . . was . . . to sink the . . . bayonet into your cousin's stomach," Farris said, his voice now a faint whisper. "You should've seen the surprised look in Crazy Horse's eyes as he stood there with the bayonet sticking through him before he collapsed on the ground, dead."

Maddy stared disbelievingly down at this man

who even while dying could not stop bragging about his terrible deeds.

She looked quickly at Black Wolf, who remained still, despite the awful words of this evil man. She couldn't understand how Black Wolf could keep such composure now, in the light of all that he now knew about Farris Boyd.

Even *she* wished that she had the courage to grab up the knife and silence him forever!

She jumped when Black Wolf suddenly leaned down and rested on his haunches close beside Farris, his face low so that Farris could see and hear him.

"Crazy man, do you not know that all along I have known who truly killed my beloved cousin, the most courageous and beloved chief of all time?" he said, smiling cunningly down at Farris. "It was most certainly not *you*."

Maddy gasped. She scarcely breathed as she listened to what Black Wolf was saying so calmly, so deliberately.

She was stunned to know that it had not been Farris, after all, who had killed Crazy Horse. For years he had carried this tale around with him like it was a trophy he had won in a game.

"You are a man who has bragged time and time again about a deed you never did," Black Wolf said, enjoying the way Farris cowered and shivered with each word as Black Wolf continued to talk.

"The man who truly took my cousin's life was a man of my own skin color," Black Wolf said.

"Yes, this man who killed my cousin was a breed, who had a white mother and a Sioux father. It was he who killed Chief Crazy Horse. He was raised by the Sioux, then acted as a scout for the white-eyes during the war. He went white in heart and deeds and wore the uniform of the white pony soldiers. It was this man who dishonored himself by thrusting the bayonet into Crazy Horse, not you, Farris Boyd! White man, your lies about having killed Crazy Horse brought *you* no honor either . . . only contempt!"

"It . . . was . . . all a lie?" Maddy murmured, kneeling down beside Black Wolf.

"This man's whole life was a lie," Black Wolf said, reaching over to place his arm around Maddy's waist. "He is experiencing now, perhaps for the first time in his life, one absolute truth in life. Death, Maddy. Death."

Maddy shuddered as Farris's eyes went wild, as though staring at some apparition above him. He seemed to be trying to fight something off, then strangled on a large spurt of blood that leapt into his throat.

His eyes suddenly froze in a death stare.

"This man's lies are now forever stilled," Black Wolf said, helping Maddy to her feet. He drew her into his embrace.

"Had he harmed you . . ." he said thickly, searching her face, then lowering his eyes to the blood on her throat. Softly he touched the slight wound.

"He did that with his knife, but I'm truly all right, Black Wolf. At least *now*, I am, now that you came . . . and . . . saved me," Maddy murmured. She leaned back and looked up at Black Wolf. "Black Wolf, is Jaimie at home? Is . . . she all right?"

"She is home, safe beside our lodge fire," Black Wolf said, refraining from scolding Maddy for having left the safety of the lodge, herself. All that mattered now was that she was alive.

"Thank God," Maddy said, sighing.

She saw Black Wolf look down at Farris again. She wondered what he was thinking, but would not ask. Surely he was recalling how the man had bragged of having killed his father.

It cut deep into the core of her being to know that he had killed *hers*. And, oh, good God, he had also murdered gentle, kind Santa!

Oh, how good it was that the man was dead, his brutal ways finally stilled!

Black Wolf stared at Farris, thinking he was an example of the worst kind of white man. It was because of men like Farris Boyd that Black Wolf no longer saw buffalo on the plains. It was because of men like him that Black Wolf would never again see his original home in Nebraska. It was because of this man that Black Wolf was denied the loving arms and words of his beloved father!

"*Hetchetu-aloh*, finally, it . . . is . . . finished," he said. Then he whisked Maddy up into his arms and walked away, carrying her to his horse, which Lone Beaver had held so that Black Wolf could sneak up on Farris on foot without being heard.

When he reached his horse, he stopped and gazed down at Maddy. Their eyes locked and held, their smiles filled with a soft, radiant peace.

"Now we have forever ahead of us," Black Wolf murmured.

Tears of joy swam in Maddy's eyes as she gazed at him. Slowly she slid a hand over her abdomen. She could hardly wait until they were alone tonight so she could talk with Black Wolf about their child. Oh, yes, they had so much to celebrate tonight.

How wonderful it was that Farris had not harmed the child. He had come close to taking that away from her and Black Wolf.

For a while there, she had thought she would never have the opportunity to give birth to Black Wolf's child.

Inside the soft, protective cocoon of her womb, the baby still breathed, its heartbeat only a faint whisper, but still there, beating out a steady rhythm until the child could be held by his mother and father, to be cherished by them.

"Let us go home now," Black Wolf said, gently lifting Maddy to the saddle.

"Yes, let's," she murmured, her eyes beaming. "Tonight we can share so much, my darling."

Imagining the child so soft and sweet inside

her, Maddy laid her head against Black Wolf's chest after he mounted behind her and swept a protective arm around her waist.

"Black Wolf, *Tay-chee-khee-lah*, I love you so," she murmured, shivering sensually when he bent low and told her that he loved her.

Tonight!

Tonight when they were alone and embracing!

Oh, tonight couldn't come soon enough for Maddy. As she closed her eyes, she could envision how it would be, the very thought of it making her insides quiver with happiness.

Chapter Thirty-six

Sudden, thy shadow fell on me;
I shrieked and clasped my hands in ecstasy!
                              —Percy Bysshe Shelley

Seven summers and winters had passed. It was now August, the Moon When The Cherries Turn Black. The Sioux people's lives had been fulfilled and happy, with many children having been born into their tribe.

Several Sioux families had arrived from various places to be a part of Black Wolf's village, until now the lodges of his people hugged both sides of the stream.

Maddy felt that life was wonderful with her Sioux chieftain husband. She had miscarried her first child, but had successfully gone the full nine months with her second child, who was now five. The spitting image of his Sioux father, the boy was named Winter Hawk.

As Winter Hawk scampered around today, playing with children his age, Maddy sat on a blanket with Raven Hair and Raven Hair's newborn baby beneath the shade of an old oak.

Maddy glanced over at Raven Hair. Not often in life did someone find a friend as special and sincere as Raven Hair was to Maddy.

And what fun it had been that first Christmas, introducing that white custom to the Sioux. A huge cedar tree had been placed in the council house. They had had a merry time making decorations for the tree, and then came Christmas Eve, when everyone learned the custom of exchanging gifts.

Maddy would never forget the joy this practice gave the Sioux people. She would never forget how they had all crowded around her before the blazing central fire and listened to the story of baby Jesus.

Each year now everyone looked forward to Christmas. Every Christmas Eve she repeated the story of Jesus.

Maddy smiled as Raven Hair openly nursed her child, slowly waving a fan of feathers over her tiny daughter to keep the flies away from her tender, copper flesh.

Then Maddy's eyes were drawn elsewhere when Jaimie's voice came to her in the wind. Maddy and Raven Hair watched a group of young braves gathering in the middle of the Sioux people, who sat in a wide circle on the ground just outside the large council house.

Today was the Test of Endurance at the Sioux village.

Normally only young braves participated. But today, to Maddy's disappointment, her sister was among those who would be challenged in ways that Maddy tried to understand, yet still found hard to accept.

"Running Deer is so pretty with her longer hair," Raven Hair said softly, interrupting Maddy's thoughts. "Maddy, you must be so glad that she finally allowed it to grow. It makes her look more . . . more . . . like a. . . ."

When Raven Hair didn't finish what she was saying, Maddy sighed. Jaimie's boyish behavior was still something Maddy disfavored. Maddy had almost given up hope that her sister would ever change.

"You were about to say that the longer hair makes my sister look more like a lady?" Maddy murmured, giving Raven Hair a wistful look.

"Well, yes . . ." Raven Hair said, her eyes wavering.

"I do wish her upcoming marriage to Eagle Wing would make her come to her senses about her behavior," Maddy said, watching Jaimie as she laughed and talked with the young braves while Eagle Wing tenderly held one of her hands, his love for her obvious in the way he looked so adoringly down at her.

"Jaimie is seventeen winters of age now," Raven Hair said, now also watching Jaimie. "Soon she will marry, and with marriage will come the responsibilities of a wife and one day a mother. She will change, Maddy. How could she not?"

Maddy laughed softly. "How could she not?"

she said. "You'll see, Raven Hair. You'll see. Just saying vows with Eagle Wing, and realizing she is a wife, will never make her become the demure woman I wish she could be. She loves horseback riding too much, and everything else that will keep her from her duties as a homemaker. I'm so afraid this behavior might jeopardize her marriage to Eagle Wing."

"But having a child should change everything," Raven Hair said, gazing with smiling eyes down at her tiny daughter, whose fingers were gently kneading her breast as she suckled from the nipple.

"Running Deer says she never plans to have children," Maddy said, her voice drawn. "Even loving her nephew so much, and spending time with him, doesn't seem to have changed her feelings about having children of her own."

Maddy watched Eagle Wing as he walked away from the group of young braves, leaving his future wife standing and talking and laughing with them. She wondered where he might be going since he was supposed to participate in the Test of Endurance today along with Jaimie and the others.

She worried so often that he might become jealous of Jaimie's closeness to the other braves. Surely he could not enjoy the way Jaimie mingled with them all as though she were one of them, when he surely would prefer having her all to himself.

. Raven Hair also watched Eagle Wing leave the

circle of people and step into the shadows of the forest. "I wonder where Eagle Wing is going," she said, giving Maddy a quick look. "Do you think he has changed his mind? That he will not participate in the challenge today?"

"I'm not sure," Maddy said, watching for Eagle Wing's return. If he was unhappy with Jaimie and decided not to marry her, after all, Maddy's hopes of her sister ever changing would be gone.

"And how are my two most special women doing as they await the ceremony?" Black Wolf said, coming up from behind Maddy and Raven Hair.

He sat down beside Maddy and swept an arm around her waist. "*Tah-wee-choo*, did you not hear what I said?" he asked softly. "Are you even aware that your husband has come to observe the ceremony with you?"

Maddy turned her eyes quickly to Black Wolf. She twined her arms around his neck and gave him a tender hug. "I'm sorry," she murmured. "I didn't mean to ignore you. It's just that I'm so worried about my sister."

"About her endurance test?" Black Wolf said, placing his hands on Maddy's arms and gently easing her away from him. "I have explained the test to you. If Running Deer experiences any pain, it will be brief."

"I still can't help but be concerned about her participating in the test, but I'm also worried about her relationship with Eagle Wing," she said solemnly. She turned her eyes back to Jaimie. "Just look at her. It's as though she doesn't even know Eagle Wing exists. She's laughing and talking to the other braves too much."

"Where *is* Eagle Wing?" Black Wolf said, searching the group of young people.

"He just walked away," Maddy said, glancing at the forest where she had last seen Eagle Wing. She nodded toward it. "He went into the forest. I can't help wondering why."

"Do you want me to go and find him and ask why he left when it is only a matter of moments before the test begins?" Black Wolf asked, drawing Maddy's eyes back to him.

"Oh, would you, darling?" she asked softly. Black Wolf nodded, but before he got to his feet, Eagle Wing came from the forest, his arms filled with clumps of wild azaleas with brilliant golden dandelions placed among them.

"My goodness," Maddy said, her eyes widening as she watched Eagle Wing take the flowers to Jaimie and place them in her arms.

Maddy smiled when she saw Jaimie gaze in wonder at the flowers, then look up at Eagle Wing, beaming.

Tears of relief came to Maddy's eyes when Jaimie held the flowers in the crook of one arm, while with her other arm she hugged Eagle Wing.

"Eagle Wing is very much in love with Running Deer," Black Wolf said, settling down again beside Maddy. "And look at her. She returns the love. She is grateful for the gift of flowers. See how your *tahn-kah* is now hugging them to her bosom?"

Maddy flicked tears from her eyes as she watched the other young braves stop talking, smiling at Jaimie as she showed them her flowers.

"Just perhaps it's beginning," Maddy whispered, then tightened inside when Jaimie took the flowers and laid them aside on the ground, seeming to forget them.

"Oh, well," Maddy said, sighing.

"The true test is whether or not she will go and get them after the endurance trial is over," Black Wolf said, placing a comforting arm around Maddy's waist.

He reached out his free hand to Winter Hawk as the boy came to him and bounced up on his lap.

"See my sister?" Winter Hawk said, pointing to Jaimie, whom he thought of as a sister instead of an aunt. "I wish one day to be as brave as Running Deer."

He turned wide, dark eyes up to his father. "*Ahte*, Father," he said, eyes wide. "This morning Running Deer explained the endurance test to me. I am afraid she is going to be hurt. Is she not brave to go ahead and do it, even knowing the sunflower seeds are going to burn clear down to her skin?"

"Yes, she is a brave sister," Black Wolf said,

giving Maddy a half glance when he heard her heave another sigh as she watched Jaimie get ready for the test.

Black Wolf then watched Jaimie, himself, but in his mind's eye he was recalling the first time he had been put through the same test.

He had been his young son's age, far too young to participate in the test. But he had been so daring as a young child. He pushed the limits of every challenge, attempting what braves much older than himself dared to try.

He smiled as he recalled the very moment the sunflower seed on his wrist had burned down to his skin. Although the fire had been scorchingly hot against his young, tender flesh, he hadn't knocked the flaming seed off. He had wanted to be the most courageous of those who were participating in the test that day.

Black Wolf turned his arm over so that he could see where the sunflower seed had lain. There was still a trace of a scar there.

"There she goes," Maddy said, her pulse racing. "I wish she wouldn't do this, Black Wolf. I wish you had forbidden it."

"Your *tahn-kah* is old enough to make her own decisions," he said thickly. "She understands what she is doing, and why. It is not for either of us to question."

Maddy frowned as she glanced over at him, and then looked at Jaimie again as she lined up next to the others participating in the endurance test.

From a distance, she looked much like the young men standing beside her. Jaimie still wore the fringed breeches and shirts that she favored over dresses. Her hair hung as long as that of the braves, but it stood out from theirs in its brilliant red.

Only up close did one see that Jaimie had turned into a ravishingly beautiful young lady, her breasts round and full, her features perfect, her lashes long and thick as they veiled her vivacious wide green eyes.

"There they go!" Winter Hawk exclaimed excitedly. "Watch, Mother! Watch, *Ahte*! See Running Deer? See?"

Maddy found it hard to watch, but she forced herself to, just in case she felt the need to run to Jaimie and stop the foolishness.

She held her breath when one of the village elders placed a dried sunflower seed on the wrist of each participant.

She covered her mouth with a hand when the elder, one by one, lit the sunflower seeds at the top.

Maddy knew the challenge . . . that each participant was to let the sunflower seed burn right down to the skin.

She had heard various warriors discussing their participation in this same challenge, and how the burning seeds had hurt them and left sores.

But to remove them was to prove oneself a coward.

Maddy silently counted the minutes as she waited for the sunflower seed to burn out on Jaimie's arm. She could see her sister cringe as she watched it burning on her arm, but she never made a sound.

The seed continued to burn, and Jaimie continued to stand there, until Maddy could no longer watch.

She was still trying to understand these tests the Sioux put themselves through! How could anyone see these people as anything less than courageous after all they had faced and lived through? Why would they need these sorts of tests to prove again and again that they were brave?

But she knew that no matter how much she tried to understand, or disapproved, these tests would go on until the end of time, for the Sioux had been practicing their various customs since the beginning of time.

Maddy had learned to accept almost everything she had been faced with after becoming a part of the Sioux's lives. These tests, too, she would learn to accept, whether or not she would ever understand them.

A sudden outburst of cheering, clapping, and chanting drew Maddy's eyes back to Jaimie and the others who were standing with her, smiling, congratulating each other, the burned-out seeds now on the ground.

"She did it!" Winter Hawk shouted, jumping from his father's lap. He ran to his sister and hugged her legs, and then her neck when she leaned down and grabbed him into her arms.

"I'm so glad it's over," Maddy said, sighing. Until the next time, she reminded herself.

She wanted to go to Jaimie and inspect her wrist, but knew that was the last thing her sister would want her to do.

She watched Jaimie smile as she proudly showed her brother the sore on her arm.

When Jaimie turned smiling eyes toward Maddy and Maddy saw the pride in their depths, she understood how wrong she had been to want to deny her sister this moment. She smiled back, knowing she would fight harder against questioning these things her sister wished to do.

Her sister was special. She was unique. Maddy was going to make herself be more proud of her sister's uniqueness!

"It was not all that bad, now was it?" Black Wolf said, drawing Maddy's eyes back to him.

"Not really," Maddy murmured, then turned her eyes quickly to her son when he came and squirmed onto her lap.

His little hands framed her face as he looked up at her.

"Mother, was not it exciting? I saw no fear in anyone's eyes as the seeds burned on their wrists. I want to put sunflower seeds on my wrist and let them burn!" he said, his voice filled with excitement. "Can I, Mother? Can I? Can I now?"

Maddy's smile faded and a coldness rushed across her heart.

Seeing Maddy's sudden alarm, Black Wolf swept his son from her lap and held him on his. "One day, Winter Hawk, but not now," he said softly. "You have many moons before you are old enough to enter such challenges as you saw today."

"But I am as brave as those who are older," Winter Hawk said with a pout.

"You must build on that bravery, my son, and not only for challenges of endurance, but for future survival," Black Wolf said thickly. "As for now, my son, run and play with children your age."

"Oh, all right," Winter Hawk said, crawling quickly from Black Wolf's lap.

"You handled that well," Maddy said, snuggling closer to Black Wolf as she saw Winter Hawk join his friends. "I hope you can handle him as well when he is Running Deer's age."

"He will grow into a wise, brave young man who will know his mind better than his mother and father," Black Wolf said, giving Maddy a gentle smile. "We must accept it when it comes, wife, this boy who will then be a man."

"Yes, I know, but it will be so hard," Maddy said, sighing.

"What you need is another child to take your mind off your worries about Winter Hawk," Black Wolf said, taking her hands. "It is time, *mee-tah-ween*, to try again to bring new life into our lodge."

"But I just can't seem to get pregnant again,"

Maddy said, smiling a goodbye over her shoulder at Raven Hair as Maddy walked away with Black Wolf toward their lodge.

She looked over her shoulder again, her eyes searching for Jaimie. Everything inside her mellowed with thankfulness when she saw Jaimie pick up her bouquet of flowers and hold them as Eagle Wing lifted her onto her horse, a beautiful bay gelding that Black Wolf had given to Jaimie shortly after Maddy's marriage to Black Wolf.

She watched as Eagle Wing swung himself in the saddle behind Jaimie, placing a gentle arm around her waist as she leaned back against him, the bouquet snuggled in her arms.

Eagle Wing wheeled the horse around and rode in a slow lope toward the forest.

Maddy knew that the two youngsters had been intimate, even though they had not yet spoken the vows that made them man and wife, but hadn't Maddy, with Black Wolf?

She knew that it was right, for she knew they would one day be man and wife. Jaimie's wedding day was quickly approaching!

"You *will* get pregnant again," Black Wolf reassured her. "I promise you that it will happen."

He swept her up into his arms and carried her inside their tepee, where soft rabbit and elk skins beckoned them to their bed. "*Mee-tah-ween*, perhaps today is the day the seed of our second child will be planted inside your womb."

"I want that so badly," Maddy said, her breath catching with ecstasy when Black Wolf lifted the skirt of her dress and splayed a hand over the soft mound of hair at the juncture of her thighs.

"We do not have long before Winter Hawk will come home to see where his mother and father have wandered off to," Black Wolf said huskily. "We will not take time to undress."

Maddy trembled with ecstasy when she felt her husband's heat enter her where she was so open, ready, and wet for him. She twined her arms around his neck and clung to him as his strokes within her came in rhythmic thrusts.

"A dream was placed over my eyes last night," Black Wolf whispered against Maddy's parted lips.

"*Tah-wee-choo*, in the dream, what did you see?" Maddy whispered back, her eyes closed with ecstasy as he so magnificently filled her with his thick, throbbing shaft.

"In the dream I presented you with a fan made of beautiful eagle feathers," he said huskily. "You were so proud to have something made of feathers that once touched the sky."

"As *we* are about to do," Maddy murmured, drawing a ragged breath as sweet currents of warmth swept through her. "Let us fly now, my love. Let us join the eagles in the sky! *Tay-chee-khee-lah*, oh, how I love you."

Black Wolf's steel arms enfolded her as his mouth closed over hers, hot and hungry.

Her hips strained upward, and she surrendered herself to the savage wonder of the moment. In her mind's eye she pictured them making that child they both desired so much.

But even if it were not possible for her to have that second child, it would always be enough that she had been blessed to have found Black Wolf, and then to have given him his son.

She had discovered that paradise was what one made for oneself by accepting what life handed out.

For Maddy, she had found paradise when she discovered Black Wolf on the floor of a cave on the day of the horrendous flood.

Although she hated the Ohio River with a passion, she had often silently thanked it for having brought Black Wolf into her life. For without him, her life would have no meaning!

She rocked and swayed with him, then clung again as their passion peaked and they found fulfillment in one another's arms.

Maddy could not help marveling how each time they made love it was the same as renewing their vows to one another.

Maddy's life was truly one of wonder . . . *savage* wonder!

Dear Reader:

I hope you enjoyed reading *Savage Wonder*. My next book in the *Savage* series that I am writing exclusively for Leisure Books is *Savage Joy*. *Savage Joy* is about the Shawnee Indians and the setting for the book is my earlier childhood home of Harrisburg, Illinois. This book is filled with much emotion, romance, and adventure.

For those of you who are collecting all of the books in my *Savage* series, and want to hear more about it, you can send for my latest newsletter and bookmark. For a prompt reply, please send a stamped, self-addressed, legal-sized envelope to:

CASSIE EDWARDS
6709 North Country Club Road
Mattoon, IL 61938

I respond, personally, to all letters received.

Thank you from the bottom of my heart for your support of my *Savage* series! I love researching and writing about our country's beloved Native Americans!

Always,
Cassie Edwards

SAVAGE PASSIONS

CASSIE EDWARDS

**Winner Of The *Romantic Times*
Lifetime Achievement Award
For Best Indian Romance Series!**

Living among the virgin forests of frontier Michigan,
Yvonne secretly admires the chieftain of a peaceful Ottawa
tribe. A warrior with great mystical powers and many
secrets, Silver Arrow tempts her with his hard body even
as his dark, seductive eyes set her wary heart afire. But white
men and Indians alike threaten to keep them forever apart.
To fulfill the promise of their passion, Yvonne and Silver
Arrow will need more than mere magic: They'll need the
strength of a love both breathtaking and bold.

_3902-8 $5.99 US/$7.99 CAN

Dorchester Publishing Co., Inc.
P.O. Box 6640
Wayne, PA 19087-8640

Please add $1.75 for shipping and handling for the first book and
$.50 for each book thereafter. NY, NYC, and PA residents,
please add appropriate sales tax. No cash, stamps, or C.O.D.s. All
orders shipped within 6 weeks via postal service book rate.
Canadian orders require $2.00 extra postage and must be paid in
U.S. dollars through a U.S. banking facility.

Name_____
Address_____
City_____ State_____ Zip_____
I have enclosed $_____ in payment for the checked book(s).
Payment <u>must</u> accompany all orders. ❏ Please send a free catalog.

THE **SAVAGE** SERIES

SAVAGE SECRETS CASSIE EDWARDS

Winner Of The *Romantic Times* Reviewers' Choice Award For Best Indian Series

Searching the wilds of the Wyoming Territory for her outlaw brother, Rebecca Veach is captured by the one man who fulfills her heart's desire. But can she give herself to the virile warrior without telling him about her shameful quest?

Blazing Eagle is as strong as the winter wind, yet as gentle as a summer day. And although he wants Becky from the moment he takes her captive, hidden memories of a long-ago tragedy tear him away from the golden-haired vixen.

Strong-willed virgin and Cheyenne chieftain, Becky and Blazing Eagle share a passion that burns hotter than the prairie sun—until savage secrets from their past threaten to destroy them and the love they share.

_3823-4 $5.99 US/$7.99 CAN

Dorchester Publishing Co., Inc.
P.O. Box 6640
Wayne, PA 19087-8640

Please add $1.75 for shipping and handling for the first book and $.50 for each book thereafter. NY, NYC, and PA residents, please add appropriate sales tax. No cash, stamps, or C.O.D.s. All orders shipped within 6 weeks via postal service book rate. Canadian orders require $2.00 extra postage and must be paid in U.S. dollars through a U.S. banking facility.

Name_____
Address_____
City_____ State_____ Zip_____
I have enclosed $_____ in payment for the checked book(s).
Payment <u>must</u> accompany all orders. ❑ Please send a free catalog.

THE SAVAGE SERIES

SAVAGE PRIDE

CASSIE EDWARDS

**Winner Of The *Romantic Times*
Reviewers' Choice Award
For Best Indian Series**

She is a fiery hellcat who can shoot like a man, a ravishing temptress with the courage to search the wilderness for her missing brother. But Malvina is only a woman with a woman's needs and desires. And from the moment Red Wing sweeps her up on his charging stallion, she is torn between family duty and heavenly pleasure.

A mighty Choctaw warrior, Red Wing is tantalized by the blistering sensuality of the sultry, flame-haired vixen. But it will take more than his heated caresses to make Malvina his own. Only with a love as pure as her radiant beauty can he hope to claim her heart, to win her trust, to tame her savage pride.

_3732-7 $5.99 US/$6.99 CAN

Dorchester Publishing Co., Inc.
P.O. Box 6640
Wayne, PA 19087-8640

Please add $1.75 for shipping and handling for the first book and $.50 for each book thereafter. NY, NYC, and PA residents, please add appropriate sales tax. No cash, stamps, or C.O.D.s. All orders shipped within 6 weeks via postal service book rate. Canadian orders require $2.00 extra postage and must be paid in U.S. dollars through a U.S. banking facility.

Name_____

Address_____

City_____ State_____ Zip_____

I have enclosed $_____ in payment for the checked book(s).

Payment <u>must</u> accompany all orders. ☐ Please send a free catalog.

ATTENTION ROMANCE CUSTOMERS!

SPECIAL TOLL-FREE NUMBER
1-800-481-9191

*Call Monday through Friday
10 a.m. to 9 p.m.
Eastern Time
Get a free catalogue,
join the Romance Book Club,
and order books using your
Visa, MasterCard,
or Discover®*

Leisure
Books

GO ONLINE WITH US AT DORCHESTERPUB.COM